ABANDONED

WOLF GATHERINGS, BOOK FIVE

BECCA JAMESON

Copyright © 2014 by Becca Jameson

All characters and events in this book are fictitious. And resemblance to actual persons living or dead is strictly coincidental.

All rights reserved.

No part of this book may be reproduced in any form or by any electronic or mechanical means, including information storage and retrieval systems, without written permission from the author, except for the use of brief quotations in a book review.

❦ Created with Vellum

ACKNOWLEDGMENTS

To my fantastic publisher and fabulous editor who spend countless hours brainstorming with me to make elaborate plots possible!

CHAPTER 1

Allison huddled in the dark corner of the closet, shivering with cold. She kept her knees tucked under her chin, and her matted hair hung around her face. She couldn't remember when she'd last had a bath or washed her hair. She'd lost track of time. She didn't know how long she'd been in this dark prison, either. Hours? Days?

She was so thirsty. If she had to guess, it had been a few days. She'd slept only in short spurts, unable to get comfortable and repeatedly jerking awake out of fear. Even the slightest noise startled her.

She'd rocked to keep warm, but dressed only in shorts and a T-shirt, she wasn't wearing enough clothes for the lower temperatures she'd experienced...*wherever the hell I am*.

A noise made her freeze. She stiffened and lifted her face as though it would help her hear better. She held her breath. Was he back? He'd never left her this long. She didn't know which fate was worse, starving to death locked in this closet or him returning to drag her out and stab a needle into her filled with whatever he repeatedly injected into her.

He rarely spoke and never answered any of her questions. She'd given up trying to communicate or reason with him months ago. But she had no idea what his intentions were. She was stuck, seemingly in the middle of nowhere in a cabin in the woods. She thought they had traveled north that first night when someone snatched her from The Gathering last year, and the cooler weather would indicate she was right.

She'd been in her hotel room alone when a man knocked on the door, sweet-talked his way inside, and then jabbed her in the thigh with a syringe.

Her last memory had been staring at him wide-eyed as her body stopped holding itself upright. He'd cradled her in his arms and set her on the bed. Even her mouth refused to omit a scream. Everything had gone black.

She didn't know his name. Nor did she know the name of the man who had been her guard here in this cabin. He'd never told her. She knew it had been over a year, judging by the change of seasons.

The only clothes she had were the contents of the small suitcase she'd taken to The Gathering. Her captor had packed up all her belongings and taken her drugged body and everything she had with her. Unfortunately, The Gathering was held at the beginning of summer in Oklahoma. Nothing but warm-weather clothing accompanied her.

And now she was stuck without proper attire for the

weather, and the asshole holding her hostage never provided her with anything else.

When she'd awoken the day after her abduction, she found herself bound and gagged in the back of a Jeep bumping down the road toward her new fate. This was not what she'd had in mind when she'd gone to The Gathering.

Sure, she'd been looking for a mate. Every red-blooded shifter between the ages of eighteen and thirty did the same thing every other year when they attended. Anyone not interested in mating usually didn't show up.

But that man was not her mate. Nor was the man who'd kept her hostage in the cabin.

Footsteps… She angled her head toward the closet door. There were too many. More than one set. Every time there had been visitors, Allison had been on the receiving end of strange drugs that altered her state of mind and stole her memory.

Stomping and shuffling…even running… Someone was in a hurry. Whispers…

Allison grew anxious. She stiffened her spine. She reached out her tongue to lick her dry lips to no avail. Her saliva was almost nonexistent. A chill ran down her arms, and she squeezed her legs tighter.

"Is anybody here?" a voice bellowed.

Allison flinched. Fear made her keep very still. Nothing good happened when that closet door opened. She knew better than to trust whoever was on the other side of that door.

"Allison? Allison Watkins?" More shuffling around.

Something large scraped across the floor. The small kitchen table? "Shit."

Another deeper voice joined the first. Neither belonged to her captor. "Do you think we're too late? Fuck."

Could it be? Had someone finally found her?

Hope crawled up her spine and landed on her shoulders, weighing them down, pressing her into the floor. She couldn't lift her body, but she still had her voice. "In here." The words came out weak and raspy. She tried to lick her dry lips and opened her mouth again. "Here. I'm in here." This time she sounded louder.

"Allison?" Footsteps came closer. Thank God. At least she hoped she should be thanking God. The good intentions of these presumed rescuers had yet to be proven.

The closet door rattled. It was locked. Of course. For a moment she wondered if they thought she was stupid. If it hadn't been locked, she wouldn't still be sitting in the closet freezing her ass off. How did the closet always manage to stay colder than the rest of the cabin?

"Ma'am, could you get as far from the door as possible? I'm going to kick it in." The voice was soothing, but urgent. The fact that he'd addressed her as "ma'am" eased some of her suspicions. She hadn't been treated with any sort of humane respect in over a year.

Allison tucked her feet farther under her and pushed herself to standing. She was amazed she had the energy to pull herself upright, but adrenaline kicked in at the thought of being rescued. Finally.

She'd given up hope long ago.

Something hit the closet door and her body jerked. She squeezed herself tighter into the corner, but it was difficult to avoid the opening. The closet wasn't much larger than the door frame.

Two more times something slammed into the door before it splintered and broke free around the lock. Large hands reached inside and tugged the splintered wood until it gave way and daylight flooded her tiny cell.

Allison flung an arm over her face against the brightness. She'd been in the pitch dark too long.

"Are you Allison Watkins?" a voice asked.

"Ye-yes," she muttered, barely able to hear herself.

"You're safe now, ma'am. You can come out."

Allison peeked over her forearm, her eyes squinted against the light of day. In reality it wasn't that bright. She just wasn't accustomed to seeing at all.

Two men stood just outside the closet, both wearing hunting gear. No, not hunting clothes exactly, but camouflage. And they were armed. Military? They were shifters. Perhaps members of the North American Reserves, then? They stepped back and gave her space, the larger one holding his hand out toward her.

She stared at the gesture but didn't reach for him. Her heart pounded so hard she thought it might beat right out of her chest. She hadn't seen many people besides her captor in over a year. The only time others had visited, they hadn't spoken. They'd simply covered her head, taken her to some sort of medical lab, and then later returned her to the cabin. No one had ever addressed her or looked her in the eye.

This man was looking directly at her and concern furrowed his brow. He dropped his hand. "We're here to rescue you, Allison. You can trust us."

I've heard that before.

Allison stepped over the debris, trying to avoid the splintered wood with her bare feet.

There were three men in the room. One stood by the door, gun drawn, eyes scanning the outside. A knife hung at his waist and a larger rifle was strapped over his shoulder.

Allison shivered. She had no idea if she could trust these people, but she had nothing to lose, either.

The largest man spoke again. "I'm Bill. Are you all right?"

Allison glanced down at herself. "I think so." She licked her lips. "So thirsty."

The shorter blond man darted across to the sink in two strides, grabbed a glass from the counter, and filled it with water from the tap. "How long have you been in there?" he asked as he handed her the cold, welcome liquid.

Allison downed the entire thing in one long draw, knowing she shouldn't, but unable to stop herself. Her stomach would hurt, but she didn't care. "Not sure," she muttered. "Days?"

"Who brought you here?" the shorter blond asked. "I'm Chuck, by the way." He thumbed over his shoulder. "That's Marshall manning the door."

Marshall didn't turn around. She barely saw his profile. He had longer dark hair, almost black, and he was taller and slimmer.

"He never said his name." Allison narrowed her gaze at the three men one at a time, still trying to decide if these men had her best interest in mind.

"How long have you been here?" Chuck asked. He took the empty glass from her and lifted it. "Do you want more?"

She shook her head. She should wait a while before drinking more. "Since The Gathering. A year?" She wasn't positive. "Have…you been looking for me that long?"

"Not quite, but close." Chuck looked her up and down. "Is that all you have to wear?"

"Yes." Allison wrapped her arms around her middle and shivered again at the mention. "He never gave me more than I had at The Gathering."

The bigger man, Bill, shrugged quickly out of his jacket and draped it around her shoulders. "It's not much, but it'll help."

Marshall nodded outside as he cleared his throat. "Let's get out of here." He glanced at Allison and then back out the opening to the outside. "When do you expect your captor to return?"

"No idea. He's been gone longer than usual. I was beginning to think he'd left me for dead." She stared at Marshall's back, attempting to keep her breathing steady. She was scared out of her mind. *They offered you water and gave you a coat. Surely they don't intend to kill you.*

"Is there anything you want to take?" Chuck asked.

Allison glanced around. "No." She wouldn't mind having at least her purse with her identification, but she had no idea where it was or even if it still existed. "Who are you guys? You don't look like police." Was she trading one problem for another? She'd been held captive for a year by one man. There were three here now. They weren't official by any means. Just three men who thought they'd swoop in and take her to another location. *Shifters, though.* That had to mean something.

But three men had come in several times and taken her to another location and then returned her. She could hardly remember the details of any of those encounters.

"We aren't with the human police. We're hired by The Head Council." Chuck stepped closer to the door and then turned from her to Marshall. "Ready?"

"Clear." Marshall pushed the door all the way open and eased outside.

"I'll explain better in the car," Chuck continued over his shoulder. "I know you're scared and I don't blame you, but I swear we're the good guys. And we don't want to be anywhere near here when your kidnapper returns."

Allison didn't think he would return at all, but that wasn't going to stop her from getting the hell out of there. She couldn't imagine a fate worse than staying right then. "He wasn't my kidnapper. Another man took me from The Gathering and brought me here. I don't know who either of them were."

"I'm so sorry, ma'am." Bill ducked his head. "Our mission is rescue. Someone else will come behind us to investigate the scene."

Allison looked down at her feet. "How far do we

have to walk? I'm not very strong." She hadn't eaten anything in days and not enough for a regular person in a year. She spotted her tennis shoes by the front door and slipped them on. At least her feet would be protected.

"We have an SUV very close. We didn't want to pull up to the door, but close enough to walk." Bill set a hand on her shoulder and she flinched.

"Let's go." Marshall took off. He scanned every direction and kept low, his knees bent as he jogged away from the cabin.

Chuck followed on his heels. "Stay right behind me."

Allison stepped outside. Her legs wobbled after so long crouched in the closet and not enough use for months. She hadn't even been outside in a long time. When her captor was home, she was permitted to use the tiny bathroom in one corner of the cabin, the only separate room it contained. When he was away and she was locked in the closet, she peed in a bucket in the cramped space. She always knew when she was dehydrated because she no longer needed to pee.

She soon saw the black SUV they'd mentioned among the trees about twenty yards away. Her legs threatened to buckle, but adrenaline pulled her along.

She couldn't imagine anyone was watching them or following them, but she felt the palpable concern of the three men flanking her.

Allison scanned in both directions. The hairs on the back of her neck prickled, and she tripped over a tree stump. Chuck reached back and swept her off her feet before she hit the ground.

And then all hell broke loose. A shot rang out. And then another, coming from the opposite direction. It happened so fast, Allison couldn't tell for sure where the noises came from.

Chuck flattened her against the ground, lying on top of her and covering her head. Her knees hit the dirt hard, and then her face. She took a deep breath and dust filled her nose.

More shots. So many she couldn't count them. She could see Marshall's boots to her side where he crouched down in front of her face and mowed the area with his machine gun.

Her chest pounded. She couldn't breathe. Chuck was pressing on top of her with too much weight. And she blinked, but dirt clouded her vision, making her eyes burn.

A loud grunt followed by a thump filtered into her awareness. Bill. Had he been hit?

Allison pushed against the ground with both hands, trying to free herself of Chuck's overpowering pressure on her back. She couldn't get him to budge.

"Go," Marshall whispered. He glanced back at Chuck and then down at Allison. She squinted to see him. "Get her to the SUV. I'll be right behind you." He motioned with his chin toward the tree line.

Chuck whisked her off the ground as though she weighed nothing. He held her against his chest, one arm wrapped around her middle. Her feet didn't reach the ground.

"Go with them," Marshall said. He must have spoken that last part to Bill. "Hurry."

When they reached the car, Bill stepped around Chuck and whipped open the back door. Chuck swung her inside. "Get on the floor," he muttered before he slammed the door. Within seconds all three men had circled to the other doors and jumped inside. Someone started the SUV and gunned the engine so fast, Allison had to brace herself against the front seat. She squeezed into a tight ball on the floor and ducked her head, expecting the glass to shatter all around her any moment.

The ride was rough at first as the SUV bounced around on the uneven ground. There were no more shots. She held her breath for several minutes it seemed, worried about a tire blowing or the gas tank exploding. Whatever sorts of things might happen to a car in a gun fight.

When she finally tipped her head up, she saw Bill in the seat across from her. His gaze kept shifting from one window to another, scanning the area behind them as they sped away. He held his left arm tight with his right hand wrapped around his bicep. Blood trickled between his fingers. He didn't seem to notice.

With a huge bounce, the SUV went over a large bump and then the drive smoothed out. They must have hit the pavement.

"I think we're safe now," Marshall said over his shoulder. "You okay, Bill?"

"Yeah, just a flesh wound. I'll live." He unwrapped his fingers from his arm and peeked at the damage, making Allison's stomach revolt. She'd never seen a gunshot wound before. And she couldn't see anything but blood on his jacket now. But the idea of what lay beneath made her swallow back bile.

"Who was that?" Allison asked, dipping her gaze down so she could avoid staring at Bill's wound.

"No idea," Chuck said from the front. "But they didn't like the idea of us taking you, that's for sure."

She breathed a giant sigh of relief. Whatever the fuck that chapter in her life had been, she hoped it was over. She lifted her gaze back to Bill. "Where are you taking me?"

~

Henry paced next to his car while he listened to the phone ringing on the other end. He'd pulled into a deserted parking lot to make this call.

He exhaled when the line connected. "Sir?"

"How many times have I told you not to call me during the day, Fairfield?"

Henry braced himself. He'd known this would happen. "It's an emergency, sir."

"What?" the older man barked.

"Something's gone terribly wrong. Several women were seized all across the country at the same time."

"What the fuck? What are you talking about?"

Henry took shallow breaths. He rubbed his forehead. "I don't know anything else, sir. It appears someone was onto us, and they organized an ambush."

"Any men?"

"No. Just the women."

"How many?"

"Not sure yet. Maybe a dozen. I'm still waiting to hear from all the guards." Henry lifted his face to the sky. "Allison Watkins was one of them. J.T. was nowhere to be found when your men showed up to pick her up. They got caught in a shootout."

"Shit." The man paused. "Was anyone harmed?"

"No, sir. They think they hit one of the men who took Allison, but when gunfire was returned in an effort to mow them down with a machine gun, they ran for safety. They think the North American Reserves were involved."

"NAR?"

"Looks that way, sir."

"Damn."

Henry waited for his boss to say something else.

"Well, keep me posted when you know more and hang tight. I'll do some investigating on my end."

"Okay."

The line went dead. Henry climbed back into his car and tossed his cell on the passenger seat. He banged his head on the steering wheel. *Fuck*.

CHAPTER 2

"They're on their way." Evan set the cordless on the counter and turned to his mate.

"I don't know why I'm so nervous." Ashley wrung her hands and then wrapped them around her mug of coffee to keep still. Her nerves were getting to her. She set her elbows on the table and couldn't stop tapping her feet. "We've known this day would come for months."

"True, but it's understandably nerve-wracking." Evan approached his mate and leaned over the table to kiss her. "Are you okay? You can still back out if you want."

She shook her head. "I would never do that. I'm sure Allison needs me. I want to be helpful. It's just stressful."

"I know. I'll be right beside you."

"What time will they arrive?"

"In about an hour. They drove all night from Minnesota. We'll see how she's doing and decide when to leave for the ranch." Evan sat next to his mate.

"Has The Head Council contacted her parents?"

"Yes. They're flying directly to the ranch in Texas. They'll meet us there."

"God, they must be so worried."

"I'm sure they are, baby." Evan grabbed her hands and squeezed them.

It had only been a year since Evan had rescued Ashley from the man who took her from The Gathering five years ago. She could remember the frantic way her parents reacted when she first arrived back home.

Evan and his team of private investigators spent months tracking and locating other missing shifters. The Head Council for the North American shifters, located in Seattle, had provided the manpower from NAR to extricate a dozen shifters simultaneously. Their hope was that by doing so, whoever was behind this elaborate scheme of kidnappings would be caught off guard and unable to move any of the women before they were rescued.

With the exception of the altercation extricating Allison from Minnesota, the plan had been flawless. All twelve people involved had been successfully recovered. None of the shifters organized to perform this elaborate sting had been killed. Several of the abductors had been taken into custody and were on their way to Seattle for questioning.

If the men holding each of these shifters were anything like the man who'd taken Ashley, Damon Parkfield, they probably wouldn't know much.

"You're deep in thought." Evan lifted one of Ashley's hands to his lips and kissed her knuckles.

"Do you think they'll be able to find out who's behind this insanity?" She lifted her gaze to Evan. "Damon was a rogue wolf. He didn't seem to know anything about who was supplying him with the drugs he used on me. What if all the others are the same?"

"It's a possibility. Hopefully there was a breach somewhere and at least one of them knows something. From my research, it seems all the shifters involved in this were loners when they were approached by whoever is leading this operation. If any of them knows more than we already do from surveillance and phone taps, it'll be a miracle."

"There could be hundreds more out there. Missing. Kidnapped. Exploited." She swallowed over the lump in her throat as she pondered the number of women who'd been taken under the pretense of mating.

Evan wrapped an arm around her shoulders and pulled her to his side. "We're doing everything we can to ensure that isn't the case. Right now I'm more worried about all the rogue wolves out there being lured into the scheme than anything. The families who frequent The Gathering every other year are easy to contact. We've called every family who's been to The Gathering in the last decade individually to ensure no one was mysteriously mated and not heard from again.

"Tracking shifters who don't attend The Gathering and have gone off on their own is another story altogether. It's nearly impossible, and we have no way of knowing how many are out there, where they live, or how many offspring they may have had in the last century." Evan squeezed her fingers and brushed them against his cheek.

It grounded her, but she also knew he was concerned. He had worked tirelessly for months tracking rogue shifters and the women they were on the run with. Circles under his eyes spoke volumes about his fears. He never said anything, but Ashley knew he was extremely concerned. Especially since no one had any idea why the women had been taken and drugged.

What was the intent? It seemed experimental.

And more importantly, it was obvious there was a mole inside The Head Council. Someone knew exactly what was going on, stayed one step ahead of Evan's efforts, and warned the wolves involved in their experiment at every turn.

Until Evan and the head elder, Ralph Jerard, had begun to keep nearly all dealings secret from the rest of The Council, they'd been spinning their wheels.

Jerard even believed one of the top five members of the Council were in on the scheme, either leading it or feeding info to someone else.

"Have you spoken to Drake and McKenzie?" Ashley asked.

Evan nodded. "Several times this morning before you got up. The ranch is ready and they're prepared for their guests."

"Good." Ashley chewed on her bottom lip before she continued, "I hope Kenzie isn't overdoing it with the new baby and all this on her plate."

"I'm sure she's fine. They have a lot of help. Remember, the ranch was already set up to accommodate large groups of special-needs children. Taking in twelve women to help them recover together from abduction isn't a stretch. They have the space and God bless them for offering to help."

Ashley glanced around the kitchen of her parents' home. They'd been staying there for a month, ever since Ashley killed the man who'd kidnapped her the same way Allison had been abducted.

When Damon Parkfield tracked Ashley down at the home she shared with her true mate, Evan, she'd gotten lucky. Damon had dropped his knife and Ashley conveniently managed to use it against him.

She couldn't go back into that house. It was for sale while Ashley and Evan looked for another place. Meanwhile they were living with her parents, Paul and Laura Rice.

"Yes. Imagine housing all those people here." She smiled.

Evan grinned back. "And I know you would if there was no other option." He kissed her forehead.

Ashley smiled. "Of course. So everyone else will meet us at the ranch?"

"Yes. Allison is the only one making a stop on the way. She's your age and she's been stuck in a cabin for over a year with no contact with the outside world. For some reason, the man holding her abandoned her several days ago."

"Why?"

"No idea. He hardly ever spoke to her, and she believes he left her for dead. All she knows is he left and didn't come back. Maybe he got wind of us moving in on him, or maybe he just gave up and decided to leave. In any case, several men came for her while our men were rescuing her. They exchanged gunfire. One of our men was hit. No one was killed."

A shiver raced down Ashley's spine. "God. Did the guys from NAR manage to kill anyone?"

He shook his head. "They don't believe so."

"Jesus, she must be scared out of her mind after all she's been through." Ashley knew they'd found Allison in a closet. Ashley was used to being in a closet. Damon kept her locked up many times during the four years he'd held her.

Something about Allison's captivity was different from all the other women. She was the only one held in the middle of nowhere and then abandoned. Ashley suspected there were other mysteries about her imprisonment that were bound to come to light in the next few days.

~

Allison jerked awake when the car lurched to a stop. She bolted upright and looked around. *You're okay. You've been rescued.*

She glanced at the two men in the front seat and sucked in a deep breath. Marshall drove and Chuck sat in the passenger seat. They had dropped Bill off with some other shifters and parted ways after her rescue. She hoped he was getting the medical care he needed.

"Sorry, ma'am. Didn't mean to startle you. We're in

St. Louis. This is where we're meeting up with the other woman I told you about. Ashley."

Ashley... Chuck had given Allison a rundown of all sorts of things after they'd driven away from the isolated cabin in northern Minnesota. Until then, she hadn't even known for sure where she was. She'd spoken to her parents on the phone between gasping sobs of relief and disbelief. They were flying to someplace in Texas to meet her.

Allison couldn't remember all the details. It all ran together in her head. She'd been dehydrated, tired, and so hungry yesterday afternoon she'd hardly managed to soak in any information. What she'd known was that the idea of heading to an airport and facing the general public had been completely unimaginable to her. So the men had driven her. St. Louis was half way, and they would leave her there with another woman who'd been abducted in a similar fashion—Ashley.

As Allison exited the car, the front door to the house opened. She was still so tired and weak she could hardly imagine making polite conversation or even socially acceptable facial expressions. But the moment Ashley appeared on the porch as Allison walked up the path, she knew she could relax.

Ashley knew. It was in her eyes. She was a sister to this nightmare. Allison was safe with her. She would have a friend.

Ashley jogged forward, wrapped an arm around Allison, and led her into the house. She didn't say a word. She didn't even make any introductions to the other people they passed. She led her straight to a bedroom and shut the door. Next she angled them into the adjoining bath and turned on the tub.

Allison slumped onto the toilet seat and moaned. It had been so long since she'd had a proper bath with hot water. Tears formed in her eyes. "Thank you," she managed to mutter.

Ashley smiled. "I'm sure you're exhausted and hungry. Relax in the water for a while. There're bubbles, shampoo, a new razor. Whatever you need. And I put a new toothbrush on the counter for you too." She nodded toward the sink. "You're about my size. I'll find you something to wear and then we can talk. Okay?"

The tears began to fall. Bless this woman. Allison couldn't remember the last time anyone had been kind to her. No. That wasn't true. She'd had a perfectly normal life up until The Gathering last year. Even The Gathering had been a wonderful weekend, right up until she met the crazy man who'd waltzed into her hotel room and kidnapped her.

Allison nodded at Ashley. She couldn't utter a word without bawling, so she let it go for now.

Ashley left the room silently, shutting the door with a snick.

Allison peeled off her disgusting clothing and dropped it in the trash. The T-shirt and shorts had been worn for so long and washed by hand so many times they were threadbare. She'd lost weight in the last year also, and her clothes had started drooping on her months ago.

She moaned as she slid into the hot water. Steam wafted up to fill the room, and she eased against the back of the tub and closed her eyes. The last twenty-four hours had been a whirlwind of crazy. Even though she'd slept all through the night as they'd driven to St. Louis, she was still tired. Bone weary from stress.

She knew she needed to eat, but after a year of barely edible food without enough nutrition, she couldn't stomach many things. Every time they'd stopped, Marshall and Chuck had gotten her food, but she'd only managed to pick at it, afraid her stomach would revolt.

Allison relaxed in the tub for a long time before reaching for the shampoo. She closed her eyes and breathed in the floral scent deeply, moaning as she remembered something so luxurious. The only soaps she'd had for the last year had been cheap and generic and infrequent.

She added hot water to the tub to warm it. By the time she was as clean as she could get and had used the detachable sprayer to rinse the grime down the drain, she felt ten times better.

She stepped from the tub and grabbed the fluffy, over-sized towel Ashley had left on the vanity. She'd been afraid to look in the mirror before, but now she lifted her gaze and stared at the woman she hardly recognized. Her face was gaunt and her eyes sunken and sad. She was glad she was meeting her parents tomorrow in Texas. It would kill her to have seen the look on her mother's face before she had a chance to at least bathe. She'd kill for a haircut, but that could wait.

Allison brushed her teeth and combed out her hair. It was so long the blonde curls had lost some of their spring. Or maybe lack of nutrition had caused that. She blinked back tears as she stared at her reflection, her sunken eyes darker blue than they had been.

Finally she turned away and exited the bathroom wrapped in the huge towel. She found a pile of clothes on the bed waiting for her, and she quickly set the towel aside and pulled on the thoughtful items Ashley had left her. Without knowing Allison's precise sizes, she'd done a fantastic job, leaving her a tank top with a built-in shelf bra, a blouse that was light enough for the midsummer heat, and a pair of khaki shorts that fit Allison perfectly.

She felt better already. Between the bath and the clean clothes, she just might live.

She left the room almost reluctantly, expecting to face a barrage of questions.

Instead she found the living room empty except for Ashley, who jumped up from the couch when Allison entered. "Oh, you look so much better." She smiled and wiped her hands on her jean shorts.

"I feel better. Thank you…for everything." She padded forward.

"Let's get you something to eat. What do you think you can handle?"

"I don't know. Do you have some chicken noodle soup? Something simple like that would be perfect."

"I bet I can find a can."

"I'm sure canned goods are all I could handle right now. Anything else would be too rich." Allison followed Ashley to the kitchen. "You have a nice place."

Ashley turned from the pantry holding up a can.

"Oh, this isn't mine. It's my parents'. My mate and I are staying here while we look for a new home."

"How long ago did you meet your mate?"

"Evan was the one who rescued me from my kidnapper last year. He kept our status as mates to himself for six months, though, to give me time to heal. And even then, I was very reluctant to get involved." Ashley giggled. "It was hard after being in captivity so long." She paused after emptying the can of soup into a pan. "I hope my experience and sharing with you will help you in some small way." She sobered and met Allison's gaze.

Allison climbed onto a bar stool. "Thank you. I really appreciate it." She cleared her throat. "What happened to you?"

"A man named Damon Parkfield showed up at The Gathering, claimed he was my mate, and swept me away without letting me say good-bye to my family. I was young and assumed he was telling the truth. By the time I realized something was way off about the situation, it was too late."

"How long were you with him?"

"Four years."

"Oh my God." Allison stiffened. She couldn't imagine a fate worse than her own. But clearly Ashley had been through a lower circle of hell than she had and lived to tell about it.

"Yeah. But I survived and you will too." She gave a half grin. "We have to stick together, not let these bastards win. I promise no matter how grim things seem right now, you will come out on the other side a survivor."

Allison watched as Ashley dished up a bowl of hot soup. She couldn't wrap her mind around four years of captivity. "I heard there are eleven others like me who were rescued yesterday. What did they want us for?"

Ashley shook her head. "We aren't sure yet. No one knows. Hopefully some of the kidnappers they picked up will shed some light." Ashley set the soup in front of Allison and handed her a spoon. "Maybe each of us will be able to pull together and come up with similarities that help The Head Council.

Allison blew on her first bite and moaned around the spoonful as she tasted the simple canned soup. It was just as she remembered. The chicken soup her mother always fixed when she was sick as a child. "I don't know how I can be of much help. I don't have any idea what my captor had planned."

"What was his name?"

"I don't even know that. He never said and he rarely spoke to me."

"Did he say you were his mate?"

"No." Allison shook her head and then took another bite. "He said I was a test subject. For what I don't know, but he injected me with some strange drugs about once a week."

Ashley nodded. "So did Damon."

"They made me tired, and after a while I didn't care. I thought he was keeping me docile."

"So you spent an entire year in a cabin in the middle

of nowhere never seeing anyone except one man who didn't speak to you?"

Allison shook her head. "Not exactly. But I might as well have. Several times other men came to the cabin." She set her spoon down, her hand shaking violently as she told Ashley what happened to her. "They would put me out with some different drugs and then transport me blindfolded to another location for a few days. It was very strange. Like a hospital, except I only ever saw men in white coats briefly when I was lucid enough. Most of the time I slept during those episodes. I can't remember much about it."

"They moved you someplace else and then took you back to the cabin?"

Allison nodded. "I was scared out of my mind yesterday when the military showed up for fear they'd been sent to transport me to that facility again. Jesus. That place made me nervous."

Ashley furrowed her brow and bit her lower lip. "God."

"Yeah. I think they were using me for some sort of experiment. But I don't know anything else."

"Can I ask you something personal?"

"Go ahead." Allison set the spoon down and looked at Ashley's troubled face, her brow furrowed, her lip caught between her teeth.

"I'm guessing you never got pregnant. How often did he—" Ashley cut herself off, not finishing the sentence.

Allison's eyes went wide. She shook her head and reached across the counter to take Ashley's hand in hers. "He never raped me." *Oh God. Is that what happened to Ashley?* Allison was right. Her fate was much less severe than Ashley's.

"Oh wow. Thank God." Ashley turned away, drawing her hand from Allison's until she faced the sink.

Allison watched the back of her head, knowing she was pulling herself together and fighting demons only she could know about.

"I'm sorry," Allison said.

Ashley turned back to face her. Her eyes were wet. "It's okay. I'm making progress every day. I'm so glad you didn't endure the same."

Allison glanced down, realizing something she should have noticed when she first arrived, and would have if she hadn't been so distracted. "You're pregnant."

"Yes." Ashley beamed now and patted her belly. "Not far along. Evan and I are so excited. I didn't think I could have children."

"Congratulations." Allison smiled back and then sobered. "It must be hard after all those years…"

"At first it seemed impossible. I fought the call to mate with Evan for months. I thought I was too damaged for him, and I went through a long period of agoraphobia and wouldn't let anyone touch me. But as soon as I gave up the battle against nature, it all fell into place. Nothing with Evan is anything like what I went through with Damon, so our reality doesn't draw me into the past."

"That's good. I hope I meet someone that special one day."

"I'm sure you will."

CHAPTER 3

Daniel Spencer ran through the back door of his family's home in Northwest Texas, letting the screen door slam behind him.

His mother stood at the kitchen counter beating eggs. She shook her head as Daniel kissed her cheek. "When are you going to learn to let that door shut softly?"

"Never, Mom." He grinned and grabbed a biscuit from the plate behind his mom.

She swatted at his hand with her free one. "Those are for breakfast."

"And I'm ready for breakfast. I'm starving."

"If you didn't run so far so early in the morning, you wouldn't be so hungry." She raised an eyebrow.

Daniel plopped down in a chair at the table and poured a glass of orange juice from the carafe. "When I joined the North American Reserves, they didn't intend for me to sleep late and sit around all day, Mom."

"I know. But I worry about how much you work out. It's unhealthy."

"I'm fine." He rolled his eyes. "I love the solitude. It's so peaceful and quiet out there early in the morning. Besides, I have to stay fit."

She padded over to the table and pinched his biceps, or tried to. "There isn't an ounce of fat on you. I'd say you're fit enough. NAR is lucky to have you." She grinned. "Go take a shower while I finish here. We have to get moving. People will arrive soon."

Daniel stood and took a deep breath. He was proud of his parents for stepping up and taking in twelve women who needed a place to convalesce after captivity. And he knew the dude ranch his family owned would work miracles toward their recovery, but he was also concerned about the safety of his parents, siblings, and now even a sister-in-law and baby.

He left the room and headed for the hall bathroom to clean up. He had his own place on the ranch now, a cabin he'd built this spring about a half mile down the road on his parents' property. But he ate almost all his meals with the family. His younger brothers, Scott and Jerrod, still lived in the main house. His older brother, Drake, had moved out years ago and also lived on the property in his own home with his mate, Kenzie, and their new baby, Aaron.

When Daniel reemerged in the kitchen, the house was bustling. The noise level always increased several decibels when his youngest brother, Jerrod, only twelve years old, awoke. The boy was a pistol, and he never stopped chattering.

At twenty-six, Daniel was in the best physical shape he'd ever been in. When he'd applied to join NAR almost a year ago, his parents had been leery. But he was dedicated to the safety of the shifter population, and his family had relaxed in their concern. His mother usually furrowed her brow when the subject of his commitment came up, but the pride on his father's face made up for it. Some serious shit seemed to be brewing among the shifter population, and Daniel felt a deep loyalty toward the protection of his species.

Scott had been talking about enlisting lately also. Daniel knew it was only a matter of time. It made his mother very nervous.

"What time will people start arriving?" Daniel asked as he filled his plate and took a spot at the table.

His father, Jerome, sat at the head of the table holding his usual cup of coffee and waiting for the commotion to die down before eating. With three male offspring still living in the house, he had to know his limbs were in danger if he reached into the fray. "The first woman is arriving shortly. Her name is Allison Watkins. Evan and Ashley Harmon are bringing her from St. Louis. They drove in the night. The rest will be trickling in during the day."

"How old are these women?" Daniel asked as he shoveled scrambled eggs into his mouth. His stomach was growling, even though he'd inhaled that biscuit before showering.

"Allison is twenty-five. The rest range in age from twenty to twenty-eight."

"Such a close age range." Daniel had not known

much about this situation until recently. He'd joined the Reserves right after The Gathering last year, but anything related to this strange rift in the shifter world had been kept quite secret until a select group of NAR had been brought on board. He still worked on his family's dude ranch most of the month, but he traveled every other weekend to train with other members of NAR. In centuries of existence, the wolf shifter population had never had such a mobilized military organization. They'd always maintained small groups in every region to keep the peace among their people, but nothing of this size. And it was growing. Concerns were rising. When he trained with the other shifters, he could feel the change in atmosphere among his superiors.

Fear. Distrust. Anger.

Daniel was fully aware something huge was about to occur. Even if other shifters, including his own family, chose to pretend things couldn't possibly be that bad. He knew with certainty now that they'd rescued so many women from captivity there was a deep-rooted conspiracy in the works. There was no telling how bad the situation was yet, but Daniel intended to be on the right side of the law when the shit hit the fan, protecting not only his family but their entire population's way of life.

Needing some time away from the commotion of his family, Daniel pushed away from the table. "I'm going to go check on the cabins, make sure we haven't forgotten anything."

His mother smiled at him with a knowing look that

told him she knew he was making excuses to escape the craziness of the noisy family.

"I'll be back in a while." Daniel kissed his mother on the cheek and left to head for a quiet zone. He checked the first few cabins, finding them in perfect shape and then made his way to the stables.

The last stall in the barn held Sadie, Daniel's personal favorite. He rode her whenever he had a chance, at least three times a week. It was hard to find time in the busiest seasons, but he at least visited her every day to escape, connect, and regroup.

He could talk to her, and she seemed to understand him. He leaned into her as he brushed her, and she took away the weight of the world. He whispered in her ear, "Some women are coming to visit, Sadie."

Her ears twitched.

"Why am I antsy?" Of course it was a big deal having twelve kidnapped women come to the ranch to regroup, but there was more. For some reason his senses were on high alert, as though something was in the air. Not just the women. Something else was about to happen. A tingling in his spine kept him on edge.

Some people said they could tell when it was going to rain or snow by an ache in their hip or a pain in their leg. Daniel felt like that now. It wasn't weather that was headed his way, but something bigger.

He knew people would start arriving at any moment, but he needed to relieve some stress. In a flash he decided to go for a ride. He grabbed his saddle and led Sadie from the stall in record time. Without turning toward the main house to check for new cars, he headed to the back pasture and took off.

Whatever was bothering him would surely loosen up after a good run.

∾

Allison stepped from the car and stretched her legs, reaching for her toes, knees locked, back arched. She'd spent two long nights riding in cars.

The screen door on the front porch opened and a woman emerged. She smiled as she approached. Allison glanced at Ashley and then Evan, the kind couple from St. Louis who had escorted her to Texas. They were both watching the blonde woman as she reached them.

"Hello." She extended a hand to Ashley first. "I'm Natalie Spencer. My husband, Jerome, and I own Spencer Ranch. Welcome."

"Thank you. I'm Ashley. And this is my mate, Evan." She pointed at Evan as he rounded the car. "And this is Allison Watkins." She nodded toward Allison just behind her.

Allison loved Natalie immediately. The warmth in her eyes as she reached for Allison made her almost cry. Her own mother would be here shortly, but in the meantime she could tell Natalie would be a wonderful support system. "Nice to meet you, ma'am."

"Please, call me Natalie." She tucked Allison's hand under her arm and led them back toward the house. "Come on inside. You three must be exhausted."

Ashley and Evan followed.

The house was inviting as they entered through the front door. Even the squeak of the front screen made Allison smile. Visions of a stereotypical farm house filled her mind. And this fantastic place fit the bill.

"Sit." Natalie motioned to the living room. "Let me get you something to drink." She headed for the attached kitchen area and returned moments later with a tray of lemonade and several glasses.

Allison relaxed into the couch cushions, her mouth watering. "I can't remember when I've had lemonade." A peace washed over her in this home. She couldn't put her finger on why, but she was more comfortable than she could ever remember.

And that was saying something. Allison was a city girl, born and raised in New York City. She'd never spent more than a week at a time vacationing in quieter rural areas. After a few days, the silence would eat at her. And after a year alone in a cabin with only one other living being around for company—her keeper—she yearned for the city. The one thing she'd craved more than anything else over the past year was noise.

Natalie handed her a glass. "Well there's plenty. So enjoy."

Allison closed her eyes as she savored the first sip. Not just any lemonade but the real kind made from lemons and sugar. "That's delicious. Thank you."

"My husband says your parents will arrive this afternoon. I'm sure you're anxious to see them."

"I am. I've spoken with them many times in the last twenty-four hours. I don't think my mother can believe it's really me."

"I can't begin to imagine what she must have gone through, dear." Natalie handed Ashley and Evan each a glass of lemonade on the love seat and settled into an armchair.

"It's so quiet here." Ashley said.

Allison glanced around, feeling the opposing sensations of calm and comfort mixed with the need for chaos. She gripped her glass tightly, wondering what on earth was going on in her head. After a year in captivity, she was out of sorts. *It's understandable. You're okay.*

Natalie chuckled. "Not usually. I have four sons and one daughter-in-law, so this place is a madhouse. But I shooshed them all out the door for the morning. They're in the barn checking on the horses right now. They'll be back in a while, and then you'll find out how not quiet it can be around here."

Evan leaned forward, setting his palm on his mate's knee. "We understand this is a dude ranch and you're used to a full house."

"Yes. We have ten cabins spaced along the periphery. And a dorm-style building we use when children are visiting. There's a cafeteria in the dorm, but each cabin is fully equipped also. Our guests can choose whether they want to eat in the cafeteria or cook for themselves."

Allison curled her feet beneath her. "And horses?" She'd never seen one up close.

Natalie turned to her. "We have eighteen right now. They're all very docile. The children we keep one week a month are challenged in various ways, so riding is therapy for them, and we have to know they will be safe on our horses."

"I've never ridden." *And I don't intend to.*

"You'll love it. It's so freeing." Natalie leaned on the arm of her chair. "Where are you from originally?"

"New York City."

She smiled. "Not many horses there. You'll find this ranch to be the polar opposite of life in New York."

Allison glanced around the room. She could tell Natalie ran a tight ship, considering how tidy the place was with four boys and a husband to contend with. The furnishings were all done in browns and blues. Everything had a western feel. "How old are your boys?"

"They aren't kids anymore really, well except the youngest. Jerrod is twelve. But the others are all grown. The oldest is Drake; he's twenty-nine and lives in his own cabin just up the road on the property with his mate, Kenzie, and their new baby, Aaron. Daniel is twenty-six. He also has his own place just down the road. And then there's Scott. He's twenty-four. He still lives here in the house. Somehow they all make it here when it's time to eat, though. And I'm so blessed."

"Sounds like it." Allison fidgeted. She had slept all the way there through the night, so she wasn't tired. She was more antsy than anything else.

The back door opened and she twisted her head sharply to see who was coming up behind her.

A vibrant woman with a huge smile entered the room carrying a baby. She had to be the oldest son's mate. She kissed Natalie on the cheek and handed her the baby before nodding at Ashley and Evan and then turning to Allison. "Welcome. I'm McKenzie, Drake's mate. Call me Kenzie." She extended a hand and sat next to Allison as she clasped her palm in a gentle grip.

"Nice to meet you." Allison glanced at the baby and then the beaming smile on her grandmother's face.

"That's Aaron. Don't let him fool you. He sleeps about ten minutes at a time and then wails for several hours." Kenzie giggled, but when Allison looked at her face, she could tell the woman hadn't slept well in weeks. Dark circles under her eyes told their tale.

"He's adorable." Allison returned her gaze to the sleeping infant, wondering if she'd ever be a mother to anything that precious.

"Would you like me to show you around? I thought I'd leave the baby here and take you and Ashley on a tour. This is Ashley's first time visiting us also."

Allison unfolded her legs. "That would be lovely." *And maybe it will alleviate some of my anxiety.*

Ashley stood. "Perfect." She kissed her mate as Allison also stood. Ashley turned to Natalie as they headed for the door. "If he wakes up, just give him to Evan. He needs the practice." Ashley quickly opened the back door and stepped out on the porch, giggling before Evan could respond.

Allison smiled at the lighthearted nature of their exchange. It had been so long.

Kenzie led them away from the main house and turned around to chat as she walked backward. "The ranch is the most efficient place I've ever been. I couldn't believe it when I first came here. You'll love it."

Allison looked around. Land extended in every direction as far as she could see, huge corrals, wide pastures. And across from the fenced areas stood quaint cabins. Allison decided to fess up. "I don't ride horses, but it's beautiful."

"I didn't ride, either, until I met Drake and moved here. I can't even remember what it was like before I had so much proximity to nature. I hated not riding for the months I was pregnant."

Allison cringed, but she didn't comment.

"I've never ridden, either," Ashley admitted. She patted her belly. "And it's not going to happen on this visit, either. Evan would have a coronary."

Allison stared across the pasture at the cabins. She held her hand up to shield her eyes. "They look like a picture. Perfect little log structures placed precisely among the trees."

"They do." Kenzie turned to face them again. "Come on. The first one is for you and your family. I'll show you the inside."

Allison fatigued as they walked. She kept looking over her shoulder as though this were all a dream and someone would jump out and snatch her again. She wasn't strong enough yet to fight off an attacker.

Ashley tucked her hand under Allison's arm. "You're safe here," she whispered. "I promise. And you'll feel so much better when your parents arrive."

"I know. I just can't shake the feeling I'm being watched." She shivered.

"I understand. I didn't sleep well for months. Almost a year actually. Until I met Evan. The first night I agreed to give him a chance, he sat up all night next to me and I slept better than I had in five years. I still have nightmares now and then. But he's always there to pull me back to reality."

Allison smiled, but inside she wasn't sure she'd ever reach that point. She'd slept in the car both the past two nights, the steady rumble of the engine lulling her every time she bolted awake, but the idea of lying down in a bed and not having to worry about what tomorrow would bring evaded her. And she didn't have a mate to lean on like Ashley.

When they reached the row of cabins, Allison was glad hers was the first because her legs were threatening to buckle. Ashley helped her along, not releasing her arm. "You must be exhausted."

"I'm just weak. I haven't exercised in forever, and I never ate well."

"You'll be feeling more yourself in no time." Ashley squeezed her arm tighter. "Promise."

"Here we are." Kenzie opened the door and motioned for Allison to enter.

Allison passed under her arm and stepped inside. The cabin was more than she'd imagined. Basic. Simple. Rustic. And so inviting. Even for a city girl, she had to admit she loved it. The cabin she'd lived in for the last year hadn't been as equipped as this one. It was more of a run-down shack.

This place was small but had everything a person could need. The kitchenette had a small stove and oven combo, a microwave, a skinny refrigerator, and a table and four chairs. The living area was an extension of the kitchen with a fireplace, a plush beige couch, and two armchairs.

Allison followed Kenzie to the attached bedroom and peeked into the bathroom.

"It's small, but it sleeps four. The couch pulls out."

Allison smiled. It was pretty, and if she were any other person at any other time of life, she was sure she would love it. But she couldn't imagine sleeping in the cabin even one night. She felt claustrophobic just thinking about it after all the time she'd been in the woods in the middle of nowhere Minnesota. Even the night sounds of animals and birds had made her cringe. Those same sounds would accompany this cabin, and she didn't think she could stomach it.

What she longed for was the noisy bustle of city life. She needed horns and flashing lights to lull her to sleep and make her forget.

Kenzie headed back to the door. "Let's go back outside. It's so nice out today." She must have sensed Allison's unease.

"I'm sorry. I'm just…"

Ashley touched her hair. "You can be anything you need to be right now. It's totally understandable. If the cabin makes you uncomfortable, you don't have to explain yourself."

Allison's eyes watered. A tear escaped and trickled down her face.

Kenzie opened the door and light streamed in. Ashley led Allison out onto the tiny porch and helped her sit on the front steps. "I'm so sorry. I know it's hard. I'm here for you in any capacity you need." She sat next to her and stroked her hair.

"Thanks," Allison managed to murmur. "I'm just

overwhelmed, and I haven't quite grasped that I'm not there anymore."

"Of course." Ashley hugged Allison's shoulders. They sat like that for several minutes. Allison was grateful for the patience of her new friends. Both women were almost the same age as her, and she knew in another life, or maybe later in this life, she could be friends with them, but today she was still so shook up she could barely focus on their good intentions.

"Would you like to see the barn?" Kenzie asked.

Allison shook her head. "Not yet. I'm not up to adding large animals with hooves to my day." She smiled, knowing it was weak.

Kenzie chuckled. "No problem. You must be exhausted. We could leave you alone if you want to nap. If not here, back at the main house or even my place."

Allison turned toward the cabin and thought about their suggestion. Lying down sounded so inviting, but alone? In a small cabin? She didn't think she could do that, either.

"Or maybe you're hungry?" Ashley asked.

Allison grinned at her. "You've done nothing but feed me since I met you yesterday."

"Well, you've been withering away for months." She smiled back.

Allison shook her head. "I'm still full from breakfast on the way. But I might take you up on that nap." She nibbled her lower lip. "Maybe if I left the door open so the outside air and light came in."

"I'd be happy to sit out here on the porch while you sleep."

"Would you?"

"Of course. My pleasure."

Allison relaxed her shoulders. "I think I'll take you up on that." She pulled herself up from the step and turned to the cabin. "I'll just lie on the couch where I can see the front."

"Anything you want. Just yell if you need something."

"I need to get back and feed the baby before my chest explodes, anyway. I'm sure the little guy is screaming. I'm surprised we can't hear him from here," Kenzie said.

"Thank you." Allison blinked back tears, ducked inside, and headed for the inviting sofa. She wasn't sure she could sleep, but she knew she could at least lie and relax her body and her brain.

The day was already growing hot, but she pulled the soft throw blanket from the back of the couch and curled up on her side facing the open front door. She closed her eyes and took deep cleansing breaths. She didn't want to sob uncontrollably, but she was a ball of emotions. Her eyes wouldn't stop watering. Partly from the relief of having been rescued and partly from the incredible outpouring of support she'd received from so many people.

For a few minutes she could hear Ashley and Kenzie speaking, and then Kenzie must have left. She watched Ashley sitting on the front step for a while until her eyes grew heavy and she fell into sleep.

Evan took a seat at the long kitchen table across from the two men who had just arrived from Seattle. Everyone had vacated the house, and he was glad Ashley and the other women had gone on a tour of the property.

Steven Wightman was one of the five members of The Head Council, and it was no small thing that he'd come to Texas to meet with Evan. He and the leader of The Head Council, Ralph Jerard, had been the only two people privy to all the information Evan had been feeding them for months concerning this investigation.

Until now. As the date approached when they would seize the captives, they had expanded their mission to include about fifty members of NAR. It had been centuries since shifters needed to mobilize the small military group they maintained, and never for use against their own that anyone knew of.

Steven furrowed his brow as he sat. "This is Alex Marshall. I've brought him up to speed and he'll be working with us."

Evan nodded at Alex and shook his hand.

"So, tell us what's new."

"The mission was a success. All twelve women were rescued yesterday morning. They're all on their way here to reunite with their families, recuperate, and hopefully shed some light on what happened in each case."

"Good. We'll be here to help interview them this afternoon. I understand some of their captors were taken into custody?"

"A few, yes. Three were transported to Seattle."

"All right. Well, hopefully this is the breakthrough we needed." Steven thrummed his fingers on the tabletop, clearly concerned with the direction this case was taking.

Evan swallowed the lump forming in his throat. He'd known this was a huge conspiracy for almost a year. And he suspected the shit was about to fling around the room. "I do have some interesting information from Allison. She's the one rescued from Minnesota, and we drove her here this morning."

Steven leaned his elbows on the table. "Is there something different about her case?"

"Seems like it. She was the only one kept in isolation with no one around except one man left to guard her. He rarely said much and didn't claim to be her mate. In fact she was never raped."

Steven lifted one eyebrow. "Really? I thought all the women had been told they were mated to the man who took them."

"I did too. But that wasn't the case here. In fact the man who guarded her wasn't even the same one who swiped her from The Gathering. And there's more." Evan swallowed. "She seems to have been used for some sort of medical experiments. Every once in a while she was moved to another location she describes as being like a hospital."

Steven sat back, running a hand through his hair. "Jesus. What did they do to her?"

"That's another interesting thing. She doesn't know. They kept her drugged, and she only has flashes of memories of the place and the people. Nothing solid. It's like she has amnesia."

"That can't be good. Does she know where the place was or how far from the cabin?"

Evan shook his head. "No. Not a clue. And in addition, they must want her pretty badly because the men who rescued her got caught in a rain of gunfire getting her off the property. They escaped on the run, but just barely. One of them was hit."

"And there were no problems with any of the other rescues?" Alex asked.

"Nope. Not a single issue." Evan sincerely hoped to find that some of the others had not been raped, either.

CHAPTER 4

Daniel finished brushing Sadie and exited the stable. He felt rejuvenated after the long run, but glanced around, wondering what sort of trouble he was going to be in with his mother for abandoning ship this morning. Luckily he didn't see too many cars out front, which meant most of their guests hadn't arrived.

Perhaps he hadn't been missed yet. He scanned the area and spotted a woman sitting on the front porch of the first cabin. She might be Allison, their first guest, but it seemed odd she would already be sitting there by herself.

Daniel headed in her direction when she waved. She stood and stepped away from the cabin to meet him. He realized as he approached she was mated and pregnant. Not Allison, then. "Hello." He held out his hand. "I'm Daniel."

She took his offered palm. "Ashley. My mate and I drove here from St. Louis with Allison Watkins."

"Ah, right. I forgot you were coming. Kenzie told us about you. How are you feeling?" He glanced at her belly. Newly pregnant shifters always made him feel awkward. They weren't like humans. Wolves knew when a woman was pregnant, so the stigma of not presuming didn't exist.

"Great. Thanks." She smiled.

He knew she'd also been kidnapped from The Gathering, and the bits and pieces of her story made him want to vomit, but she looked so healthy and happy he tried to ignore her plight. If she could move on with her life, he needed to get over himself too. After all, twelve women were about to descend on the ranch, all of whom would have horror stories of their own. He needed to be supportive.

"Why are you out here by yourself?" He noticed the door open behind Ashley.

"Allison's napping. I told her I'd sit out here while she slept to give her peace of mind."

"Ah. Very nice of you."

"She's pretty shook up. Understandably so."

"And your mate? Evan, right? He's with you?"

"Yes. He's in the main house. I assume some of your brothers are there now."

"Probably. I've been out riding." He nodded at the house. "I'd better go check in before they send out a search party. It was nice to meet you."

"You too."

Daniel turned and started to walk away, but after two steps, he froze. He lifted his chin to the air and closed his eyes as he inhaled long and slow. His body went rigid, and he fisted his hands at his sides as he inhaled again.

Someone behind him gasped. And a tiny voice he hadn't heard before spoke. "Shit."

Daniel spun around.

Ashley was still there, but her eyes were huge and wide, and her mouth hung open. "Oh," she muttered. She glanced back and forth between Daniel and the woman who'd approached from behind Ashley.

His gaze slid to the newcomer. She stood on the tiny porch as rigid as he'd felt, her arms at her sides, her brow furrowed, the sweetest red line running down her pale cheek from sleeping on that side. Gorgeous blond curls hung down her back, some falling over her shoulders. She was underweight, frail, scared, shaking. Beautiful. And his.

"Shit," she repeated under her breath.

He smiled at her. Ashley stepped to the side several paces and ceased to exist.

"Unexpected, yes. But surely you can come up with something more enthusiastic than 'shit'," he teased.

Her mouth opened and her eyes widened. "I didn't realize I'd said that out loud."

He nodded. "You did." He stepped closer, but she backed up a pace into the doorway, so he stopped. "You must be Allison."

"I am." She took a deep breath. And held it. Her eyes fluttered closed on her exhale. "Shit."

"You have a rich wealth of vocabulary." He grinned at her.

Her eyes popped open again. "I— I'm sorry. I—"

"No worries. I'm kidding you. It's shocking. I agree. I'm Daniel Spencer, by the way."

Ashley cleared her throat to his side. "I'm going to go back to the main house. I think..." She turned and left without finishing her statement. Daniel didn't glance her way.

"This can't be happening," Allison said. She fisted her hands together in front of her and squeezed one with the other. She eased forward until she plopped down on the front steps of the cabin.

Daniel worried she would fall before she sat, but he gritted his teeth and let her lower herself to the step on her own. She wasn't remotely ready for him to approach.

She set her elbows on her knees and her head in her hands.

"It's not exactly what I had in mind for today, either. I'm sorry to shock you." He shook his head to clear his mind. *This is a woman who's been held hostage for a year in the remote woods of Minnesota. You're freaking her out.*

He couldn't bring himself to walk away, though. And besides, no way would he just leave her sitting there alone.

Her entire body shook.

He ached to hold her and tell her everything would be okay. But for her, the world was not okay right now, and the last thing she needed was a man getting in her space and pressuring her.

Deep breaths, Daniel. Think.

Unchartered territory had him floundering for words that wouldn't come. He opened and closed his mouth several times before he spoke again. "Don't panic." He backed up a step. He could tell she was close to hyperventilating. "It's going to be okay." *Somehow. Right?*

He wasn't sure he believed his own words. Suddenly nothing was okay. Not even for him. He wasn't in a place in life to take on a mate. He was committed to the North American Reserves for the foreseeable future. Having a mate didn't fit into that plan. Too much was happening in the world today. He felt a calling to help the cause, not to mate.

Except there was no denying what lay in front of his eyes. Her scent would haunt him. He had no choice. This was what Fate had dropped on his doorstep, and he had to face his new reality all wrapped up in the least tidy of packaging ever.

She lifted her face, her eyes red and huge. "Nothing about me is 'okay'. I haven't even wrapped my mind around the fact that I've been rescued. I haven't seen my parents yet."

"We'll deal with it. Everything. One minute at a time." He crouched in front of her to bring his face to her level. He remained several yards away, though he ached to inch closer.

She shook her head. "There can't be a 'we'. I'm not ready. I'm not even sure who I am right now." She looked away.

His chest squeezed tight as though she'd gripped it with her fist and yanked his heart out. Common sense told him she was in pain and unable to deal with this explosion of information right now. And she had every right to be. But still he swallowed the hurt. *Man up, dude. This mate of yours needs space and time. Don't take it personally.*

Voices behind him made him stand and back up several steps. He turned to find his mother approaching, Kenzie behind her holding the baby. He kept backing up. Allison would get the comfort she needed from his family. He had no choice but to step away and let them take over. For now. His legs literally ached with each step, but he forced them to move. He met his mother's gaze as she approached and pleaded with her to help his mate.

She nodded, a wan smile that didn't reach her eyes expressing her sorrow at his predicament.

Words weren't needed. Ashley would have told them what had occurred. And even if she hadn't, any wolf would smell the mating call on approach.

As his mother passed and took a seat next to Allison, Kenzie touched his arm with her free hand. He lifted his gaze to meet his brother's mate. She had the same look on her face as his mother.

He swallowed. "I'll be at my place." And he turned and walked away, desperately trying not to think about the fact that he'd left his heart behind on that porch.

~

Allison shook. She couldn't control the shivers that climbed up her spine and down her arms. She trembled as if she had a fever. She crossed her arms to hold them against her body and tried to breathe through the intensity of emotion washing over her. Natalie said something next to her, but she couldn't hear a word.

She felt like she was underwater. Perhaps Natalie was speaking to Kenzie, who stepped closer and kneeled in front of Allison. She held the baby close to her chest.

Allison only knew one thing. Daniel was her mate and he'd just left. In fact she'd chased him off with her mouth. Relief and sorrow warred inside her, fighting for control.

Part of her wanted to run after him and breathe in his scent some more. It was calming. Even though she was scared out of her mind, his presence had been soothing.

Another part of her demanded she run in the opposite direction. Get in a car and drive away to anywhere but here.

Natalie set a hand gently on Allison's shoulder and her words penetrated. "Honey?"

Allison turned her gaze to the kind woman who would be a part of her life forever now. *At least you know your mate's family is nice.* If Natalie was a good representative of the rest of the clan, Allison could be sure of good in-laws.

She shook her head. What was she thinking? She couldn't mate now. It was absurd. She swallowed. "I'm fine. I just need…" She had no idea what. A reverse in time to five minutes ago before she met her mate would be a good start.

"I'm so sorry. I know this wasn't in your plans for today," Kenzie said. She reached forward with her free hand and set it on Allison's knee. "You have so much on your mind."

Natalie nodded. "Let's deal with one thing at a time. Your parents will be here any minute. Why don't we head to the main house, and then when they get here, you can spend some time with them alone. I'll talk to Daniel. Tell him to give you some space for now. Okay?"

Allison turned to face Natalie. "Is it that simple?" Somehow Allison's racing heart and sweaty palms knew better.

The woman smiled. "No. It's complicated. But like I said, let's take it one step at a time. You need time with your family first and foremost." She stood, taking a limp Allison with her. She was so kind, keeping her arm around Allison on the walk back to the house.

When they entered through the back door, the place was quiet. The only person inside was a man who looked like an older version of Daniel.

He beamed when he turned to Allison. "Allison. So nice to meet you. I'm Jerome." Instead of taking her hand in greeting, he pulled her into his huge embrace and held her.

It was awkward. Her own father wasn't as affectionate with her as Jerome. But the discomfort she expected never came to surface.

He pulled her back to arm's length and met her gaze. "Welcome. Anything you need, you let me know, okay?"

She nodded, silently. Tears threatened again for the millionth time in two days. She glanced down.

"I'll leave you women alone." With that he released her and stepped out the back door.

Now that Allison was back in the main house, she could smell Daniel's scent everywhere. She almost moaned. There would be no escaping him. "I think I'll go out front and wait." She stepped away from Kenzie and Natalie without looking at them, heading through the kitchen and living room and out onto the front porch. She finally inhaled slowly, long and deep. At least in the open air she was able to breathe easier without the world filling her senses with her mate's pheromones.

Kenzie joined her, still cradling the baby. She sat on the porch swing.

Allison decided to sit next to her.

"Would you like to hold him?" Kenzie offered the squirming bundle to Allison.

For the first time Allison peered into his sweet face and almost melted. Babies could bring a person to their knees. Aaron's puckered face and baby scent would do wonders for her rattled nerves. "I'd love to." She took the swaddled child from his mother and held him against her chest. She brought her lips to his forehead, inhaled deeply, and kissed his soft newborn skin. "How old is he?"

"Four weeks tomorrow."

"He's so tiny." As she spoke, his hand broke loose from the blanket and flailed in the air. Allison set her index finger in his palm and he gripped her tight. She smiled. God, it felt good to smile. Her face hurt from so many months with nothing happy to live for. "Aren't you a strong little fellow?"

"He likes you."

Allison giggled. "How would you know that?"

"He isn't screaming," Kenzie teased. "You're a winner."

Allison lifted her gaze. "Thank you." She sobered. "For everything."

"Anytime." Kenzie touched her arm. "I'm here for you. I know I can't begin to imagine what you've been through, and there will be twelve women here shortly who can relate, including Ashley, but in the long run, we'll be like sisters, and I can't tell you how relieved I am to have someone else around to commiserate with against the testosterone."

Allison swallowed. "I can't stay here," she muttered. She shook her head. "It's too…quiet. I'm a city girl. I need my noise. Car horns. Screaming children. Flashing lights."

Kenzie didn't comment. She set her hand over Allison's and rested it there on top of the baby.

"Can I ignore the calling?" Allison lifted her gaze.

"I don't know. I attempted it myself and failed. Moving here wasn't on my short list of things to do last year, either. But denying my feelings for Drake wasn't possible."

"But people do it, right?"

"I guess. I've not met anyone who did, though."

Tears fell down Allison's cheeks unchecked and blurred her vision. "This wasn't in the plans," she whispered. "I had a life and I want to go back to it. To New York. To my family. To my job… Hell, I probably don't have a job anymore. What am I talking about?"

"What did you do?"

"I was a nanny to two sweet kids. More than a nanny. I was their teacher too. Their parents were bigwigs on Wall Street and had more money than time. I loved them." New tears broke free. Ashley finally wiped them on her shoulder.

"Sounds like the best job."

"It was. Obviously they would have replaced me by now." *Not that losing my job would stop me from returning to New York.*

Just then a car pulled up the long drive and stopped in front of the house. Allison willed it to contain her parents. So much so that she was stunned to find them actually exiting the vehicle. When they spotted her on the porch, they both froze. Her mother released a sob.

Kenzie took the baby from Allison. "Go." She nodded toward Allison's parents.

Allison bolted from the porch swing and raced down the steps. She flung herself at her mother and squeezed her. Even her father wrapped his arm around the women as they hugged and cried.

When her mother finally released her and held her at arm's length to look at her face, Allison smiled. "I can't believe you're here."

"We can't believe *you're* here," her mother replied. "We've been so worried for so long." She stepped back a pace, not releasing Allison's arms. "Are you okay?"

"I'm fine."

"You've lost weight."

"I'll gain it back." She was hurting, but right now she needed to reassure her mother she would live. And she knew she would.

Her mother threaded her fingers in Allison's curls. "Your hair is so long."

Allison nodded. "It needs a cut. That's for sure."

"I like it. You've never worn it this long."

"Tames the curls, that's for sure." Why were they discussing hair?

The front door opened behind them, and Allison turned to find Natalie approaching. "You must be Geoff and Holly Watkins." She extended a hand to Allison's father. "Welcome. Nice to meet you."

"Thank you for having us here." He glanced around. "It looks so serene."

"Thank you. We love it. Come inside. I'll get you something to drink."

Allison balked. No way could she endure the scent of her mate inside that house right now, and she wasn't ready to tell her parents what had happened this morning. She wanted to enjoy them all to herself for a while first. "I was thinking we could go for a walk maybe." She looked toward Natalie. "Which direction would be good?"

Bless the woman for reading her mind. She nodded and pointed to the right. "If you head down this path, you'll come to Drake and Kenzie's house first, and then you can circle around toward the cabins. Why don't you show your parents where you'll be staying? I'll have one of the boys bring their luggage up there. Jerome or Scott," she added.

So far Allison had only met Daniel, but Natalie understood her predicament and that's all that mattered. "Perfect." She wrapped her mother's arm in her own and headed toward the gravel road next to the house. "Daddy. You coming?" she called over her shoulder.

Daniel paced the living room of his house until he figured the hardwood floor would be worn under his feet. He didn't care.

A knock at the door jarred him from his path. He yanked the door open and found his father standing on the porch. "May I come in?"

Daniel stood back. *Would it matter if I said no?*

"Your mother told me what happened."

Daniel nodded.

"I thought you might want to talk about it."

"No."

His father sat on the black leather couch, leaned back, and crossed his legs. "I could send Drake."

Daniel moaned. "God. Please no." He faced his father and took a seat in the matching black leather armchair. "The thought makes me want to vomit."

His father chuckled. "I know it's been a crazy year adjusting to him mating, but at least it's happened to him recently enough he might have some advice."

"I don't need advice. And Drake would have way too much to go around." For months Drake had spoken of little else besides mating. Not that McKenzie wasn't a fantastic woman, but it got old after a while.

"Allison is in a tough situation."

"No shit." Daniel set his head in his hands and threaded his hair through his fingers.

"So, if you don't need any advice, what's your plan exactly?"

"I don't have one. It seems pretty cut and dry to me. There's no way Allison is in a position to be claimed right now, and to do anything toward that aim would be crass."

"I'm not suggesting you pressure her in any way, but you could at least woo her. Court her."

Daniel laughed as he lifted his face to see his father's expression. "Did you just say 'woo' and 'court'? What year is this?"

"Laugh all you want, but women like to be pursued in a way that doesn't make them feel like they have no choices. Is the timing good for Allison? Hell, no. But Fate has her reasons. The timing is rarely ideal for anyone. All I'm suggesting is for you to make yourself available to her in a way that isn't threatening or pushy. Get to know her. Let her get to know you. You'll need to take things at her pace. She's hurting right now."

Daniel nodded. Maybe his father's advice was sound. Sitting there feeling like punching Fate in the face wasn't doing anyone any good.

"Her parents arrived. Why don't you go introduce yourself and give them a tour of the stable or something? Three other families arrived also. It's going to get busy around here."

"Was that Mom's suggestion?" Daniel lifted an eyebrow.

His father shook his head. "Not even close." He grinned.

Daniel smiled. "Did she send you?"

"Yes, with specific instructions about what to say. I might have altered it a bit."

"I can imagine." Daniel shook his head. "I think I'll give it a day or two. Let her get her bearings."

"And you should talk to Drake. Not just Drake, but Kenzie. I know the idea of getting girl advice from your brother makes you cringe, but they've only been mated a year. The memory of meeting each other is still fresh in their minds."

"Yeah." Daniel hung his head. He dreaded the idea of discussing how he felt with his brother, but his dad was right. However, there was another side to this coin. "I have obligations to the North American Reserves. Besides the fact that I'm committed to protecting shifters and our way of life, I'm not at liberty to just bail now. Bringing a mate along for that ride seems cruel and distracting."

"People do it every day, though, Daniel. Humans and shifters marry and mate in the midst of military obligations. Even those who don't have Fate choosing their loved ones make it work. And you can too."

It was true. Daniel couldn't deny the logic. But he worried about the level of distraction a woman would pose for him. Physical and emotional. Already after spending just minutes with her and not even touching her, he needed her like he needed oxygen. He wasn't stupid. He knew that drive to mate would increase over time. He could control himself, but it wouldn't be easy.

Henry grabbed his cell before it finished the first ring. "Yes." That was all he needed to say. The caller ID told him the call was from his superior, whoever that was. All he knew was the guy worked at the headquarters for The Head Council. He was their main inside man. Perhaps he was even *the* main leader.

"I've done some digging. These bastards at The Head Council organized that sting. They have gotten very powerful, and they're expanding. They're enlisting more shifters to NAR every day and mobilizing as we speak. I don't want this shit to get out."

"I understand, sir." *I understand, but what the fuck do you want me to do about it?*

"It's too soon. We aren't ready... Fuck." He sounded winded, as though he hadn't thought this out before he called.

"What would you like me to do, sir?"

"Get a man out to get a visual on Allison Watkins. She's at a dude ranch in Texas. I'll send you the address. We need to go in and get her ASAP. Figure out exactly where she's staying and all the details surrounding her location."

"Get her? You want us to kidnap her back?" *What the fuck?*

"Yes. But for now, just gather the information. We don't want to alert anyone to our plan. She's vital to the mission. We need her and we need her damn mouth shut. The longer she's with those people, the better the chance is she might remember details we don't need exposed. And Henry…"

"Yes, sir?"

"Get on this fast, Fairfield. Time is of the essence. I'll get you the manpower. You get me the deets."

"Okay, sir."

"The rest of the women taken from us should be there also. I want Allison Watkins back. We'll decide about the others soon."

"I'm on it, sir."

The line went dead.

Henry dialed the next number and drummed his fingers on the desk as he waited for Tarson to pick up on his end. It wasn't until the fourth ring that the man finally answered. "Hello?"

"Tarson. You had me worried there for a moment."

"Sorry. I was in the other room. Is everything okay?"

"Not even close." He stretched his neck to both sides as he continued. "I need you to do a job, and I need you to keep it completely to yourself."

"Okaaay." Tarson dragged that word out as if it were absurd to even question his allegiance. "Have I ever let you down?"

"No. But this is important and confidential." Henry had spoken many times to his superior and thought long and hard before choosing Tarson for this job.

The fact that Tarson had been working for the Romulus for several years and had an impeccable record made the selection that much easier. The man had always been trustworthy and reliable. Hiring him had been a good decision.

"There's a dude ranch in Texas I need you to spy on. I need some information about who's there and what's happening."

"Sure thing, boss. When?"

"Immediately."

"Okay. What am I looking for?"

"A dozen women. I'll send you information on all of them—pictures and data. The most important one is a woman named Allison Watkins. I need to know if she's among the others. A visual is mandatory."

"Got it. But why the hell would anyone care about a bunch of women?"

The one bad thing about Tarson was his inquisitiveness. Henry would love it if the man would simply do a job, no questions asked. But that wasn't his style, so Henry had called prepared. He knew Tarson well enough to play into his hand perfectly.

"These women banded together to conspire against their mates and abandoned their homes and their duties."

"Are you fucking with me?"

"Nope. They even stole money from their mates to get away. And now they're gallivanting around living the high life on a ranch in Texas."

"God damn. The gall. How did you find them?"

Henry smiled to himself. "They're women. They're too stupid not to leave a paper trail. Several of the men found evidence of their plot."

Tarson gave a sardonic chuckle. "Of course. Ignorant. All of them. No worries. Send me the details and I'll be on my way."

"Good. Oh, and Tarson?"

"Yeah."

"Be super careful. I'm not sure who they may be with or what they may have told the shifters they're with. After all the lies they've woven, I wouldn't be surprised if they've come up with some damn sob stories about being abused. They may even have protection."

"Got it. I'll make sure no one sees me."

"I knew I could count on you."

"Absolutely."

CHAPTER 5

Allison sat on the steps of the front porch of her cabin, cupping a mug of coffee and watching the steam rise in the cooler morning air. It wouldn't stay that way. If today was anything like yesterday, it would be hotter than hell before noon. And she loved it. After spending the last year in the middle of nowhere without enough clothes to keep her warm in the cooler climate of Minnesota, she couldn't get enough of the heat. It seemed to be metaphorically warming her soul from the inside out.

She lifted her gaze to scan the horizon. It was early, but several people were already outside their cabins. All the cabins were full now that the other women and their families had arrived. And several people were staying in the dorm. It had been easy for the Spencers to choose. The ten families with fewer than four people occupied the small cabins and the two larger families were in the dorm.

Ashley and Evan were staying with Kenzie and Drake. They would only be there for the first week. The others were welcome to stay as long as they'd like.

Allison could see the appeal. The Head Council had provided several counselors to work with the women and families, and Allison had spent the entire day after her arrival in large and small group meetings getting to know the others. There was no doubt the plan to bring everyone together had been sound. The solidarity was healing in and of itself.

Each woman had a different story and experience, but in the end, they were united in the fact that they'd been taken against their will or under false pretenses and drugged.

All the woman had given blood samples the first night to help determine what was in their bloodstream, but apparently no one expected the results to be surprising.

Everyone had also met individually with Evan and two members of The Head Council. Until then, Allison hadn't been quite sure what his role was in this grand scheme other than being the mate of a previously rescued victim.

The reality was Evan was heading up the investigation to determine what underlying conspiracy was at work. He'd been the one to rescue Ashley in the first place, and he'd worked for months for The Head Council to track other missing women and organize the collective rescue this week.

What Allison hadn't done yet was allow herself to deal with the reality of Daniel. She had yet to tell her parents. Thankfully no one in the Spencer family had breathed a word of her predicament. But Allison knew she needed to tell her parents. She couldn't hide out forever, even with good reason. And Daniel couldn't be expected to stay away forever, either. She could feel the weight of her mating pressing in on her.

She'd spent two days with her parents. It was time to come clean.

Daniel deserved a face-to-face confrontation, even if in the end she told him to take a hike. To do otherwise would be unimaginable. Already she was impressed with him for giving her time and space to reacquaint herself with her parents.

The door behind her squeaked as it opened and closed. She could sense her mother without turning around. The woman eased next to her on the step. "You're up early." She also held a cup of coffee.

"I'm not fond of the inside of the cabin, to be honest."

"I see."

"It makes me feel like I'm strangling."

They sat in silence for a few minutes. Allison listened to the gentle noises of the farm. It was nothing like the city and still too quiet for her, but she did have to recognize the appeal of the sounds of the birds, the trees rustling, the whinny of horses in the distance. "I need to tell you something."

"Okay, honey. Anything." Her mother put an arm around Allison and squeezed before releasing her again to hold her coffee with both hands.

Allison took a deep breath. "I met my mate."

Her mother gasped. "When? Where?"

"Here. As soon as I arrived. He's Natalie's second oldest. Daniel is his name."

"Oh. No wonder I haven't met him. Where is he?"

"Not sure. But God bless him for letting me have this time with you. I couldn't have faced him that first day. He backed off and has given me space. At least that's what I'm imagining. Probably Natalie had a hand in it."

"That is kind. But isn't it tearing you up inside?"

"Yes." Allison ducked her head and stared at her feet. There was no denying the physical reaction she'd had to him and still did, even though she'd only seen him for a few minutes two days ago. She'd been busy every minute since her parents had arrived, and that had kept her mind from straying to the sexy man who'd kneeled in front of her and smiled so warmly. That one image kept her awake at night, tossing and turning.

"Don't you think you need to go talk to him?"

"Yes." She shuffled her toe against the bottom step. "I've been sitting here building up the courage. I wanted you to know where I was going before I left."

Holly turned to face her daughter. "Go. We'll be here if you need us. We can only stay a few more days, anyway." Her voice lowered. "I hadn't considered you not returning to New York with us, but…"

"And I can't, either." Allison lifted her gaze. "I need to go home. I crave the chaos. It's too quiet here and I miss my busy lifestyle."

Holly smiled. "Well, Fate sometimes puts a wrench in things."

"I see that." Allison stood. She wiped her hands on her jean shorts. She stared at her mother for several seconds before she backed away with a short nod.

When she turned to face the stable, she took a deep breath. She knew instinctively he was in there. She hadn't seen him since that first morning, but Kenzie had told her he was often with his horses and would use the barn as a refuge to escape his problems.

One foot in front of the other and minutes later Allison stood outside the entrance to the stable. She paused, lifting her face to the rising sun. Nothing about this situation was in her realm of comprehension. She wasn't fond of large animals. Had never been on or near a horse. And didn't want a mate this week.

The moment her mate stepped out of the barn, however, she knew it immediately. She lowered her gaze to his and bit her lower lip between her teeth.

He stood still for several seconds before he shuffled forward a few feet. "Hi."

"Hi," she repeated, feeling like a middle school student with a crush. Her heart pounded, and she wiped her sweaty hands on her shorts again. She glanced down at herself and wondered why she hadn't taken a moment to make herself at least somewhat more attractive for this second meeting.

The clothes she wore came from Kenzie, bless her. The woman insisted she'd never be that small again after delivering Aaron. Allison doubted that, but she was still grateful. It was already hot for nine o'clock in the morning, and the pale blue tank top Allison wore hugged her body so tight she worried her nipples were visible.

Daniel approached slowly until he stood about three feet away. He stuffed his hands in his jeans pockets. His boots were worn and scuffed. His black T-shirt was tight around his chest. He looked like a total cowboy, and while Allison never would have imagined herself attracted to a man in boots, she lusted after this one full force.

So…masculine.

He cleared his throat. "I was going to come find you this morning."

She finally lifted her gaze to his face. "Beat you."

He softened at her words, the wrinkle in his brow evening out. When his mouth turned up, a dimple made itself present on both cheeks. He was tan from spending time in the sun, his hair just a shade darker than her own blond curls, probably bleached from the sun also. And his eyes, when she met his gaze, pierced her with their deep blue depths.

He nodded behind him. "Can I show you around?"

Allison took a step forward. "Yes, but I have to warn you, I know nothing about horses or any other farm life."

"No worries." He turned and she followed.

He says that now…

As they entered the wide-open doors to the barn, Allison paused to adjust to the lower light. She braced herself for the onslaught of what the barn would smell like, but she was pleasantly surprised. Either barns didn't smell as bad as she expected, or Daniel's personal scent was overpowering her senses and blocking out all else.

Probably the latter, since Allison knew only one thing—Daniel Spencer flipped her world upside down. As he walked in front of her, she stared at his ass. Firm and sexy. She wanted to grab it, and she clenched her hands into fists to keep from doing so.

His back was all rows of muscle and strength. His T-shirt did nothing to hide his physique.

When he turned toward her, she almost ran into him. She'd been so focused on his body. A flush heated her cheeks as he reached out a hand and grabbed her shoulder to steady her. He grinned. "You okay?"

It was the first time he'd touched her. *Hell no, I'm not okay.*

Electricity zinged down her spine from his contact. She squeezed her legs together at the immediate jolt to her sex. And she had to concentrate to breathe evenly. Every inhale brought more of him into her lungs and spread through her system.

He released her with a jerk as though he'd been shocked. "Wow." He stepped back and leaned against the stall next to him. "My brother mentioned what it was like, but I didn't believe him."

"Yeah, I've spoken to Kenzie a few times myself." Allison stepped back a pace, as much for self-preservation as anything. If she could just remove herself from his personal space…

Nope. That wasn't working. He'd gotten not just under her skin, but inside her somehow. She couldn't put words to the sensation. What she wanted to do was lean into him and bury her face in his neck. She wanted to grab his shirt with both hands and pull him closer.

But she wasn't that kind of girl. Or hadn't been.

Daniel righted himself and pushed off from the wall. He reached for her hand slowly and covered it with his own. She thought he was going to pull her along with him down the row of stalls, but instead he lifted her hand to his cheek and stroked his face with the back of it.

Allison sucked in a gasp. Touching him again wasn't helping. The shock was still there. Maybe worse. Her entire body shook, tremors she couldn't control.

He pulled her closer, seemingly unable to stop himself, his gaze locked on hers. When her chest landed on his, she braced herself against him with her free hand. And God, his pecs…

He was a wall of muscle. Solid.

"I couldn't shake your scent from my mind after we met the other day," he whispered. He inhaled deeply and set his forehead against hers until their eyes were too close to really see each other properly. "I haven't slept well. I know the timing sucks, but…"

But what? She held her breath.

He didn't finish. Instead he held her shoulder with his free hand and stepped back. "Let me show you around." He'd already said that. So far all she'd seen were his pecs and his fine ass. If there was a barn surrounding her, she was nearly oblivious.

He didn't release her hand. He threaded his fingers between hers and started shuffling backward. Allison followed. It took forever. "So, this is the barn…" she teased.

"Yep." He winked. "There are some horses in each of these stalls we pass."

"Figured that."

"The last one is Sadie. She's my favorite. We're going to ride her."

"We?" Allison stopped, her arm pulling tight when Daniel didn't.

He tipped his head to one side and gave a wry grin. "Yeah. Don't worry. I'll hold on to you."

She shook her head, almost without meaning to. "I, um…not so much." She bit her bottom lip, curling it between her teeth.

Daniel chuckled. "No worries. Sadie is the gentlest soul you'll ever meet." He tugged, forcing her to continue forward. "You'll love her in no time." He finally stopped at the last stall in the back of the barn.

Allison was vaguely aware of other people around her, undoubtedly working, but she never glanced in their direction. She looked to the left when Daniel released her hand and opened the half door to the stall. As he entered, she gripped the wood across the top of the door and watched him.

Sadie was huge as far as Allison was concerned. And gorgeous. But that didn't make Allison want to ride her. Or even climb up onto her back.

She was a solid dark brown and her ears twitched when Daniel rubbed her back. He made a click with his tongue and took her reins to lead her from the stall.

When he had her in the center of the aisle, Allison plastered herself against the wall.

She wasn't exactly afraid of the horse. More like uninformed. Up close and personal like this, she couldn't breathe. She was majestic and barely flinched while Daniel put a saddle on her and cinched it tight. He glanced at Allison every few seconds. "You really aren't fond of horses."

She shook her head and then licked her lips. "It's not so much that I don't like them. It's just that..." *What, exactly?*

"Trust me?" He reached for her again.

That was a loaded question. In her soul she knew she trusted this stranger with her life, but he was really asking her to trust Sadie, and she wasn't as sure about that.

As though he'd read her mind, he spoke again. "Sadie hasn't ever met a person she didn't like, and she's never tossed anyone yet."

Good to know...

"Ready?" He didn't give her time to think. He wrapped his hands around her waist, and before she knew it, he'd swung her up onto the saddle. She held her breath and grabbed the horn between her legs. Seconds later, Daniel swung up behind her. *Oh God.*

Allison squeezed her eyes shut and stifled a groan. She was barely aware of the horse. All she knew in that moment was Daniel's firm body pressed against her back and her pussy against the saddle horn.

Daniel wrapped one arm around her just under her breasts and held her closer. His nose met her ear. "On second thought, maybe this wasn't such a good idea. Your pheromones are driving me crazy, woman." He nipped her ear with his teeth and then kissed it.

Allison thought she would faint. She held the horn with both hands, squeezing so tight her knuckles turned white. She didn't know for sure if she held on to avoid falling or to keep her pussy from rubbing against the leather.

"Next time, maybe not sandals for riding," he said, nudging her legs and pointing at her feet.

"I didn't exactly leave the cabin with riding in mind."

"What did you have in mind?"

She didn't answer him. Her hands lurched from the horn to his thighs as he clicked with his tongue and Sadie headed for the door.

He was touching her in too many places. Her mind went to mush as she tried to concentrate on how high off the ground she was and the clip-clop motion that made her body sway back and forth as they left the barn. It was useless. All she knew were the places Daniel touched her. Her breasts bobbed above his arm, grazing his forearm over and over. His fingers kept touching her bare arm as he held her. His chest was like a rock behind her, and she couldn't avoid plastering herself to him without rubbing her clit into the saddle.

And that maddening horn was doing a number on her. What the hell did they put those things there for?

She held his thighs with both hands, digging her nails into his jeans for support.

Allison tried to look around as they left the stable and turned to head toward a trail behind the building.

The day had been hot. Now she was steaming. And she doubted it had anything to do with the temperature.

"You okay?" he whispered.

She nodded, a brief, sharp jerk of her head.

"Tell me about yourself."

Now? She couldn't think, let alone talk.

He chuckled into her ear. "I know you're from New York and you don't care for horses. What else?"

She swallowed and released his thighs to hold on to his forearm. "My favorite color is purple?"

He laughed again. She loved the sound of it, his chest rumbling at her back. "Okay. Okay. You can elaborate on that later."

Thank God.

~

Daniel held his mate tight, far tighter than strictly necessary, but he couldn't help himself. She smelled so fantastic, like summer. Her shampoo was fruity and only masked her personal scent slightly. Her skin was so soft on her neck he couldn't stop from rubbing his nose and lips across the space behind her ear. And she shivered every time.

She held him with iron fingers. He couldn't decide if she was afraid she might fall or afraid she wouldn't. Either way, his idea of taking her riding was one of his best-laid plans.

Now if he could just convince her to relax a little.

When he had cleared the area around the barn, he tapped Sadie with his ankles to move into a trot.

Soon the breeze blew across his face and cooled his heated skin. He was burning everywhere he touched his little mate, and he had no interest in alleviating that burn.

"She's so calm. Gentle." Allison patted the horse's mane awkwardly with one hand.

"She's used to working with children with disabilities. All of our horses are gentle and tame."

They came to a clearing. "Whoa, girl." He patted Sadie as they came to a stop.

"What's the matter?" Allison asked.

"Nothing." He kissed her temple and then swung his leg over the saddle to dismount. When he reached for Allison's waist and lifted her down, her eyes widened. "I thought this would be a good place to relax. Get to know each other. Without being interrupted." He turned back to the saddle, releasing Allison and regretting it immediately.

But he couldn't very well continue to hold her and retrieve the blanket he'd secured to the back of the saddle. He lifted it into the air and shook it out so that it fluttered to the ground, spreading open enough for them to sit on it.

When Daniel glanced back at Allison, he found her rigid and biting her lower lip. Her legs were crossed, pinched together. "Allie? I didn't mean to imply I intended to claim you right here right now. I just thought it was peaceful here."

She didn't move, but her gaze landed on his.

He lifted both hands in surrender. "I swear. I won't pressure you in any way."

"What if that's what I want you to do?" she muttered, her face going red.

He smiled and sat on the blanket before his legs gave out and caused him to fall. He leaned back on his hands. "Well, there is that. Not here, though. I mean, that's not what I intended anyway." He couldn't seem to draw in enough oxygen, as though Allison were sucking all of it out of the air and leaving him none.

She finally eased up to him and sat cross-legged at his side, facing him. At that proximity with her legs spread open, he could smell every nuance of her. She was aroused. Not that he wasn't. His dick had started aching the moment he'd found her outside the barn.

But it was different for Allie. She was wet. And the smell of her sex permeated the clearing.

He tried to breathe shallower to no avail. He reached for her face and tucked a lock of hair behind one ear. "May I call you Allie?"

Allison smiled. "Just you. No one else calls me that. But I like it coming from you."

He melted a little more. Seconds ticked by while he stared into the depths of her sky blue eyes. They were such a clear color he thought he could see into her soul. And it poured out of her gaze in any case. *Is this how it is for all mates?*

She opened her mouth to speak, and when she finally broke the awkward barrier between them, she spilled a litany of words into the space separating them. "I'm conflicted. There are so many thoughts racing through my mind, I can't grab one long enough to ponder it.

"On the one hand, I'm so attracted to you, I can't see straight." She glanced down at her lap and fiddled with the bottom edge of her shirt.

Daniel held still, letting her get it all out.

"Everything they say about mates is true. My heart is threatening to beat out of my chest. My hands are sweaty. My brain is fuddled. You smell fantastic, like clean straw and whatever soap you used." She flushed as she spoke, not looking at him directly most of the time.

"I want to do things I've never wanted so bad in my life." Now she fisted her hands in her lap. "But…"

Ah, the gauntlet. Daniel stiffened.

"I can't picture where we end up after the frenzy. I mean it's so beautiful here and it's your home. But it's not my home. I need noise and traffic and crazy people fighting in the street. I've never spent this much time in such silence. It's…disconcerting." She lifted her gaze to his. "You belong here like the Mona Lisa belongs in the center of Leonardo da Vinci's canvas. This is your home. You wouldn't be you if you left." She bit her lower lip again, and he wanted to kiss it, stroke it with his tongue until she relaxed.

Daniel watched her shoulders ease marginally as she finished, like a small piece of the weight of the world had been lifted by spilling all her thoughts into the air.

He cleared his throat. "You haven't said anything that hasn't gone through my mind. Believe me. And I don't have all the answers. And I know you've been through a lot. Hell, I don't even know the entire story of where you've been and what happened to you. But I have spoken to my brother Drake, and I do know that trying to avoid the Call will get us nowhere fast.

"It isn't something we can ignore. So all those questions we have, we're just going to have to sort through them together one at a time and find the answers."

"Do you have to be so damn practical?" She grinned.

He chuckled. "If by practical you mean, please let me claim you before I explode and we'll deal with the rest of the questions later, then yes."

She sucked in a breath but didn't shy away. In fact, she lifted her small hand to his cheek and pressed her palm into the side of his face. "I can't believe I would say this, but yes. I don't see any way to avoid the claiming. I haven't slept well since I met you, and that was only for a brief few minutes. Now that I've touched you, spoken to you, I don't think walking away is an option."

"Good." He put his hand over hers and twisted his mouth to kiss her palm. "When was the last time you shifted?"

She lowered her gaze. "Over a year, before…The Gathering." She carefully avoided stating the obvious. "I'm guessing the drugs he used on me didn't really leave me with the energy to shift. I've been sort of out of it forever. My mind is slowly coming back to me. I think I was dazed."

"I'm so sorry." He sat up straighter and pulled her into his lap, not with any sexual plan in mind, but because he ached for her, and the best way he knew to let her know how he felt was by holding her in his arms.

"I'd give anything to take the last year back and have you whole."

She lifted her gaze to his. "If I hadn't spent the last year in a cabin in Wisconsin, chances are I wouldn't be here today and we still wouldn't have met. Who knows if we ever would have?"

How the hell could she find a bright side to this coin?

Daniel swallowed his glass-half-empty attitude as he gazed into her eyes. She was the one in captivity. If she could find something positive about the experience, who was he to deny her?

"Do you want to talk about what happened?" He stroked her back with his full open palm, loving the feel of her body beneath his hand. "You don't have to now, if you aren't ready, but I'd like to be someone you can come to whenever you need. I know you have your groups here and your own counselor, but I just want you to know I can listen too, if it ever helps."

Her eyes watered and she blinked, but one tear sprung from each eye to trail down her face.

He reached with his thumb to brush them away. "I'm sorry. I didn't mean to make things worse." He felt like a heel, his chest tightening.

She smiled through the watery gaze she held on him. "I'm just emotional these days. Don't misread my tears. They aren't the product of some mislaid sorrow about the last year. Not that I'm not angry as hell and mourning my previous life, but the way you look at me and touch me and listen to me makes my emotions even stronger. How did I get so lucky?"

He shrugged. "Yeah, I'm a bucket of roses all right," he teased. "I'm lucky I haven't stuck my foot all the way down my throat yet. I'm not known for being glamorous with words."

"Well, today you're doing great."

He stared at her, memorizing every line of her face, every freckle sprinkled across her nose, every crease in her forehead. "Run with me."

"What? Now? Here?"

He chuckled. "There's no better place in the world to shift than right here in these woods on my parents' property. We're safe here and secure from human eyes."

She glanced around, and he watched her chew on the inside of her cheek as she pondered his suggestion. Finally she returned her gaze to his with a coy grin and narrowed her eyes. "Is this just some ploy of yours to get me naked?"

He laughed, his entire body shaking and making Allie wiggle on his lap. "I wish I had thought of that. It's a good idea. Now I really want to run with you." He held her tighter and took her face in both hands. "May I kiss you first?"

She nodded, her face transforming from jovial to serious in an instant. Her gaze landed on his lips. She licked hers.

It undid him watching her tongue jut out to moisten her mouth. His cock swelled further, and he hoped it wasn't pressing embarrassingly into her thigh. It was all he could do to keep from ripping her clothes off and taking her right there. But he wasn't an asshole. What he needed right now was a small taste from her lips.

He leaned in slowly and let his mouth settle over hers, trying not to grip her face too hard with his hands.

He groaned into her the moment their lips met. She tasted like heaven. On the surface were hints of her morning coffee and the minty toothpaste she'd used, but underneath was all Allie. His mate. His heart. His soul.

He deepened the kiss when she didn't protest, tracing the edge of her lips with his tongue and then dipping inside to duel with her tongue. She met him with every stroke, her hands coming up to grasp his forearms and hold him tight.

She didn't pull away. In fact she put all her effort into getting closer to him. Daniel had to be the one to release her lips. He was growing closer and closer to the edge of sanity, his cock straining in his jeans and his heart beating out of his chest.

Daniel tipped his head back and took a deep breath, as though the air from the sky above him would be less tainted by her scent. It wasn't.

She let go of his arms and stood abruptly, wiping her hands on her shorts and stepping back. "That was…"

"Intense." He lowered his gaze to hers. "Let's go for that run before I can't keep myself from mauling you." He tried to grin to soften his words, but Allison was smiling at him anyway.

"Promises, promises."

Before he could respond, she stepped behind Sadie, stripped off her clothes, and shifted. And before he could even gather his wits, she sauntered over to him in wolf form. She was breathtaking. Her fur was golden blonde and so soft to the touch when he reached out to stroke her head.

He held his breath, trying to pull together his thoughts. It all happened so fast, he hadn't gotten the chance to see her naked. She'd stood sideways behind the horse, giving him no more than a glimpse of the pale skin of her hip. Her top half had been concealed by the horse's belly.

Daniel finally managed to pull himself to standing, keeping his hand buried in his mate's fur. She even trotted along beside him as he stepped over to Sadie. He had to let go of Allison to tie Sadie to the lone tree she stood under for shade. "There, girl," he said as he secured her, patted her neck, and then turned back to Allison.

He pulled his T-shirt over his head and then hopped on one foot to remove each boot. He kept his gaze on Allison, watching as she sat on her rear haunches and tipped her head to one side. No way was he going to hide behind the horse, and apparently Allison had no intention of turning away. Good. He liked that she was bold enough to watch.

When he popped the button on his jeans, his cock pushed itself free, peaking out of his underwear. Still gazing at his mate, he lowered both his pants and his underwear and shimmied out of them. Lastly, he tugged off his socks and dropped them on the pile.

He gave Allison a moment to stare at his body before he shifted, and then he let nature take over, lowering himself to the ground and quickly transitioning to his wolf form.

He blinked several times and pawed at his mate when she approached. He was almost twice her size, his fur a shade darker. He thought they looked picturesque together.

The shift didn't lower his libido, but he shook thoughts of sex out of his head and tried to concentrate on the allure of running full speed through the trees. Both activities were on the short list of things he wanted to do with his mate today. One at a time. Starting with the run.

He nudged her with his muzzle and nodded behind him. And then he took off toward the trees. Allison followed on his heels. He could sense her behind him even though she barely made a sound. She was light on her paws. But her scent in wolf form was even stronger than in human form.

Daniel dashed through the trees as fast as he dared, knowing she was undernourished and wouldn't be able to endure as much as normal. He wished he could run with her for hours. And he could. Later. But now he used the exercise to burn off energy, hoping his need to claim her would tamp down enough to make it back to his house and perhaps wine and dine her a bit before sex became a forgone conclusion.

Who are you kidding?

~

"Jackpot," Tarson mumbled to himself as he watched Allison Watkins run past him through his binoculars. At first he'd panicked and nearly fallen on his ass when she'd shifted and taken off into the woods with some man he didn't know.

He'd been watching them from a perfect distance until the moment they'd headed in his direction unexpectedly. But then a smile had spread across his face as he realized they were mates. They were oblivious to his existence, probably due in no small part to their raging need to mate. At least that's how Tarson had always heard it went when a shifter met his mate. He wouldn't know, and he didn't give a fuck since claiming a goddamn female was the last thing he intended to do in this lifetime.

So this bitch had left her mate with a dozen other women and traipsed halfway across the country to meet up with another shifter at this ranch? She sure didn't waste any time.

If he'd had a gun on him, he might have shot her on sight just for being a whore. He suspected that wouldn't please his superior, however. The man had asked for a visual and intended to kidnap her back ASAP. Tarson doubted the Romulus wanted her dead. They had some use for her apparently. Fucking female.

As soon as his target was out of earshot, Tarson pulled his cellphone from his pocket and pressed speed dial.

"Tarson. Give me good news."

"She's here. And she's about to fuck some guy."

"Great. I don't care who the hell she fucks as long as you know where she is."

"Yep. I'm following them now." He stepped forward, his cell in one hand his binoculars in the other. "They're heading to his place, it looks like." He'd seen the man come and go several times from a cabin on the property. He had to be a permanent resident.

"Great. Get back to me on that exact location when you can, and then you can get out of there for now. I'll send someone else in to retrieve her."

Thank God. Tarson had no great desire to kidnap some bitch today.

CHAPTER 6

Allison chewed on her lower lip as she followed Daniel up the front steps of his home. She loved the log cabin look of the outside, modern and well-built, but right now all she wanted to do was let him claim her. Any other concerns could wait. They had to. She could think of nothing else. It consumed her. Her blood was pumping fast through her body, and she felt as though she had a fever.

The run in wolf form had been glorious, but it had only fueled her need. Seeing Daniel naked as he shifted whetted her appetite for more. When they'd returned to Sadie's side, they shifted and dressed quickly and silently, seemingly in agreement it was time to end the mating dance.

At least Allison was ready. And from the scent of her mate, she would guess he needed her just as bad. And his cock… Jesus he was built. Her pussy hadn't stopped pining for him since he'd lowered his pants and released his impressive length to her gaze.

Daniel turned around at the door. He took her hand and brought it to his cheek as he leaned against the wood. "I'll be honest with you. I want you more than I've ever wanted anything in my life. I didn't bring you here for a tour."

"Good. Can we go inside now?" She leaned into him, took his shirt in her fists, and lifted on tiptoes to kiss his lips.

Daniel grinned into the kiss. She could feel his mouth curving upward. He twisted the knob of the front door behind him, and they both almost fell into the house. As they righted themselves, Daniel kicked the door closed and pressed Allison into the solid wood.

Like a randy teenager, she grappled with his T-shirt, tugging on it until she had it over his head. He only released her to lift his arms, and then his hands were all over her, molding her shoulders and neck and then her breasts.

Allison moaned and bucked her chest toward him. The light was dim inside the house, but she didn't care. As shifters they could see fine in the dark. And she wanted to see more of him again right now.

Her nipples tightened as Daniel squeezed her breasts. When his warm hands worked under her tank top and lifted it above her chest, her fingers started to shake. She gripped his biceps and leaned into his chest. She needed to taste his skin. Before he could protest, she closed her lips over one of his nipples and flicked her tongue over the tip.

"Oh, baby." He let his hands wander to her back and flicked open her bra. In a flash, he yanked her shirt and bra over her head together and dropped the items on the floor. Her nibbling on his chest was only disrupted for a moment.

She drew her hands toward his chest and ran them over his pecs and down to his abs. He was rock solid. And she continued to lick his chest, unable to get enough of his taste, a mixture of his soap and the salty residue of his sweat from the heat.

Daniel lifted her face away from his chest and took her mouth in a kiss that demanded surrender. He inched even closer, pinning her to the door and holding her head, his fingers threaded in her hair. When he released her lips, he was breathing heavily. "You okay?"

She nodded. "Please…" An ache that had built for the last several hours in her belly threatened to explode out of her. She craved more of him. She couldn't control the drive.

"I'm going to claim you. If you aren't ready for that, you need to tell me." He stroked her cheek with his thumb and ducked enough to meet her gaze, his brows lifted in question.

"God, Daniel. Like now already. You're taking too long."

He smiled.

She couldn't believe how brazen she was being, but nothing about her life had been ordinary since Daniel had first approached her. It seemed she was ruled by a new power. No matter what her rational mind might argue was reasonable, all she knew was the overwhelming desire to become one with her mate.

She would never mock the stories of mated couples again.

Daniel swooped in and took her lips again. His tongue dueled with hers, and she met him stroke for stroke, craving more with every taste.

He angled her head back and forth as he deepened the kiss. And then abruptly his lips were gone and she was left gasping for air as he lowered to his knees and sucked a nipple into his mouth. It happened so fast. She gripped his head, needing any form of contact and using him to keep from falling.

Her breasts swelled as he switched from one to the other, suckling her. Every time he moved, her wet nipple puckered harder as it met the cool air. "Daniel…" Her voice was raspy, unidentifiable.

Without stopping, he went to work on her shorts, popping the button and then lowering the zipper.

She squirmed as he eased both her shorts and panties to the floor and helped her step out of them. She kicked off her sandals at the same time. She'd been naked in his presence earlier when they shifted, but nothing compared to this. She felt more exposed than ever, especially when Daniel released her nipple and set his forehead against her belly.

He inhaled long and slow. She knew he was taking in her essence.

His hands moved to her thighs. He was so much larger than her that his fingers encompassed her legs and spread them open, forcing her to step out wider.

Allison slipped her hands from his head to his shoulders. *Oh God.*

"You smell so fucking good," he muttered, but his words drifted off as he dipped his face between her legs and stroked his tongue between her folds.

OhGodohGod. She dug her nails into his shoulders, surely leaving marks. She didn't care. Couldn't.

When he flicked his tongue over her clit, she came up on her toes. *Shit.* She was going to come. Even that brief contact was pushing her to the very edge of sanity.

Daniel spread her folds with both hands and then dipped his thumbs into her channel while he rapidly flicked her clit with his tongue again.

That was it. A loud moan filled the room, coming from Allison as she bucked forward, begging for more, smashing her pussy against his face. Her orgasm shook her entire body. Her pussy pulsed around Daniel's thumbs. Her clit throbbed. And she held on to his shoulders for dear life.

As she came back to earth, he slowed his motions and tipped his head back to make eye contact. "That was so beautiful, baby." He rubbed her thighs.

She swallowed. The orgasm had taken only the edge off. She needed him inside her. "Daniel...now." She released his shoulders and molded her palms around his cheeks. "Jeans off. Now," she demanded.

He chuckled and stood. When he released her, she swayed and had to plaster herself to the door to keep from falling. She watched as he struggled to pull off his boots and socks and then his jeans. It might have been comical how he wiggled free of his clothing so haphazardly, another time. But not this time. She needed him worse than before the orgasm.

When he was finally naked, he took his cock in his hand and stroked it from the base to the tip.

Allison licked her lips and dropped to her knees in front of him. She needed to taste him as he'd just done to her. Daniel stepped into her space and planted his spread hands on the door behind her, leaning in. His enormous erection bobbed toward her face as though it knew just where she was. Precome dripped from the tip, and Allison leaned in to lick the drop from the head.

She moaned around his flavor, taking in the salty sweet taste of him for the first time and wanting more. Without pausing, she gripped his hips and sucked his cock into her mouth. God almighty he was large. She could barely fit half of him inside her, bulging her cheeks to accommodate his girth.

When she sucked, he groaned. "Baby, slow down. I don't want to come in your mouth."

She wanted exactly that. She wanted to swallow all of him as though starving.

Instead, Daniel pulled back, letting his cock pop out of her mouth. He righted himself and pulled her to standing.

When he took her mouth again in a wild kiss, she pressed her body into his, trapping his cock against her belly.

Finally, Daniel broke the kiss and spoke again, staring into her eyes. "My mind is swimming with all the ways I want to make love to you, but this first time I want to see your eyes while I claim you."

She nodded. As long as he meant right now, she didn't care what position he chose.

Shocking her, he swung her into his arms and carried her away from the front of the house. In a few strides he nudged a door open with his hip and made his way across another room until he dropped her onto a bed. It would be the master bedroom, she assumed, but right now her gaze was locked on his, nothing else.

He climbed over her, spreading her legs with his knees as he crawled. And then he was at her entrance. "Eyes on mine," he growled. His hands landed on both sides of her head, and his cock nudged her entrance.

She was so wet, he needed to do nothing to prepare her. *Please, just come into me.*

Allison reached for his cock with both hands and held it while she lifted her hips to meet the tip. It was all the invitation he needed apparently, because he slid into her sex on the next breath.

She gasped at the fullness. Tighter than anything she'd ever experienced. And he was hers. "More," she pleaded, bucking up to meet his cock and force him deeper.

Daniel groaned as he pushed the rest of the way home, never loosening the grip he had on her gaze. She couldn't look away, as though caught in a trance. The deep blue of his eyes darkened. So full. She never wanted to be anywhere else. If they could freeze this moment in time, she would forever be grateful.

Seconds passed before Daniel began to move in and out of her. She thrust up to meet him with each stroke, grabbing his hips as though she could control the pace. He was twice her size and above her, so it was a farce, but she loved the feeling anyway.

"Touch yourself." It was the first thing he'd said since they'd entered the bedroom.

Allison shook her head. No way in hell.

"Please. Rub your clit with your fingers so you can come with me. I want to see your eyes when you come."

As if she were under a spell, her hand strayed from his hip to the space between them. She'd never masturbated in front of anyone. She felt her flush deepen, knowing her face was bright red.

"That's it, baby. Stroke your clit for me." His thrusts had slowed, his breathing raspy as though he were running a race. "I won't come until I see your eyes glaze. I need you with me."

Emboldened by his words, Allison let her fingers land on her swollen nub and she stroked the tip gently. She wasn't sore, but the mating had made her ultra-sensitive to any contact.

When she finally pinched and plucked at her clit, she instantly went to the edge again. She lost his gaze when her eyes rolled back.

"Yes, baby. Like that. God you're sexy. Don't stop." He increased his pace, thrusting deeper with each stroke, filling her so full she thought she'd burst. And then she came, her pussy grasping at his cock with intent to contain him. As each pulse washed through her, he held himself steady deep inside her.

She lowered her eyes again to his and watched as he gritted his teeth and released his orgasm against her cervix. On and on he came, long and hard, each pulse felt by her still quivering pussy.

When he finally stopped and his gaze returned to normal, he smiled. "You're mine."

She grinned back. "It would seem that way."

He slumped to one side of her and drew her body with his, not letting his cock pop out. "That was unbelievable." He breathed in shallow gasps, and she caressed his chest with her free hand as it rose and fell with every deep breath.

"Beyond words." She was physically exhausted, but at the same time mentally alert. She needed him again. "What else you got?"

He chuckled and met her gaze, his arm wrapping all the way around her shoulders. "Give me a minute to recover and I'll think of something."

She flushed and bit her lip. How brazen. But she didn't care. He was hers. Forever. And she wanted him inside her as much as possible in the foreseeable future.

She set her forehead on his chest and closed her eyes.

∼

When Allison's eyelids fluttered open again, she froze for a second, stiffening before she realized where she was and why she was so warm. She smiled and snuggled into her mate's chest.

"Ah, the princess awakes."

"Was I asleep long?" she questioned without lifted her head.

"Most of the day."

"What?" She jerked upright until she was sitting and

stared down at him. She glanced around the room, noticing the dim light of the sun coming in through the window. It was already evening? "Oh my God."

Daniel stroked her back and then took her hand and pulled it to his lips. "When was the last time you slept?"

She met his gaze. "Over a year ago," she admitted. "Solidly like that, anyway." She'd been kept in a state of exhaustion from the drugs for the entire year, but she had only slept fitfully, fear always on her mind.

Daniel lifted both hands and cupped her breasts. "You have goose bumps," he said as he rubbed his thumbs over her nipples. In less than a second she went from sleepy to aroused.

She batted at his hands. "How could I not with you doing that?"

"I missed you."

"I was right here," she teased, pointing at the bed.

"You were comatose."

"I'm not now." She flung a leg over Daniel's torso and straddled him, and then she leaned in to kiss his lips. "What did I miss?"

"A glorious rendition of me watching you rest peacefully for hours."

"I'm sorry," she muttered against his lips.

"I'm not." He lifted his hands to her face and pulled her closer to deepen the kiss.

Her pussy came to life quickly, the goose bumps on her chest chased away and replaced by the heavy feeling of her breasts and her firm nipples. She lowered them to sway against Daniel's chest, heightening her sensitivity.

Daniel released her head to skim his hands down her body. When he reached her pussy, he stroked several fingers through her folds. "So wet, baby."

She moaned and lifted herself enough to give him space. He gripped her hips, settled her over his cock, and lowered her onto him until she was fully seated.

"Oh God." She sat upright on him, using his chest to support her body above his. And then another thought occurred, and her eyes shot wide. "We didn't use protection."

He caressed her ass with both hands. "It's okay. You aren't fertile right now."

She exhaled. *Right. Of course he would sense that.* But she still hadn't ever had sex without a condom. It felt fantastic having his cock bare against her.

As shifters, they didn't have to worry about STDs. They were immune. Their only concern would be pregnancy.

Daniel lifted her hips as she relaxed, easing her on and off his cock. He controlled the pace and the intensity from under her. She gripped him tight with her pussy, feeling the build of an orgasm inside her even though she hadn't touched her clit yet.

Luckily she didn't have to. She was having enough trouble holding herself up. Daniel drew his hands to her belly and then lowered his fingers to her clit. He pinched the nub between both thumbs and pressed into her.

Allison screamed, an unexpected orgasm ripping through her, tightening her pussy and making her clit throb.

"That's it, baby. Let it go. I love watching you come."

As her brain fluttered back to earth and she was able to put two thoughts together, she took control of their mating. She batted his hands away and he smiled, his eyes turning a deeper blue. She rode him at her pace now, lifting and lowering over him while her clit pressed into his torso with every pass. Her arousal rose to a new high quickly, but she concentrated on the feeling of his cock filling her, stretching her tight.

When he stiffened and then shot his come into her, she lowered herself onto him fully, pressing her clit into him and shocking herself with her ability to come again and without direct stimulation from her hand or his.

She finally collapsed on top of him, nestling her head in the crook of his neck. She stared at his nipple and grazed one finger over the tip while her breathing came back to normal in sync with his.

"You must be starving. I know I am." His voice was raspy and deep, and it vibrated through her.

She nodded against his chest. "I haven't eaten since breakfast. God." Her stomach picked that moment to rumble.

"Well, me neither. Someone was having the nap of a lifetime against my chest."

She lifted her face to see his. "And it was the best sleep of my life."

"Good." He set a finger on her nose. "Now, let me feed you before you collapse on me." He sat, taking her with him, still buried inside her.

Their faces met at the same level in this position and Allison took his head in both hands. "How did I get so lucky? It's like the universe is making up for a year of bad luck in one day."

He set his forehead against hers. "I don't know, but I'm not questioning it. I've never been this happy. And I'm a happy kind of guy." He grinned.

She lifted off him, wishing she could stay locked in that particular position forever, but knowing they needed to eat soon or they wouldn't have the energy for round three.

Daniel eased from the bed, setting his feet on the ground and then padding to the bathroom. He flipped on the shower and then stuck his head back into the bedroom. "You coming, lazy?"

He watched as his sweet mate pulled herself reluctantly to standing and approached on wobbly legs. He knew he'd worn her out, but in addition she wasn't back in full swing yet from lacking good food for so long.

He took her hand and led her into the shower. He'd built this cabin himself, intentionally ensuring the shower was large and luxurious so he could share it one day with his mate. That day had come, and as he pressed her against the wet tile and took her mouth, he thanked God for the delivery of this woman into his life.

They had ten thousand issues to overcome in the near future, but they would work things out because there was no other choice. She was his and he would follow her to the ends of the Earth if necessary to make her happy.

Fleeting thoughts of his obligation to NAR made him pause for only a moment. He chased that hurdle from his head, preferring to deal with reality later.

He released her lips, leaving her with pink cheeks and deep breaths. He loved how easy it was to bring her to such a heightened aroused state. But now they needed soap and then food.

Reluctantly he grabbed the shampoo and poured it on his hand.

Allison stepped under the hot spray of the shower and let it cascade down her long hair. He paused to watch it drip over her pert nipples. Her breasts weren't huge. They were less than a handful, but they were gorgeous and he knew they would fill out more as she gained some much-needed weight.

When she lifted her hands to run them over her head, he sucked in a breath watching her nipples rise higher. He had to close his eyes a moment to control himself.

His hand shook, and he glanced to see he still held a pool of shampoo. "Come here, baby." He tugged her from the spray with his free hand and proceeded to wash her hair. The thick locks eased between his fingers as he massaged her scalp.

Allison moaned and tipped her head back, turning at the same time to face the wall so he would have a better angle.

Daniel rubbed the suds into her shoulders next and then reached around to caress her breasts with both hands, the slippery shampoo making her feel slick and smooth. She leaned her back into his chest and sighed, her eyes closed to avoid the soap running down her face.

He had to release her and finish the shower, but it took a grand effort.

While she once again stood under the spray, he grabbed the bottle of body wash. He had to disassociate to run his hands over the rest of her body, her gorgeous pale skin making his cock rock hard. When he finished with the soap, he handed her the conditioner. "I'll let you finish before I can't control myself." He looked away so he could wash himself without nailing her sexy body to the wall. His cock wanted her again already. Hell, his brain and his heart did too, but she needed a break.

And they both needed food.

As if they did this every day of their lives, he stepped from the shower, handed her a towel, and they dried themselves in silence.

Daniel secured his towel to his waist and nodded toward the door. "Dinner first. Then we'll talk."

He didn't want to talk. He wanted to fuck. But they hadn't mentioned the details of their future yet, and soon that would have to be faced. At least the immediate decisions. Like the fact that he didn't intend to let her out of his sight even for a moment.

"Can I borrow a T-shirt?" she asked as she followed him back into the bedroom, her towel wrapped around her body.

Daniel padded to the dresser and pulled out a T-shirt for Allison and a pair of loose shorts for himself. While he stepped into his shorts, dropping his towel on the floor, he watched his mate set her towel on the foot of the bed and shrug into his shirt. It was way too big for her tiny frame, hanging halfway down her thighs, but he figured it would give her some semblance of modesty while they ate.

He kissed her soundly and then took her hand and drew her from the room. "It's not a huge house," he said as they walked. "But I built it myself and I love it." Hell, he'd only finished it this past spring, doing most of the work himself.

She released his hand and wandered around the open living room-kitchen area, her eyes soaking in every aspect of his home. "I love it. It's so...open. I love the space. Even though it's not very big, it feels open."

He watched her face. She meant what she said. He knew she was uncomfortable with tight spaces after being confined for so long. "I'm glad you like it. If you want to change anything, it's your home now too."

She smiled at him but then resumed perusing his belongings. He watched as she wandered from the stone hearth to the dark black leather couch. She ran her fingers across the end table. "You don't have a television?" She lifted her gaze.

"I do. It's inside that cabinet." He pointed at the rustic armoire in the corner. "I just don't like to see it all the time. Something about the modernness of it doesn't suit the space."

She twisted around, her gaze roaming over the real

wood logs that made up the walls. "You're right. It doesn't really fit in."

Daniel left her to explore and entered the kitchen area. The room was all one great room, so he could see her while he pulled food out of the refrigerator and began to cook. "Do you like hamburgers?"

"God that sounds delicious."

He set about making patties and then grabbed a bag of precut fries from the freezer to stick in the oven. Anything more elegant would have to wait for another day. Right now, he just wanted to eat and wrap himself around his mate again.

She wandered over to the island he worked at and leaned on her elbows. "Feed me." She grinned.

"Working on it." He grabbed a pan and set it on the stove. "Cheese?"

"Yum." She licked her lips, and he couldn't resist leaning over the island to kiss her again. "What can I do to help?" She righted herself and propped her hands on the granite surface.

Daniel turned to the refrigerator again and pulled out lettuce, tomatoes, and pickles. "Want to cut the tomatoes?"

"Sure."

He handed her a knife and a cutting board, and they worked in silence for a few minutes. When he set the burgers in the pan, the smell filling the room made them both groan.

"I've never been this hungry. Even though I haven't eaten well in months, I feel like a weak, starving refugee right now."

"Mating will do that to you."

She flushed. Her cheeks grew pink as the heat rushed down her face and neck.

The dinner was easy. They devoured everything. He loved the way she didn't worry overly so about manners or filling her mouth too full or getting ketchup on her lips.

When he finished, he set his elbows on the table and watched her eat the rest of her food. "You're beautiful."

She swallowed a bite and rolled her eyes. "I'm eating like a pig."

"I love it. You're too skinny."

She grinned. "There's a line men don't usually use." She glanced at the window. "Shit. It's dark. I haven't spoken to my parents all day."

"Do they know where you are?"

"Yes. I told my mom when I left this morning. About you, I mean."

"Then they know." Every wolf who'd ever mated understood what happened in the first few hours, days, weeks. "When are they leaving?"

She turned back to him. "We were supposed to leave together in a few days."

He took her hands across the table and held her gaze. "Will you stay?"

"Twelve hours ago I would have told you hell no. I don't see how that's an option anymore. But I haven't been home yet. I need to go back to New York and take care of my things."

"Were you living with your parents?"

She shook her head. "No. But my belongings are at

their place. I was living with a family as their nanny." Her gaze lowered as she inhaled.

"I'm so sorry. That must have been hard."

"Yes. They were sweet kids. They had to scramble to find another caregiver when I disappeared. They're also shifters, and the family has been very kind to my parents, providing them with a shoulder to lean on when they realized I hadn't just run off with my mate but had been taken against my will."

"What made them think you had gone on your own accord?" He gripped her hands tighter. He ached deep inside for what she'd been through.

"I texted them several times the first few days to let them know I was with my mate and the happiest person alive."

"Why did you do that?" He furrowed his brow, confused.

"I didn't." She tilted her head to one side. "But they thought I did. My kidnapper acted as though he were me. It took several weeks before they grew suspicious enough to contact The Head Council. They knew from the start the matter would need to be handled by the shifter community and not the local human police. The way my kidnapper spoke to them by text tipped them off eventually that it wasn't me making the communications, and his jargon solidified that he was a shifter."

"God. That must have been awful for them. And you of course, but…"

"Yeah, they were very relieved when Evan was assigned to the case and worked night and day to track me down. My mother cried a bucket of tears when she got here."

"I'm sure. And you were in Minnesota?"

"Yes, somewhere in the middle of nowhere in the mountains. Very far from anything. At least that's what I was told. I spent the majority of the last year in a tiny, one-room, rickety, old cabin with a man who was like my guard. He barely spoke to me, and the only food we had was delivered by a group of shifters about once a month."

"But they took you someplace else a few times?" He cringed inside, knowing he needed to discuss this with her and not wanting to upset her or make things worse. But she was his mate, and she needed validation right now, from him. It didn't matter how many counselors she met with or how many group sessions she attended with the other women. She needed to tell Daniel what happened in her own words. He knew that.

"Yes." She sighed. "And that part is very foggy. I was always drugged. My memory of what happened at that place is spotty. It was a sterile, white, hospital-type location. Shifters shuffled all around me at all hours of the day and night, but I was usually strapped to a table with an IV in my arm. I rarely woke up. It's a blur."

His chest beat harder. He knew all this. Evan had spoken to him. But it still hurt to hear it from her. "Come here." He tugged her hands, and she stood to come around the corner of the table as he scooted his chair back from the edge. He pulled her into his lap and held her tight, threading his fingers into her damp hair. He inhaled her scent deeply and exhaled slowly until he could recoup some of his calm. "It's over." He stroked his other hand down her back, feeling every bump in her spine.

"I hope."

"Maybe you'll recover more of your memory about the times you were at that facility."

"I hope for that too. Evan needs that information. The Head Council is counting on me to remember. I know doctors were in the room discussing things around me, but I can't come up with anything specific. It just sounds like mumbling when I attempt to recover words."

He kissed her temple. "Don't stress over it. It will come in time or it won't. It isn't your responsibility."

"Isn't it? What if other women are there right now? What if more are taken?" She lifted her gaze. "It scares the shit out of me."

"I know, baby. I know." He kissed her forehead and trailed a line with his lips down her cheek to her neck.

She stretched her neck longer for him, tipping her head back and gripping his biceps as he worked his way to her shoulders.

Leaving the dishes where they were on the table, Daniel lifted his mate in his arms and carried her back to the bedroom. He lowered her onto the bed and climbed in beside her. As bad as he wanted to have sex with her again, her eyes were heavy with sorrow and lack of sleep. Even though she'd slept for hours all day while he watched her, she needed weeks of sleep to let her body heal and come back to herself.

Daniel tucked the comforter around his mate and

held her loosely until her breathing evened out and he knew she was once again at peace in sleep. He eased from the bed and watched her for several minutes before leaving her to slumber and shutting the door to the bedroom to return to the kitchen.

CHAPTER 7

"How's it going?" Evan asked when Daniel finally called him a few hours later. He'd cleaned the kitchen and put everything away and then headed out to sit on the porch and make contact with the rest of the ranch.

"Good. She's sleeping. She slept most of the day and now she's at rest again."

"I'm sure she needs the z's."

"No doubt. So she told me about the weird hospital place she was taken. I wanted to punch a hole in the wall."

"Yeah. Don't we all. Did she add anything new?"

"No. She seems to have amnesia about the entire thing. Not sure if it's a result of self-preservation or the drugs."

"Could be a combo."

"We may never find out more from her."

"I know."

"I'll let you know if anything new comes to light." Daniel rubbed the back of his neck, hating the chill that raced down his spine. Something niggled at him. Worried him. Reasonable or not, he wasn't the kind of man to ignore premonitions. He stared into the darkness as if he might see something out there between the trees. He didn't scent another shifter, but nevertheless he felt like he was being watched. He shook the thought from his mind for a moment. "I need to make a few more calls. Talk to you later?"

"Of course. Later." Evan hung up.

Daniel dialed his father next.

"Son," he answered.

"Dad."

"Everything okay?"

"Yep. With the exception of the fact that my mate was held prisoner and drugged mysteriously for the last year. Peachy otherwise."

His father exhaled loudly. "I'm sorry for that."

"Are her parents okay?"

"Yes. They're here at the main house with us this evening. They're fine. They know what's up."

"Please tell them I will speak to them as soon as possible. I don't mean to be disrespectful, but I can't leave Allison here alone, and she's exhausted."

"They understand, Daniel. Don't worry. Why don't you and Allison come to the main house for breakfast tomorrow, and I'll have the Watkins join us."

"Sounds good."

"Good night."

"Thanks, Dad." Daniel pressed the end button and set the phone in his lap. It was still blazing hot out, even in the late evening air. He stared into the darkness again. He could see quite well even at night, and he peered into the tree line as though someone were going to pop out at any minute and try to ruin what he'd just solidified today.

It wasn't reasonable, but the feeling persisted. He finally dragged himself inside and joined his mate in bed, wrapping himself around her and holding her tight against his chest.

Whatever else they had to face would be there in the morning.

~

Henry's hands shook as he answered the phone. Receiving more than one call within a few days from his superior was never a good thing. "Yes." His voice squeaked and cracked on that one word.

"Did you get a man out to that dude ranch?"

"Yes, sir. He got a visual on Allison Watkins. I've already dispatched a team to retrieve her. Shouldn't be tough. She's alone in a cabin with some guy from the ranch."

"Good. Act fast. I don't want Allison Watkins slipping away, dammit."

"I understand, sir." Henry drummed his fingers on his thigh as he spoke.

"And Henry. I need you to pick up the pace on your end. This means war."

"Pick up the pace?" *Is he crazy?* As it was they'd been working around the clock trying to meet the demands of his superior and whoever was above him.

"Did I stutter?" The man's voice rose. He was angry, but Henry heard a thread of fear in it also. *So, there is another man above this guy. There has to be. He wouldn't be so nervous if he were the end of the line.* The man didn't wait for Henry to respond. "How many subjects are ready to fight?"

"Maybe two dozen, sir."

"Only two dozen? Fuck." His voice rose. "I need more than that and I need them ready within a week. Do you understand how critical this is?"

No, I don't have the foggiest clue how critical this is? Why don't you tell me?

The man continued. The more Henry spoke to him, the more he realized by his voice the man was older, significantly older than Henry. "Do you think NAR has just two dozen men ready to fight against us?"

"No, sir. I'm sure they are far more prepared than that." Henry cringed. NAR was mobilizing. They surely had hundreds of men at the ready. But what NAR didn't know was that the Romulus was coming. The Romulus was stronger. The Romulus would take them down unexpectedly and take over the entire shifter government system so fast they wouldn't know what hit them. But Henry needed more time. At least a few weeks. Maybe more. No sense telling his superior that, though. The man needed to be placated right now before he had a stroke.

"Are you with me on this, Fairfield?"

"Of course, sir." As aggravating as his superior was, Henry was totally on board. One thing he agreed with wholeheartedly was that The Head Council needed to be taken down and destroyed. Those bastards had ruined his life and he would get them back. When he'd come to work for the Romulus, he'd been giddy. Finally, a group organizing to take out the mother fuckers who thought they ruled the universe.

Henry would be on the winning side in this history lesson. And he intended to make that clear as soon as possible. Nothing would make him happier. He didn't give a flying fuck what his superior's motives were. All he cared about was that their goals were the same. Take out The Head Council and end their rule for good.

When Henry hung up the phone, he leaned back and closed his eyes for a few minutes. A quick nap would refresh him. He didn't expect it to be long before the phone rang again.

~

Something yanked Daniel from a deep sleep. His eyes shot open wide. He had no idea what it was. A noise? He couldn't recall, but he wrapped himself tighter around Allison and listened closely, his heartbeat thumping in his ears loud enough to raise his blood pressure.

There it was again. Definitely a noise. He jerked upright, his hand still on his mate as he recognized the sound of someone trying to open the front door. The distinct noise of a rattling doorknob that wouldn't turn.

"What is it?" Allison whispered.

Daniel set his finger against her lips, glancing only briefly in her direction.

Another noise. Coming from the kitchen. The

window? Had he locked it? Hell, he'd never even locked the front door before tonight. His instinct must have been well-founded.

He couldn't remain impassive any longer. He needed to act. Allison was naked, as was he. As silently as possible, he slipped from the bed, grabbed a T-shirt from the floor and slipped it over his mate's head.

She trembled, her breaths coming in loud pants. She gripped his hand and pulled him closer.

Daniel set his mouth against her ear. "Get under the bed." He pulled her to the edge, and she crouched down when her feet hit the floor.

"Daniel?" Her whispered voice was shaky and filled with fear.

Daniel grabbed his cell off the bedside table, dialed his father, and set the phone on the floor. "Don't say anything. Just leave the line open." He pressed her head and pointed at the floor. He needed her under that bed immediately, where he could at least hope she was safe from gunfire.

Allison squirmed her way under the low mattress, holding her breath, her eyes wide when he glanced at her.

He slid the phone under next to her, praying his father would answer if he hadn't already and gather there was danger.

The rattling in the kitchen had ceased, but that only made Daniel more nervous. At least when there had been a noise, he'd known where the threat was located. Without that warning, he had no idea what direction to head first.

He crept to the bedroom door and listened carefully, hoping someone didn't crash through the bedroom window as he exited. His hands were fisted at his sides as he inched the door open and peered through the slit.

Nothing. Whoever it was wasn't inside. He'd be able to smell them, human or shifter, if they were. He held his breath, attempting to detect any noise at all. Leaving his mate unattended wasn't on his short list, but sitting in the bedroom waiting to be attacked didn't give him warm fuzzies, either. He hoped if he left her, he might be able to lure the bastard with him.

The front doorknob rattled again. Why? Did the asshole think it might have gotten itself unlocked in the last few minutes?

The second Daniel made a step into the hall, a crash behind him made him spin on his heels. Something had come through the bedroom window, shattering the pane. A brink clattered to the floor.

Allison let out a short scream.

"Fuck," Daniel muttered under his breath. That meant there was more than one person outside. No way could the same man who'd rattled the front door also throw a brick through the bedroom window on the other side of the house so quickly. "Allison, stay down," he whispered as he stepped back into the room and shut the door behind him.

Whoever was out there was determined. Without backup, there was no way Daniel could keep them safe.

A gunshot sent Daniel to the floor. He flattened himself on the broken glass and rolled toward the bed.

He had no idea where the shot had come from or who it was aimed at, but he wasn't taking any chances.

Silence. He breathed so heavily, it almost covered the whimpers of Allison under the bed. She reached out with one hand and grabbed his arm. "Are you hit?"

"No, baby. I'm fine," he whispered.

Two more shots rang out in succession. This time he thought they came from the front of the house. He prayed whoever was doing the shooting was on his side and successful. He rolled over onto his back and then his front again, assuming it would be safer against the glass than crawling over it.

Reaching up with one hand, he managed to open the drawer on the bedside table and retrieve his gun. He set it on the floor under his chin and then reached back in to grapple for the box of bullets. The gun was loaded, but he had no idea how much ammunition he might need if he left the room.

"You have a gun?" Allison gasped.

Honestly, Daniel had never owned a pistol until he'd joined NAR. Now he'd never been so glad to have military experience in his life. He didn't answer her rhetorical question. Instead he looked into her eyes and reached out to stroke her cheek. "Stay as quiet as you can, Allie. I need to check this out."

She gripped him again, harder. "No." She shook her head. "Don't leave. Please," she pleaded in a voice so low he knew she was struggling to hold on to her sanity. Her nails dug into his wrist.

Another shot. Daniel ducked his head to hers and set a hand on top of her hair to hold her closer to the floor.

If anything happened to her, he didn't know what he would do. It wasn't an option.

She pleaded with him with her eyes, her bottom lip between her teeth, her hand holding his wrist in a grip he was surprised she was capable of.

"I'm going to shift." He knew he could scent better in wolf form, and he needed all his senses on high alert right now. He handed her the gun, pushing it across the floor toward her. "There are six rounds in there. Use it if anyone comes through that door you don't know."

She shook her head. "I've never shot a gun in my life."

He turned the grip toward her and wrapped her hand around it, settling it in her palm the way she would need to fire a shot. He flipped off the safety. "It's ready to fire. Just pull this trigger."

"No," she muttered. "Stay." Tears ran down her face. "I can't do it."

"You can, baby. If it's you or them, you will." Daniel released her, praying she could gather the courage to save her own life if need be. He scooted back a few inches, wincing as glass cut into his naked body in several places.

He closed his eyes for a brief moment and shifted, emitting an unsolicited growl as he bounced up onto all four paws and bounded for the broken window first.

A glance at the ground showed one man lying in the bushes. Daniel sniffed the air and held his breath a moment. He heard no breathing sounds. The asshole was a shifter, but he appeared to be a dead one. That was a good sign.

He turned to the bedroom door, wishing that fucking window didn't leave Allison unprotected. With his front paws, he opened the door and then he nosed it ajar enough to stick his head out. Nothing else was inside the house yet. Keeping a keen ear on the bedroom, he widened the door and padded into the hall. He moved from room to room, peering out every window into the darkness.

Still nothing. Who'd fired the shots? And where was the other intruder? All he could do was hope his father had gotten his call and sprang into action. Any other choice was unimaginable. But where was he now? Someone had killed the man at the window. Had his father been somehow incapacitated in the altercation?

Allison screamed and Daniel bounded back to the bedroom just as a wolf came flying through the window. It wasn't anyone Daniel knew. His scent was unfamiliar, which meant he was as good as dead.

Daniel jumped, landing on the intruder almost before his paws hit the ground. Daniel growled as he slammed the shifter into the floor, skidding them both across the hardwood until they hit the wall under the window.

The bastard clawed at Daniel, trying to get out from under him. Daniel pounced again, getting his entire body over the slightly smaller frame of the asshole with the mess of gray fur.

The shifter slammed his jaw over Daniel's leg, biting down hard and forcing a loud squeal from Daniel's mouth. Daniel gritted his teeth together and twisted his neck until his gaze landed just where he wanted. He had the fucker on his back, pinned. A quick lift of his hind leg and he struck hard against the shifters balls, nailing him with enough force that the guy released Daniel's leg and curled up in a loud whimper.

Something blocked Daniel's view as it flew through the open window to land at his back. Keeping one paw on the piece of shit under the window, Daniel jerked his gaze behind him, expecting his fight to double. Instead he found his father standing behind him, a gun lifted in the air. "Not another move, if you value your life, you son of a bitch."

Daniel jumped to the side, leaving the shifter in his fetal position. For a moment he thought they were safe and it was over, but then the goddamn maniac jumped up onto all four paws and bared his teeth. He leaped into the air, straight toward Daniel's father.

Luckily his dad was quicker. He fired one shot and the shifter landed in a heap on the floor of the bedroom, barely emitting a squeal as he died almost instantly.

"Shit," Jerome muttered.

Daniel shifted quickly back to human form, grabbed a pair of jeans, and shrugged into them. "What? You're mad?"

"Well, I wanted that asshole alive. He's not going to answer any questions dead."

Daniel kneeled on the floor and set a hand on his mate's leg from the opposite side of the bed he'd left her. "It's okay, baby. It's over." He leaned in farther as she shook. "Come here." He didn't want to drag her out, but she seemed to be in shock. When she twisted her head around to see him, her eyes were huge and glazed over. Again he thanked God for his incredible vision. So much could be determined from just a look, and in the dark that meant the world to a shifter.

Instead of pulling on Allison at the risk of scaring her to death, he let go of her leg, flattened himself to the floor, and wiggled under the bed to join her. When he reached her side, he pulled her into his arms and held her tight. He threaded his fingers in her hair and tucked her head against his chest. He knew he was bleeding from several cuts, but he didn't care. All that mattered was calming her racing heart and reassuring her she was safe.

∼

Two hours later, Allison stood at the kitchen table, still wearing nothing more than the long T-shirt, her eyes narrowed as she examined another cut on Daniel's chest. "I think you got half of these crawling under the bed after the fight."

He winced when she applied antiseptic to another bloody spot. He didn't respond.

"I don't think any of them need stitches. If you take a shower and rinse away most of the blood, you'll probably look much better."

He raised an eyebrow. He hadn't released his grip on her since his father had flipped on the bedroom light, filling the room with the bright glow that snapped her out of her trance and set her into motion.

She'd climbed out from under the bed on her own on the side not currently occupied by a giant dead shifter. Daniel had been right behind her, his hand on her the entire time. He'd led her into the bathroom and set her on the toilet while his two oldest brothers and Evan entered the house and disposed of the intruder. What they did with the body and that of the shifter under the window outside, she didn't know. Hell, she didn't want to know.

What she did know was that she was alive, and she owed that to Daniel and his quick thinking when he'd called his dad. She'd heard the man answer on the other end and managed to mutter into the phone. It didn't matter what she'd said. The important thing was he'd told her he'd be right there. And he'd come. Armed. Bless him.

Daniel wrapped his arm around her middle and pulled her close again, her belly against his cheek. He fisted her T-shirt at the back. "If anything had happened to you," he repeated for the tenth time.

"It didn't." She lifted his chin and stared into his eyes. "Nor to you. We're safe."

In the two hours since all hell had broken loose, several shifters had arrived on the scene, sent by NAR. They now surrounded the house and were scattered around the property. Unfortunately they'd found no other unwanted guests, and the two who had been shot weren't talking. Dead had a way of preventing that.

Allison still shook, her hands not returning to anything close to steady, but she tried to keep her chin up.

"And tomorrow you're going to learn to fire that gun."

She scrunched her nose at him. Shooting a weapon had never been on her bucket list, but neither had being kidnapped or shot at, so she needed to alter her frame of reference and buck up. She nodded and sighed. "I guess there's no other option."

Daniel stood. He twisted his left arm in every direction as he held her steady with his right. Luckily it was just a sprain. Nothing seemed to be broken. A few hours in wolf form would speed his recovery and help heal his wounds also. "I think I need you to wash me. I feel a little weak." He grinned at her, and she rolled her eyes as she led him from the room toward the master bath.

"That's the dumbest line I've ever heard." But the opportunity to bathe him made her knees weak. She wouldn't turn it down for anything. She might need to pay extra special attention to every inch of his skin, in fact, just to be sure they didn't miss any cuts…

∽

Allison opened one eye and moaned at the bright light filling the room. She realized where she was upon awakening and snuggled into Daniel's warm body, pulling the covers over her head to block out the sun.

His chuckle shook her. He ran his hand up and down her back, giving her chills even when surrounded by his warmth. "We have to get up."

"Oh God no." She lifted her chin and set it on his chest, shrugging the blankets away from her face to see him. "We have to face people today?" She'd had enough company in the night to last a lifetime. And they'd only slept a few hours after his family had graciously swept the bedroom free of glass and covered the window with a large sheet of clear plastic. She was tired.

The only thing that had allowed her to slow her heart rate and relax into Daniel's arms was knowing there were so many military trained shifters surrounding the property now. No one would get by them without making a lot of noise.

His teasing smile made her heart beat faster. "Unless you want to hide out here forever. I'm okay with that too. But your parents, and mine for that matter, might express opposition. They're expecting us for breakfast."

She scrunched up her nose. "A family gathering? Ugh." She ducked back under the covers and wrapped her arm around his chest. She hadn't known he'd planned that.

"It is customary for newly mated couples to occasionally leave the house. And I agreed to this plan yesterday evening. If I'd known we would have been attacked in our sleep, I'd have told them we couldn't make it." His chest vibrated against her cheek as he spoke.

"How about later," she mumbled as she caressed his abs and then lowered her hand to surround his cock with her palm. He wore shorts, but that didn't stop her from wrapping her fingers around him through the loose material.

She'd kept her hands to herself in the night while they'd showered, recognizing the wince that repeatedly crossed his face as she soaped his body, but all bets were off this morning. Now that she was awake and his pheromones were filling her nose, she needed him. "You should have shifted for a while," she muttered as she nibbled his skin. The cuts were fading anyway, but they'd be completely gone if he'd spent time in wolf form.

"I didn't want to stop touching you even for a moment," he whispered, his breath hitching as she stroked her hand up and down his shaft through his shorts.

"Uh-huh."

When she grazed her thumb over the head, Daniel groaned. "You imp." He lifted the leg she had straddled and pressed his thigh against her pussy, taking her breath away. She was wet, probably had been in her sleep. She'd been wet since she first walked up to him yesterday. Had it only been twenty-four hours?

Before she could catch her breath, Daniel turned the tables. He lifted her off him, set her on the bed on her belly, and climbed over her, nudging her legs apart with his knees and settling between them.

She squealed, but even her sharp sound was cut off as he pushed the T-shirt she wore up her body and over her head to tangle with her wrists. His mouth landed on her ear, and he nibbled a path down her neck and across her shoulders. "I want to take you from behind. Is that okay?"

She couldn't breathe, let alone answer. All she knew was her nipples rasped against the sheet and her pussy begged for him to remove his shorts and press into her without the material between them.

Daniel lifted onto his knees. She assumed he was squirming out of his shorts. And then he ran his hands down the sides of her body, grazing the edges of her breasts, and lifted her hips off the bed. He stuffed a pillow under her belly and nudged her knees farther apart. When his fingers landed on her pussy and spread her lower lips to swipe through her folds, she shot up onto all fours and rocked back into his touch.

"So wet, baby. Always so ready for me." He pushed two fingers into her. "And so tight..." His voice trailed off as he grabbed her hip with one hand to steady her and fucked her with his other hand.

God. She burned for him. She needed to move. But he was too strong and held her still, his arm slinking under her stomach to brace her against the thrusting of the fingers of his other hand.

Allison moaned, letting her head dip toward the mattress. When her arms began to shake, she set her forehead on the pillow, leaving her ass in the air.

"God you're sexy, Allie."

She was so close. He hadn't touched her clit, but just the position she was in heightened her arousal. Just as she was about to come, he released her. *No!* She bit her lip to keep from protesting and wiggled her rear toward him, pleading with her body for more.

And then he was back, his cock pressing into her, his hands on her hips to keep her from leaning away from him. He thrust into her so fast, she came.

"That's it, baby. Let it go." His voice soothed her, his hands trailing away from her hips and caressing her back.

Her entire body shook, a chill racing down her spine as her pussy milked his cock, grasping it as though pleading with him to never exit her body.

Before the pulses of that first orgasm subsided, Daniel reached around and stroked her clit with his fingers while he eased out of her and then thrust back in.

So intense. So…natural…to be taken this way by him. No man had ever taken her from behind. She loved it.

His thrusts increased, and he doubled his efforts on her clit until he finally held himself deep inside her, his orgasm jarring his body against her ass. As he came, he pinched her clit between two fingers, sending her over the edge right behind him.

He held her still as their orgasms spiraled down, his fingers pressing into her hip.

When her knees began to shake, threatening to give way, he drew her against him and collapsed onto the bed sideways, spooning her into his chest.

She hated that his cock popped out of her during the fall, missing the feeling of fullness immediately. But the hand he settled over her breast, molding the globe and flicking her nipple, distracted her. He kept her on edge so easily, making her crave more, not less.

His lips landed on her temple. "That was so…"

She smiled. "Perfect."

"Yes. Perfect."

"You're so distracting. Are you going to feed me now or what?"

He hugged her tighter, his hand squeezing her breast. "Me? Who started this?" he teased.

Allison just smiled. How had she gotten so much luck in such a short time? If he kept it up, he could almost erase the disastrous year behind her.

∽

When they stepped into the main house half an hour later, both sets of their parents were already seated at the breakfast table eating. All four stood at once. Allison's heart swelled at the reception. Daniel's parents each hugged her while her parents shook hands with Daniel. They hadn't even met him until now.

Allison's mom hugged her tight. "Are you okay?" she asked as she pulled back to look her in the eye. "We were scared out of our minds when we heard the gunshots."

Allison nodded. "I'm fine, thanks to Daniel and his father." She turned toward Jerome and smiled.

Jerome shrugged. "I'm glad I got there in time and we're safe now. There are so many Reserves on the property, no one could possibly get by them."

As the six of them took their seats, Natalie glanced at her nearly empty plate. "We started without you. We weren't sure if you were ever going to make it." No one would fault newly mated couples for tardiness. They would have a free pass for months. And after the night Allison and Daniel had experienced, everyone was lucky they'd gotten out of bed.

Allison was starving, again. Seems she was always

hungry lately. She filled her plate from all the serving platters in the middle of the table and tore into her breakfast, savoring every bite and nearly moaning at the taste of Natalie's cooking.

Their parents had been just finishing and chatted around her, small talk that helped them all get to know each other over coffee.

"I spoke to Evan last night before all hell broke loose," Daniel said between bites. He set one hand on Allison's knee and squeezed. "He didn't sound as relieved about this successful rescue endeavor as I would have expected. Obviously his concerns were well-founded."

Daniel's father, Jerome, nodded agreement. "I know he works directly for The Council and can't share everything he knows, but the look on his face and the furrow in his brow tells me there's a lot more we don't know. It's scary. I hope the women staying here can regain their lives somehow and work together, leaning on each other for support to get over what they've each been through. But there's more to come, I fear. Last night was just a taste."

Allison swallowed her last bite. It went down hard, as though it were gravel instead of pancakes. "I hate that you all got dragged into this. Your home. Your ranch. Your peace."

Jerome shook his head. "Don't go there. We wouldn't have it any other way." He grabbed Natalie's hand and brought it to his lips. A glance in her direction told Allison the woman was distressed. "Scared the dickens out of all of us, but it won't happen again. Not unless this group of thugs has an entire army at their disposal." His words trailed off. No one commented. They all feared that was exactly what might happen.

Daniel squeezed Allison's knee tighter. She set her hand on top of his, her nails digging into his knuckles. Her other leg bounced.

She cleared her throat and changed the subject. "Do you think there're more women being held?"

Her father spoke next. "Not sure, sweetie. It's possible."

Her mother nodded. "I've heard a lot of young men are joining the North American Reserves. It scares the bejebus out of me." She twisted her napkin, her elbows resting on the table top.

Natalie agreed. "Yeah. I've heard that too. Not sure if they're joining out of some sense of duty or if they're being recruited by The Council. We live so far out, it's harder for me to know what's happening in bigger cities."

"Well, in New York we have a lot of friends in the shifter community. It seems like a little of both. Some recruiters were in the area and then some of the young men's friends heard and joined with them." Allison stared at her mother as she spoke. She'd never seen her so concerned.

Allison had been so worried about herself for the last several days, she hadn't stopped to ponder the broader implications of what was happening in the shifter world. It wasn't just that she had been kidnapped and rescued, but some mysterious secrets were definitely occurring that went far beyond her situation.

"It would freak me out if anyone I knew joined NAR right now. I don't think I could sleep." She set her head on Daniel's shoulder and wrapped her hands around his arm.

No one spoke for several seconds, and then they all resumed chatting on top of each other, changing the subject. Good. She needed a generic discussion about the ranch, or even the weather.

~

Daniel cringed when his mate spoke her mind. A collective breath-holding filled the room with silence. Every person in the room knew Daniel himself was enlisted with NAR, except Allison. It wasn't that he'd intentionally kept the information from her. It just hadn't come up yet, and right here in front of both sets of parents wasn't the place to lower the bomb after what she'd said.

Great. He gritted his teeth, hating the sensation that he was lying to her. He didn't need this wrench in his relationship that started only yesterday. He tried desperately to remain calm next to her and not stiffen with her words.

After several minutes of chatter about the workings of the ranch and its normal operation under ordinary circumstances, someone knocked at the front door.

Daniel's father scooted back and excused himself to answer, though they could all see the door from the long table.

It was Evan, and he apologized for barging in. "So sorry. I was hoping I could speak with Daniel."

Daniel's brows rose as Evan stared at him. He turned to Allison and kissed her brow.

She smiled up at him. "I should go join the other women this morning, anyway. They must be pretty freaked out about what happened in the night. Go." She released his arm and nodded toward Evan. "I'll catch up with you later."

He hated leaving her side. He feared for her safety, even with the increased security. But mostly because they'd just mated and he wanted her in his presence. When he wasn't touching her, breathing in her scent, watching the way she moved, hell...listening to the sweet melody of her voice, he felt the loss. But he knew she needed to talk to counselors and continue to make progress toward healing. And the look on Evan's face suggested it was urgent.

Daniel rose from the table and stepped out of the house with Evan.

"Sorry, man. I know the timing of all of this stinks," Evan said as they headed down the front steps and away from the house.

Daniel followed as if Evan knew all the best places on the dude ranch to talk instead of Daniel. The man walked at a clipped pace, on a mission.

When they reached the fence surrounding the pasture to the left of the main barn, Evan leaned against the top and turned toward Daniel. "I wouldn't ordinarily involve you in everything happening behind the scenes, but considering the circumstances surrounding your relationship with Allison, I feel you must be kept informed."

Daniel nodded. His gut tightened, threatening a revolt against the huge meal he'd just consumed. Evan's face spoke volumes about the seriousness of whatever he had to say.

"I've spoken with the head elder, Ralph Jerard, and he agrees you need to be brought up to speed. The fact that you joined the North American Reserves last year didn't hurt in making this decision.

"The reality is that someone working high up for The Council is a mole. Even though we whittled down communication to just myself, Jerard, Steven Wightman —another of the elders—and my assistant, Alex Marshall, somehow information still filtered to the Romulus months ago. Of course many more shifters are involved now, but something is still not right."

"What the hell is the Romulus?" Daniel asked. "Never heard of it."

"Right." Evan nodded. "When we seized the twelve women, we also managed to snag three of their guards. They've been in questioning in Seattle in an undisclosed location since then. To be honest, the amount of information they have provided is paltry and disappointing. I truly don't believe they know much. However, we have learned the organization heading up this drug trial calls itself the Romulus."

"Drug trial? Is that what you think this is?"

Evan nodded. "Yes. All of the women were given a strange combination of Rohypnol and Scopolamine. However, the dosages weren't the same, nor were the methods. Some were injected. Some were given pills. Others didn't even know they had been drugged at all. Theirs must have been stirred into their food.

"According to the women, Allison is the only one who recalls being taken to another location for testing of some sort."

Daniel nodded. That much he'd known. "So these men, how is it possible they can't tell you anything?"

Evan shook his head. "I think the hierarchy of the group is very tight. The men on the bottom don't seem to know anything happening above them. They get phone calls from mysterious members of the Romulus giving them instructions without knowing who they're talking to."

"What the hell is the incentive?"

"Money. And promises of mates. The Romulus must be quite wealthy. They bank roll these guys. They're all rogue shifters who were on their own, lured in with the promise of a mate. That's what had happened to my mate, in fact. The asshole who took Ashley insisted he was her mate."

"God." Daniel swallowed. "But that's not what happened to Allison. What the fuck?"

"I know. It's very strange. The man guarding her wasn't the same man who took her, and he never insinuated she was mated to him or anyone else. And that leads me to the reason I'm talking to you now. I'm particularly concerned about Allison. And even more so after what happened in the night. It's like they targeted her specifically. I'm afraid she means something more to them than the others."

"Why? She seems to be in a better position than any of the others you rescued."

"Yeah. That's what worries me, to be honest. She served another purpose for the Romulus. And we fucked with whatever that was."

"How do you suppose these Romulus assholes found her here?" Daniel stiffened.

"I have no idea. But I think we need to be diligent. They might not be satisfied with last night's results. Especially when their men don't report back. I'm not sure what kind of manpower they might have to retaliate."

"Shit."

Evan continued. "After questioning the three men in custody, we've determined her case assuredly doesn't match any other. No idea why, but if they fear she knows anything or they weren't done with her, they may not give up."

"Fuck." Daniel turned to lean on the fence. "Do you suppose they'll return?"

"I don't presume anything with regard to these assholes. No matter how tightly we've operated, they've thwarted every effort. The fact that we managed to stay one step ahead of the Romulus and rescue those women is a miracle."

"What do you think we should do?"

"For now, sit tight and be diligent. I don't trust the safety of any of the women. I'm going to meet with your parents in a few hours and beg asylum here." He chuckled wryly. "I know it isn't what your family had in mind when you let me come here, but the stakes are higher than anticipated, and a safe refuge is what we need for everyone involved. I'm hoping to stay a while, if it's okay with your parents, and conduct my investigation from here. I'd rather be close."

"Of course. I'm certain you will have the full support of my family. We always assumed the women would stay for an extended time period anyway, for counseling. The ranch has made no other guest reservations for several weeks still." He wished Steven Wightman and Alex Marshall had stayed also, in light of this information. But both men had only been there for a few hours. They had more pressing matters to deal with from their headquarters in Seattle.

"Thank you. Your cooperation is appreciated, and your hospitality. The families of the women will all leave within the next few days. I'd like to move the women to the dorm building so members of NAR can provide the best protection against whatever we may face."

"Yeah, about that, Allison isn't aware of the fact that I enlisted last year. I'd appreciate it if you'd not mention that detail until I've had a chance to speak to her. She isn't going to like my involvement."

Evan nodded. "Of course."

CHAPTER 8

Steven Wightman stood at the front window of his secluded home sipping his coffee and staring out at the rain. It wasn't different from many other days in Seattle, but his hackles were up this morning. Sundays were usually quiet days for Steven. Sundays were the only day he didn't go in to The Head Council offices to perform some duty as one of the five head elders.

But times were changing, just like the weather. He closed his eyes and thought about everything that had transpired in the last year. After hundreds of years living in peace, the existence of shifters was threatened. He didn't know yet who posed the threat, but he was certain turmoil was coming, racing toward him like a steam engine.

Few humans had ever been privy to the secrets of their shifter friends and neighbors. Now, Steven felt he couldn't even trust his closest friends. Someone he worked with every single day—someone he ate lunch with, shared drinks with, exchanged stories with—one of those someones had betrayed the shifter community and put them all at risk. He feared that someone was another member of The Head Council.

Ralph Jerard was out. No way could he believe that for a minute. That left Melvin Cunningham, Earl Johnson, and Lucas Sheffield. And it chilled him to the bone to consider any of those possibilities. It had put a strain on their collective relationships with each other knowing what Steven knew and keeping it to himself.

There were no more Sundays for Steven. Every day was another day he had to tackle this problem head on. It was early still. In another hour he would leave the house to meet with the head elder, Ralph Jerard. The man was older, but he was wise, and Steven trusted him with his life.

Of all the possible shifters he knew, Ralph wasn't a suspect in his mind. For any of the other employees of The Head Council, all bets were off. Every other shifter was a suspect.

And the problems they were facing seemed to be piling up incrementally each day. If they couldn't find the leader of the mysterious Romulus soon and put an end to its pyramid of followers, there would be no way to keep the existence of shifters from the rest of humanity much longer.

Eventually war would break out among the shifter community. A war Steven never expected to see in his lifetime.

A faint whine met Steven's ears. He opened his eyes wide and squeezed his coffee mug tighter. As a shifter, his sense of hearing was better than the average human. The whine could be anything. It may not even be close.

He peered outside. The rain came down harder, beating against the picture window of his living room. Even with his increased eyesight, he could see nothing out of the ordinary. In fact, he couldn't see much past the porch between the dense storm and the water running off the roof to form a sheet of clear liquid that cascaded like a waterfall over the rain gutter and onto the railing. He needed to clear the gutter out again. It had been a year. Hell, he needed to pay someone younger and spryer to do it. He was getting too old for that kind of work.

The whining happened again, and he tipped his head to one side as though making his ear more available to the noise.

It came from behind him. The backyard. Steven set his coffee down on the end table and turned toward the kitchen. Just as he stepped from the carpet to the tile, his senses went on full alert. The whine switched to a scratching noise. Someone was at the back door. Not just someone. A shifter, in wolf form. Now he could smell the distinct scent of his species.

Steven froze for a moment, staring at the back door, wondering—hoping—his imagination was getting away from him. He'd lived alone and had for many years, ever since his mate had passed away too young.

Thankful no one else was in the house with him, he inched closer to the door. It wasn't common for shifters to paw at a fellow wolf's door in their natural form. Unheard of. First of all, even though Steven's home was blocked from the view of neighbors, this was still a community. No one shifted this close to homes. It wasn't safe. But more importantly, why on earth would anyone come calling in wolf form?

Steven set his hand on the knob and took a deep breath. When he opened the door, he kept his gaze low, knowing a wolf would be there to meet his gaze.

What he found startled him. The dripping wet muddy creature crouching on the small back porch was pitiful. He was male, and large, but he kept his head low, his jaw almost touching the ground in a stance of submission.

Steven furrowed his brow and opened the door wider. If the wolf meant to harm him, there was nothing Steven could do to prevent it. "Come inside. Are you injured?"

The wolf crawled into the kitchen, dripping water all over the floor. He was filthy and tired, but Steven didn't see evidence of blood or a broken bone.

Steven crouched down in front of the wolf and breathed deeply. Shit. He was related. Steven had no idea who this was, but his scent indicated he was a relative.

"Can you shift?" Steven stood. "Hang on a second. I'll get you a towel." He left the tired, matted ball of fur in the kitchen and headed for the bathroom. When he returned thirty seconds later, a man sat in the location he'd left the wolf. Not surprising.

Steven handed him the towel, and the lanky, exhausted man stood on wobbly legs to dry himself.

"Sorry about the water," he muttered as he wrapped the terry cloth around his waist.

"Who are you?" Steven stepped toward the coffee pot and poured his unexpected guest a steaming mug.

"My name is J.T. My father is your brother Johnathan."

Steven handed J.T. the coffee. "Johnathan? I haven't seen him in over thirty years."

"I know." J.T. ducked his head and took a sip. "Thank you so much. I was chilled to the bone out there."

"Come." Steven motioned behind him with a nod. "I'll get you some clothes. You can shower and clean up and then tell me what you're doing here."

J.T. followed and Steven eyed him from top to bottom. He was taller than Steven and skinnier. Which was saying something because Steven was a tall, slender man himself. Nevertheless he grabbed a pair of sweats and a T-shirt from his bedroom and handed them to J.T. as the man entered the bathroom and flipped on the shower.

"I'll wait for you in the living room."

"Thanks. I appreciate it."

Steven paced. What the hell was his brother's son doing at his home out of the blue? Johnathan had run away from home at eighteen and never returned. Steven's poor parents died a few years ago, never knowing what had happened to their oldest son. He'd been a free spirit and had been in many screaming matches with their mother and father. And now, over thirty years later, a man shows up claiming to be his son?

It wasn't as though Steven could deny their relation. J.T. could pass for Steven's own son. He imagined once the boy cleaned up and shaved, they'd look very similar. Not to mention the obvious scent declaring them to be relatives.

Steven startled from his thoughts when J.T. emerged quietly and took a seat on the couch. "I know it must be a shock to see me after all these years. You probably didn't even know I existed."

Steven shook his head. "Not a clue. Johnathan?"

"He and my mother died several years ago. I've been on my own since then. Rogue I guess you would call it. Well, my parents were rogue also. They didn't want to have anything to do with wolf politics or maintain relationships with anyone they'd known." J.T. balled his hands into fists.

"How old are you?"

"Twenty-five. I was seventeen when they died." He glanced down at his fists in his lap. "They were shot. Killed."

"God. I'm sorry. That must have been terrible. Do you know why?"

J.T. shook his head. "Not really. But a few days after they were left for dead in front of our house, three men came to see me."

Steven lifted his eyebrows. Somehow he knew the rest of this story was important. The look on J.T.'s face alone told him he should take a seat and listen carefully. He sat in the armchair facing J.T. "Go on."

"We lived out in the wilderness in Minnesota. No one around for miles. My father built our cabin himself, and we lived a very simple life. Occasionally we went to scavenge for supplies in nearby towns. Without accompanying my father on some of those missions as I grew older, I would be completely ignorant to the rest of the world.

"After my parents were killed, these men who arrived were very sympathetic. I thought they had my best interest at heart when they took me in and gave me a place to live, clean clothes, food… For a while they acted like perfect hosts. And then they started asking me to do things that were very odd."

"Like what?" Steven inhaled sharply, wishing he hadn't interrupted.

"Like spy on people and shifters. They would take me to various towns and ask me to gather information. It was strange, but I was alone and didn't have many other choices. At least I didn't think I did. I've been with them for seven years. Was, anyway…"

Steven held his tongue as J.T. paused and fiddled with his sweats, picking at imaginary lint and then wiping his palms on his thighs. "I'm not formally educated. My mother taught me at home. But she did a good job in my opinion. She didn't want me to be uneducated. However, I learned a lot more about the world quickly living with the Romulus."

"The Romulus?" Steven jumped to his feet. He leaned forward.

J.T. cringed back into the couch cushion. "Yeah. That's what they called themselves."

Steven ran a hand though his hair. This nephew of his was oblivious to many things. Steven needed to get a grip on himself and let the boy finish the tale. "I'm sorry. You shocked me. Please continue."

"I spent most of my time living in their main bunker. I'd say they were molding me. Now that I think back, they may have even been the ones to kill my parents. That idea began to enter my mind years ago. But I didn't have any place else to go. And I hoped it was just my imagination.

"Why would they kill my parents and then take me in? It didn't make sense. Unless they needed bodies and they thought a seventeen-year-old boy living a rogue life was the perfect kind of shifter to fill a vacancy in their strange hierarchy."

"You lived with the Romulus for seven years?"

"Yes. Except when they placed me somewhere else and gave me a job." J.T. cringed. "That's why I'm here. I left my last assignment without informing them and went out on my own. They kept calling me on my cell and demanding I return to the fold. Eventually I realized whatever they were doing was huge and dangerous. They couldn't risk losing me and having me tell anyone everything I knew.

"I know my father ran off to be on his own when he was just a kid, but he was like a hippy, I guess you would say. A mountain man. He didn't mean anyone any harm. He just didn't want to live in society. He was a good man. And so was my mom. They raised me to be respectful and polite.

"When I was a kid, they told me about you on many occasions and had me memorize your address in case I ever needed anything. I'd say I need something pretty bad right now. I'm scared out of my mind that these guys from the Romulus are going to hunt me down and kill me. And I'm sure my fate will be worse than that if they find out I contacted a member of The Head Council."

Steven took a deep breath. He couldn't believe this was happening. "What was your last assignment?"

"Right. That's part of why I'm here. These guys are conducting some sort of experiments at their main bunker. Medical experiments. And they have a lot of test subjects. Most are volunteer, but I now realize not all of them are. They placed me at a cabin in the woods to guard a woman for over a year."

"Who?"

J.T. cringed. "Her name is Allison. That's all I know."

Steven bit his cheek. "Go on." He needed to be patient and get every piece of information he could from his nephew.

"She was about my age. A tiny sweet blonde who clearly came from wealth. Not someone on the run who'd been living rogue like other people who come to the Romulus. Allison had been kidnapped. They told me it was for her own good and to guard her and make sure she didn't escape.

"I had grown leery of the Romulus by then, but I was afraid they would kill me or at least toss me out on my ass with nothing if I didn't do as they said. So I guarded that poor girl for the last year. We barely had enough to eat and never anything very good.

"Hell, the Romulus was probably trying to keep me weak also to ensure I was malleable. I hated that job. I couldn't even bring myself to speak to the girl because I didn't want to befriend her in any way. It made me sick, though. And the Romulus were drugging her. Using her for a test of some sort. They left me pills to give her, and sometimes they took her to their main bunker for more tests."

J.T. dipped his head. "I'm afraid in my efforts to keep her alive, I may have caused her death."

"How was that?" Did J.T. not know Allison was alive?

"I knew it was wrong. I knew everything I'd done for years was on the wrong side of the tracks. It kept getting clearer to me. I stopped giving Allison those drugs. I buried them in the woods instead. But that probably only made things worse, because she wasn't responding the way the Romulus wanted, so they grew tired of her.

"When they called and told me she was useless to them, I was relieved, thinking I'd succeeded. But then they lowered the bomb and told me I had to kill her."

Steven gasped. "They told *you* to do it?"

J.T. nodded. "There was no fucking way I was going to kill anyone. Ever. It was bad enough what I'd done in the first place, keeping her there. So I locked her in a closet like I always did when I was away and ran. I shifted and left the state so fast there was no way anyone could track me.

"At first I didn't know what to do. I just kept moving and worrying about Allison. When I wouldn't answer my cell, the Romulus started texting me. Threatening me eventually when they realized I'd gone rogue and then promising to kill me when they found out Allison had escaped and not been killed. I hope to God she's okay."

"She is."

J.T. flinched. "You know that?"

He nodded. "There are a lot of things I know, J.T. But what I need from you is every single detail of the last seven years so that we can track these bastards and put an end to whatever they have going on. It's dangerous and threatening the entire shifter species."

J.T. flopped his head back on the couch and stared at the ceiling. "I will tell you everything I know. I'm just sorry it took me so damn long to break from them and run. I was naïve and stupid."

"Well, you're here now. And I'll get you to a safe place where the Romulus can't find you. But I will tell you now, you can expect to spend every waking hour of your life filling us in on everything you know until you may wish you'd just stayed rogue."

J.T. shook his head. "If I can be of any help saving anyone, I'll do everything I can."

"Good. I'm glad you came to me. And I'm sorry to hear about your parents and everything else that has happened to you. You've gotten a bad rap in this life. I hope we can get you straightened out so that the rest of your life is on track."

～

"What the fuck happened, Henry?" The voice of Henry's superior was shrill.

"I'm not sure, sir. I sent two men in to retrieve

Allison. We knew exactly where she was located on the ranch property. They didn't return." He cringed. The man was going to freak.

"That's it? Just, they didn't return?" His voice grew louder. Wherever he was, the entire area would be able to hear him screaming at Henry.

Henry swallowed. "That's all I know."

"Well get your spy back the fuck in there and find out what's going on."

"Already sent him, sir. I'm waiting to hear back from him."

"Is this guy reliable?"

"Yes, sir. Definitely."

"More reliable than the two assholes you sent for the retrieval?"

Henry didn't get to respond to that question because the line went dead. His boss had hung up on him again.

Henry tossed his cell on the table and ran a hand through his hair. If he didn't get this mess cleaned up pronto, his boss was going to have him hanged. Perhaps literally.

He stood and paced the room. Waiting to hear back from Tarson this time was going to turn him prematurely gray. The guy was a follower, and Henry trusted him implicitly. But he didn't trust the bastards on that ranch. He feared the worst with regard to the two men he'd sent in to capture Allison.

They'd either been captured or killed. And sending Tarson back to get another look had been Henry's only viable option.

CHAPTER 9

Allison leaned on the top of the stall, watching Daniel brush Sadie. It was mesmerizing watching him work. When Daniel was in business mode, he was all serious, stern man, but when he was devoted to the animals or Allison, he was soft and gentle. Her heart beat a fast rhythm. She was falling in love with him hard and fast.

Daniel lifted his gaze to hers. "Are you okay? I know it was hard on you seeing your parents off this morning."

"Yeah. It wasn't long enough, but obviously any aspirations I had of returning with them were shot to shit when you came along." She grinned at him.

Daniel eased over to stand face to face with her, the wooden gate the only thing between them. He kissed her lips leisurely. "Mmm. Hope I can make it worth your while," he muttered as he stepped back. "I promise we will visit them first chance we get."

"I know." She fiddled with the rough wood, picking on a sliver sticking out.

Most of the other families had left today too. A few were leaving tomorrow. All of the women were staying. Allison expected them to prefer to return to their homes and be with their families, but in the end that hadn't been an option.

Allison was the only one who didn't move into the bunkhouse with the others. And Daniel hadn't let her out of his sight for over twenty-four hours. She wasn't stupid. She just wished Daniel would tell her what was going on himself instead of her having to ask. He hadn't spoken to her about anything of consequence since he'd wandered off to speak with Evan.

He cooed at Sadie and then stepped from the stall. "Ready?"

"Sure." *For what? More following you around the ranch doing odd jobs that can't possibly be as helpful as you insinuate?*

Daniel entwined his hand with hers, and she walked alongside him toward the exit. They wandered slowly toward his house.

"When are you going to tell me what's going on?"

"With what?" he asked, glancing at her briefly, just long enough for her to see his eyes widen. He didn't meet her gaze, which told her there was definitely something happening.

She yanked her fingers free of his and stopped walking, forcing him to turn around and meet her stare. She pursed her lips.

Daniel sighed. His shoulders slumped, and he toed at the dirt with one boot. "I'm sorry. I've been trying to protect you."

"From what? I'm a grown woman, Daniel. I deserve to know anything that concerns me. And I strongly suspect all the women aren't staying here for a long-term visit just to attend counseling sessions and bond together in sorrow. Do you think we're still in danger?"

He lifted his face, thankfully giving her that. "I don't know."

"But you suspect?"

"Yes."

"Based on what?"

"Information we've gathered from the guards who were caught about who they worked for and why." Daniel stepped toward her and set his hands on her shoulders. "I really don't want you to have to worry. The ranch is safe."

"Is that why there are so many more NAR members here? Because you think it's super safe? Daniel, be straight with me. I deserve to know everything you know. It's my life on the line. Obviously someone is after me." A chill raced down her spine to say that out loud. "I'm clear on that. Do you think the other women are just as at risk?"

He shrugged. "We don't know."

She lifted an eyebrow, making him shake his head.

"No. I don't think anyone is as at risk as you. Happy?"

"Of course not." She shook herself free of his grip on her shoulders. She glanced around, noting the various Reserves lurking everywhere.

Daniel reached for her again, and she stepped back. "They make me nervous. Please tell me you won't enlist." She stared at him, praying he wasn't a fighter. But she didn't know him well enough yet to be sure of that. She'd seen him fight in wolf form. And he owned a gun. But he hadn't mentioned teaching her to use it since that night. For that she was grateful.

Daniel didn't say a word. He turned toward the cabin, grabbing her hand and tugging her along at a quicker pace.

Allison gritted her teeth, fear climbing up her spine to stiffen her back. He was thinking of joining. She could tell by his reaction. Could she stop him? And was that even a good plan if his heart was set on enlisting?

They reached the front porch and entered silently. Daniel led her to the sofa and sat, pulling her alongside him. "We need to talk."

She didn't move. She let him hold her hand, and he jiggled it loosely in his grasp as though weighing it.

"I enlisted with NAR a year ago, baby." He paused and looked her in the eye.

She gasped.

"When you mentioned your aversion at breakfast the other day, I didn't want to say anything in front of our parents."

"And you couldn't find another opportune time since then?" She gripped his hand tighter, not letting her gaze leave his.

"I was putting it off. I wanted us to have a few days together first before I laid that burden on you. It was selfish. And I'm sorry."

She swallowed the lump in her throat, trying to hold herself together. "So what do you do for them?"

"I train two weekends a month. Or at least that's what I have done so far. I suspect The Head Council will be calling many of us into active duty if the shit hits the fan."

"Oh God." Now her hand actually shook, and she tugged it free to ball it up with her other hand.

He lowered his face. "I wish to hell it hadn't happened like this. But I'm not sorry I enlisted. As crazy as that sounds, if I hadn't enlisted last year, I would do so now in a heartbeat. No way could I sit back and let other people protect our way of life, especially not after mating with you. You mean the world to me, and if I have to go to battle to keep you safe, I will."

"And you don't think I'm safe here? Daniel, you haven't left my side for two days. How could I be any more safe? I can't even go into another room without you shadowing me. We're surrounded by Reserves, and no one has tried to get through since that night. Don't you think whoever sent them gave up?"

He shook his head. "Not for a second. And it would be foolish to even entertain the idea. I don't know what those sons of bitches were doing to you, but they obviously weren't done."

She leaned toward him and held his face with both hands when he scowled. "Well, no one is going to get to me now. You're attached to me like glue."

He lifted his gaze again and gave a half smile. "That's not entirely altruistic, you know. I like being around you. No..." He shook his head, erasing that statement. "I can't stand to have you out of my sight, regardless of the circumstances. You've woven a spell around me that makes me crave your presence."

She smiled back. "Well, at least it's not one-sided. It makes my chest pound when you follow me around. I had hoped it was because you were drawn to me like a magnet. I admit to being a bit dismayed to find you're chasing me out of duty."

"Never." He grabbed her waist and pulled her onto his lap. He stroked his hand down her arm until he reached her fingers and then set them on his growing erection. "Does that feel like duty to you?" He grinned. "Your damn pheromones drive me fucking crazy all day and all night. Most of the time I forget we're under a bit of a siege here because all I can think about is how sexy you are under those clothes and wonder when I might be able to lure you back here to take them off again without appearing crass."

He released her hand to run both of his under her tank top. "And then to make matters worse, you wear these damn tight shirts that leave nothing to the imagination." He lifted her shirt as he whispered those words until his thumbs grazed over her nipples. "These little peaks poke out all the time, making me drool with want."

He whipped her shirt over her head and pulled the cups of her bra down to expose her breasts.

Allison whimpered. He was so good with words, she could barely remember why she was supposed to be upset or stressed.

When he lowered his head and sucked one tight bud into his mouth, she bucked her chest and grabbed his biceps. "God. You send me from zero to infinity in moments." She watched as he released her nipple and flicked his tongue over the tip.

She squirmed. Needing more. Now. She loved how aroused he could make her by just fondling her chest, but it wasn't enough. She released his bicep with one hand to grab his cock, squeezing it through his jeans, her thigh making it difficult to get a good grip.

Daniel shocked her when he grabbed her waist and stood her in front of him, immediately popping the button on her jean shorts and dragging the offensive denim off her body, taking her panties with them. When he reached her ankles, she kicked off her sandals with the shorts.

Allison reached behind herself to pop the clasp of her bra and release her swollen breasts to finish the unveiling. She nodded at his crotch. "A little help here."

Daniel smiled. He yanked his shirt off and squirmed his way out of his jeans and underwear in record time. His cock sprang free, engorged as always, the tip wet with precome.

Allison lowered to her knees in front of him, needing to taste him, even though she knew he wouldn't let her do it for long. She couldn't resist. Every flavor she sucked from his body was ambrosia. She'd spent hours tasting his skin and nibbling around his cock.

She took a deep draw on him, causing him to moan at her unexpected quick move. She could feel the vibrations from his throat all the way to his cock. And he stiffened, his thighs going rigid where she grasped them.

"Allie…"

She loved the sound of her nickname on his lips. It always meant he couldn't come up with any other words at that moment. She swirled her tongue around the head and then sucked him back in deeper than the last time.

Daniel threaded his fingers in her hair, rigid fingers that desperately tried to keep from pushing or pulling on her head.

She always ached for him, but knowing the effect she had on his body heightened her arousal. God how she loved this. The fact someone on this planet felt the same way about her made her heart swell.

She spread her fingers on his thighs and held him firmly, sucking harder, deeper, as deep as she could manage without gagging. All the while she breathed in his musky scent, her body having memorized it and aligned with him in a way that her pussy grew wet just from the memory of Daniel's smell.

Daniel groaned louder, stiffened his rigid body further, and tugged on her hair. "Baby…stop."

Not this time. Instead of obeying his demand, she hollowed her cheeks and held him deep, gripping him with her palms and pressing her face as low as possible.

A rumble escaped from deep inside him, coming out of his mouth as more of a growl than anything else. Animalistic in nature, just as they both were in their natural form.

She needed to swallow him this time. Craved the taste of his come on her mouth, not just the dribble that leaked out the tip, but the whole thing.

Daniel stopped protesting and released her head to grab the couch cushion with both hands. He lifted his torso into her mouth, helping her suckle him in rhythm with her own thrusts. In moments he emitted a deeper growl and bucked toward her. As he came, she sucked, swallowing everything as fast as it hit the back of her throat.

She continued to milk him until his body shivered from the pressure. And then she released him to nibble around his sac and tease him with her breath and her lips until he relaxed beneath her.

"Jesus, Allie..." He pulled her by the shoulders up to meet his gaze.

Allison lifted herself and climbed up to straddle him, sitting on his lap, his still semi-firm erection pressing into her pussy.

Daniel pulled her head down for a kiss, quickly accelerating the contact until she was panting from the simple lip lock. She needed more. The ache low in her belly she'd felt almost nonstop since meeting Daniel was tight and demanding.

Daniel broke the kiss and held her a few inches away from him by her shoulders. He lowered his hands to her breasts and molded them with his palms. He held her gaze as he spoke. "Touch yourself."

Now? She widened her eyes.

He nodded. "Masturbate on my lap, baby. I want to watch. Rub your clit with your fingers and use my cock against your pussy."

That ache doubled at his words. Allison stared down where their bodies met. It was one thing to help herself along when he was inside her. It was another thing entirely to fuck herself with his full attention on her, watching.

"I can smell your arousal. Do it, baby." He released her breasts to grab her hands, drawing them to his face. He shocked her when he sucked both her index fingers into his mouth at once. He licked them, and then he let them pop out and lowered them to the place where her pussy met his cock. "Play with your clit, baby. I want to see you."

A part of Allison was somewhat mortified at the idea, but the rest of her was so aroused she didn't care if he took pictures right then. She just wanted to feel more, harder, faster…anything to ease the pressure.

Allison set her fingers on her clit, held the hood up with one, and flicked the other over the swollen nub. Her stomach hollowed as she leaned back enough to get to her pussy. She stroked a finger through the wetness and drew it across her clit. She flinched, her own fingers surprising her with the intensity of the sensations.

Daniel wrapped his palms around her ass and held the globes, massaging them. Every time he pulled them apart, she stiffened, sensing the exposure, even though no one could see behind her. Still he teased her butt. She could see him gauging her reaction by holding her gaze with his.

She moaned when he gave up the pretense and held her wide, his fingers inching closer to her rear entrance.

"Breathe, Allie. Keep your fingers on your pussy and clit. Let me make you feel good."

How did he propose to do that?

Allison watched his face. She doubled her efforts, her clit bulging now, demanding release. And she would have come right then if Daniel hadn't been distracting her with his fingers spreading her rear. The combination heightened her senses.

When he reached under her to stroke two fingers through her needy pussy and draw her wetness back to her other hole, she dug her toes into the couch cushion.

Daniel rimmed her tight hole and she stiffened. *OhGodohGodohGod*. Her eyes blinked shut and she tilted her head back, unable to decide if she liked what he was doing or not. She tried to reason with herself that society had put the stigma on her tight bud. That stigma was manmade, not real. It had to be because she loved the feelings he was evoking, sharpening the experience of masturbating herself.

Daniel wrapped one hand around her back and held her steady against his lap as he inched a finger into her.

Allison stopped moving, setting her head against his shoulder and holding her breath as she concentrated on what he was doing to her emotionally and physically.

Sensations fired. Good ones.

She stilled her fingers to focus on Daniel's movements. His finger fucked her in and out, slow and easy. When he added another finger, she flinched.

"Easy. Just feel."

She clamped down on her bottom lip to keep from moaning at the unusual feelings as his two fingers scissored in and out of her, stretching her.

"Touch yourself, baby," he muttered against her temple.

When she resumed stroking her clit, she nearly shot off the couch at the combined sensation.

Daniel held her steady, pressing his fingers in deeper.

Allison moaned, her mouth falling open as she sat up straighter and looked between their bodies. His cock rested completely stiff again against her pussy, and she dug her heels into the cushions to lift herself a few inches and insert his length into her pussy. She settled fully seated again, his cock deep and hard inside her, making her groan around the fullness combined with those damn fingers in her rear.

"Allie."

She lifted her gaze to his once more.

"Touch yourself." His words, repeated again, were firm, and a tingle raced down her spine until she shook with pleasure.

Holding his gaze, she lifted her hand to her mouth and sucked two fingers inside to moisten them again. And then she hollowed her stomach again, pulled back the hood of her clit, and swiped her wet fingers over the throbbing nub.

Her vision clouded. She didn't allow herself to lift and lower over him. The fullness of his cock was enough combined with what he was doing to her from behind and what she did to herself over her clit. Anything more would give her heart palpitations.

She flicked her fingers rapidly, enjoying the rise of arousal. But the instant Daniel started pumping his hand tight against her ass, she shattered. She gripped his cock hard with her channel. Her clit pulsed against her fingers as she pressed them tight against the little organ.

She moaned, a low sound that she couldn't imagine herself capable of.

When it was over, she released her sensitive clit and leaned against Daniel's chest, her knees shaking and her body weak.

Daniel pulled from her ass slowly, a shiver wracking her entire body as he exited. It felt so good, so naughty and fantastic at the same time.

Daniel grasped her by the butt and stood, lifting her with him and effortlessly carrying her across the room to the sink without letting his cock slip out of her pussy.

She held him tight, her arms wrapped around his neck and her feet locked behind him as he washed his hands at the sink with her body between him and the faucet. How she managed to come up with the energy to hold on was beyond her. When he finished, he set his wet hands on her back and trailed cool water down her body.

She squirmed, a giggle escaping her. "That's cold."

"Yeah, I thought you needed it. You were getting tired on me."

"We could nap." She nibbled his ear and licked the lobe.

"My cock disapproves of that idea."

She smiled against his neck. It was true. His cock was rock hard inside her, even though she'd sucked him off minutes ago.

Daniel carried her to the kitchen table and set her

ass on the edge. He eased her back to lie on the smooth surface and then stretched her arms over her head and danced his fingers over her nipples.

Allison arched her chest into his touch, her arousal shooting to full speed in a heartbeat.

She watched him pluck her buds with both hands, pinching and twisting just enough to make her squirm.

"You're so sexy, Allie." His voice was deep, a tone she'd begun to recognize as his aroused pitch. And his need fueled her own. "Your skin is so soft." He stroked the undersides of her breasts with his pinkies. And then he released one nipple and sucked his pointer into his mouth. When it popped out with a dramatic noise, he set it on her heated bud and flicked it with his wet finger.

Allie moaned. Her eyes rolled back. She couldn't hold his gaze.

"You ready for me?"

"Uh huh." She nodded. How could she not be? He was already impaling her. What she needed was for him to move. Now.

Changing the pace from lazy and slow to hot and passionate, Daniel released her breasts to grab her hips. He held her still on the edge of the table and withdrew his cock only to thrust back into her. Again and again. His grip was tight, and she loved the sensation that he was keeping her from escaping.

Her arousal rose with each thrust, his cock nudging her G-spot with every entrance from this position.

"I'm. Gonna. Come," he said as he plunged deep and

held himself against her cervix. His hand flew from her hip to her clit and pressed hard.

Allison's entire sex reacted as she came with him. She came hard, as if she hadn't just come from her own hand on the couch.

And then she lay like a noodle on the table, her arms still above her head, but limp. She couldn't lift herself if she had to. She'd be content to nap right on the hard surface naked.

Through the post-orgasm haze, she heard Daniel chuckle. He lifted her body against his again and carried her to the bedroom. When he laid her on the mattress, he disappeared.

She couldn't move. In fact, she was almost asleep when she felt a warm wet cloth against her thigh. She sighed as he washed her and curled onto her side when he pulled the covers over her and kissed her temple. "Sleep, baby. I'll be in the other room."

She might have nodded or moaned. She wasn't sure.

CHAPTER 10

Daniel felt his mate easing up behind him before she'd even entered the room. He'd grown to sense her every move in the last few days. He didn't flinch, knowing he had things he needed to tell her as she wrapped her arms around his middle and stared out the front window alongside him.

She wore one of his T-shirts again. He stood in nothing but his jeans, the heat of the day keeping him from wanting to put on a shirt after Allison had fallen asleep earlier.

The cabin was air-conditioned, but it was working overtime lately to keep up with the temperature outside.

He waited, his heartbeats aligning with Allison's as she held him tighter.

Finally she spoke, her voice hoarse from just awakening. "Mind telling me why there are wolves circling out front?"

He smiled down at her and squeezed her against his

side with an arm around her shoulders. "What? You've never seen a wolf before?"

She didn't respond. He was stalling. She wasn't stupid.

He let his gaze wander back to the window. "It's weird. We never shift this close to the ranch. There are always humans on the premises." A slight chill went down his spine.

She set her head on his chest and watched with him. "Do you normally have full humans working on the ranch?"

"Yes. We have several. Most are shifters, but some are human. We gave them the month off with pay when we decided to take in the women. Plus, most of our guests are usually human."

"I see."

Did she?

"So where's the fire? Suddenly the Reserves are prancing around shifted. I'm not dumb, Daniel. If these men are in wolf form, they must be needing all their heightened senses."

He nodded, holding her tight.

"You can't prevent every eventuality, Daniel. And I wouldn't expect you to. Just talk to me."

He glanced back down at her face as she tipped her head up to meet his gaze.

He stepped back a few paces, taking her with him, and sat on the couch with her at his side. "Evan got a call from Seattle. It seems the man who held you for the last year turned himself in."

She gasped and sat up straight. "Are you serious?"

Daniel nodded. "Apparently his uncle is Steven Wightman, a member of the head council. His name is J.T. He's been in questioning for a few days. He knows a few things, including the fact that whoever took you isn't happy about you being rescued."

"What's different about me? Does he know?"

"No, but the people who run that place where you went for medical testing call themselves the Romulus. They called J.T. for many days after he left you, trying to bring him back into the fold."

"He left me for dead then."

"Well, it could have been worse. His instructions if he ever had to abandon his post had been to kill you first."

Allison inhaled sharply. "I don't think he had that in him."

"Apparently not. And the Romulus aren't happy about it, either. Either they're afraid you know too much or they aren't done with you. Either way, they want you back." He stroked a hand up and down her back. He hated having to tell her this, but keeping it from her wasn't fair, and it was becoming impossible under the circumstances.

"We can't hide out here forever keeping your family's ranch like a fortress."

"No. We can't." He reached a hand to brush a lock of hair away from her face. "We have to go to Seattle." He waited for her reaction, his heart beating.

She swallowed hard, keeping a brave face. "Of course." She looked back toward the window. "If we don't, we're putting the other women at risk."

God, he loved her.

"Exactly. In Seattle The Head Council can keep you safe and hidden."

"Me? What about you?" She hesitated, about to say more, and then clamped her mouth shut and jumped to stand in front of him. She crossed her arms. "You're going to join the fight."

He nodded, leaning his elbows on his knees and clasping his hands. "I don't have a choice. And even if I did, I wouldn't take it. But the only way for me to do my job well is if I know you're safe."

Allison walked away, her hands falling to her sides.

He watched her pad to the sink, grab a glass, and fill it with water. She drank the entire contents and set it on the counter without turning around. "When do we leave?"

"We have a flight in about three hours."

She nodded, keeping her back to him, and left the room.

Daniel set his head in his palms. This wasn't how he ever envisioned mating. When he pictured himself with a mate, it always involved the ranch, the horses, this cabin filled with her laughter. Not a race across the country when all hell was about to break loose for shifters everywhere.

She was angry. He knew that. But she was strong. And she would pull it together.

When he heard the water running in the bathroom, he stood and headed toward his mate.

He leaned against the doorframe for a moment, watching Allison through the glass shower door as she lifted her face and let the water cascade down her body. She wasn't as skinny as she had been a few days ago. Even in that short time, she was gaining strength.

Daniel pushed off the edge of the door and unbuttoned his jeans. He lowered them to the floor and stepped out. Allison didn't flinch when he entered behind her and wrapped his arms around her body, holding her tight against his chest.

He kissed the top of her head, her shampoo leaving bubbles on his face. "I love you."

"I love you too."

"I know you hate this arrangement, and I'm sorry."

"I know."

~

Two hours later, Allison held Daniel's hand as he led her through the airport toward their terminal. He tried to look nonchalant as he scanned the area around them every step of the way, but she knew him well enough to recognize the stiffness of his steps and the way his eyes shifted back and forth with every move.

When they reached their gate, they sat. He squeezed her hand. "It's going to be okay."

She grinned at him. "Who are you trying to convince?"

He moaned and kissed her gently. "Both of us, I guess."

"Where are we going when we get there?"

"I don't know. Someone will pick us up at the airport."

Allison slumped into the seat. "I can't believe this is happening." She kept her voice low. "The last week has been like I'm in a blender or something. I'm getting pulverized."

Daniel brought her hand to his lips. "I wish there was something I could do to make it better for you."

"You're doing it." She set her head on his shoulder.

Minutes later their flight was announced, and they made their way to the plane. When they took off, the low hum of the engines soothed Allison's nerves. She hadn't flown in over a year and hadn't been willing to only a week ago. But things had changed since then. Necessity forced her to get over herself in a hurry or put herself at risk for worse than she'd been through so far.

There was a fate worse than spending a year in a log cabin with little food and only one silent man for company. If this strange group called the Romulus got their hands on her again, they would surely kill her or subject her to worse.

Allison closed her eyes, and when she opened them again, they were landing. Daniel still held her hand. She knew he had never released her.

The next hour was a whirlwind of activity, grabbing their luggage, meeting their driver, and being shuffled to an undisclosed location.

Allison stared out the window of their room when they were finally settled in a military facility outside Seattle. She didn't know for sure where they were since it had been dark when they'd arrived. The base's location wasn't public knowledge, not even to the shifter community.

The man who'd driven them had said very little and had not introduced himself. He nodded after seeing them to their room and shut the door behind him.

Allison folded her arms as though hugging herself. Seattle weather was a far cry from Texas. Even though it was dark, she could see the rain falling outside, and both times she'd dodged the raindrops to get to and from the car, she'd felt the chill in the air.

Daniel wrapped himself around her and set his chin on her head. She could see his expression in the window.

Allison swallowed. She didn't know how much time she had with Daniel before he would go. She didn't want to ask. She just wanted to enjoy whatever she could get. She knew he would leave her here soon, a place where she would be safe. And she would do it —for him.

The last thing she wanted right then was to be left alone. For some reason she felt lonelier about the prospect than she had for the last year. Now that she'd met her mate, separating from him was unimaginable, especially after such a short time.

But he would worry less knowing she was safe, and stressing over a situation she couldn't control wouldn't help either of them. She needed to be strong now. She couldn't even call her parents. She'd spoken to them cryptically earlier in the day before leaving for the airport. They understood the basics, but any other information would have to wait. Lives were at stake.

"I need you," Daniel whispered. His arms tightened around her, his hands on top of hers wrapping her in a cocoon.

She needed him too, as bad as her next breath. Just hearing those words from him made her belly clench. Already the room they were in had filled with his scent.

She turned in his arms and lifted her lips to his. The solemnness of the situation only heightened her arousal. The clock was ticking. Urgency filled her, and she grappled with his shirt, tugging it haphazardly to get it over his head.

Daniel helped her before he stepped away for a moment to pull the blinds closed. He was back seconds later, his hands working as feverishly to divest her of her clothes as she was with his. Finally they both let go in unspoken agreement and stripped out of their own jeans. When they were naked, she watched his chest rise and fall with each breath.

She stood transfixed as he circled her, gazing at every aspect of her body. It would have made her uncomfortable, but not today. She knew he needed to memorize her as she needed to do with him.

When he returned to her front, he held his cock in his hand, stroking it lightly as he watched her. "You're so beautiful, Allie."

She didn't flinch, her hands remaining at her sides, fisted loosely as she waited for his next move.

He inhaled slowly, tipping his head back and sucking the air from the room. "Your arousal humbles me every time. I love your scent. I've memorized it." He dropped his cock and led her to the bed. She'd paid very little attention to the room. It was a standard hotel-type room with a kitchenette and a love seat. A place someone could stay indefinitely. The colors around her were bland beiges that caused her to notice nothing.

She focused on Daniel's gaze as he turned her to face him and lifted her to sitting on the edge of the mattress. "Lie back, baby. I need to taste you."

She shivered as she did as he asked, the sheets cool beneath her spine and her ass.

He spread her legs wide and held them open as he leaned in to kiss each of her nipples in turn. His cock lined up with her pussy and pressed against her, making her moan with desire.

Her breasts swelled as he flicked his tongue over first one nipple and then the other. A squeak escaped her lips.

Daniel kissed a path down her body until he reached her sex. With his hands on her thighs, he opened her even wider and nuzzled her pussy, his nose buried in her folds, scenting her as she'd done him earlier. She understood the need. Since the claiming, she'd wanted to breathe this man's essence every hour of every day. She couldn't get enough of him.

Daniel tipped her thighs, opening her wider. His tongue darted out to stroke through her folds, gathering her moisture but not touching her with enough pressure in any one spot.

She squirmed.

"Lie still, baby. I need this. Please." He licked her again, his tongue torturing her outer lips and then dipping inside to draw out her arousal.

Allison bucked her hips, forcing his tongue deeper until she groaned in frustration as he pulled back, not letting her control the pace or the depth.

He moved higher until he wrapped his lips around her clit and circled the tip with his damn tongue. "So sweet." He sucked her into his mouth, her clit engorging as he forced it to come to attention.

Allison lowered her arms to grasp his head. She threaded her fingers in his dark blond hair and held his head against her pussy. *God that feels good.*

Her eyes rolled back in her head as she focused on his tongue and his lips, letting her torso rise and fall with his suction. He was going to make her come without his fingers. She was so close.

Oh God. She squeezed her thighs, but he held them tighter, not giving her an inch.

She released his head to grab the sheets next to her, afraid she would pull his hair out.

Suddenly he rapidly flicked his tongue over her clit and then bit down on the swollen nub, not hard enough to injure her, but just enough to make her shoot off.

She squealed as her pussy gripped at nothing. He flattened his tongue against her clit, the pressure reaching deep enough to push her into a second orgasm right on the heels of the first.

Before the pulsing stopped, Daniel pushed her farther from the edge of the bed and climbed up over her. In an instant he was inside her, his cock filling her needy pussy to the hilt.

She gasped, having trouble sucking in a breath as she grabbed his forearms and held on. Her eyes flew open, and she found herself staring into the deep ocean of his gaze. His brow was furrowed—in concentration or aggravation?

He took her hard and fast. She loved the rough edge. She loved the way he held her gaze intently. She loved everything about him, and her body lifted to meet every thrust as he poured himself into her.

When Daniel finally slipped from inside her and headed to the bathroom, she remained on the bed in the same position, limp and sated. He returned with a wet wash cloth, cleaned her up, and slipped into the bed with her. She wanted to stare at him, soak him in every moment she could, but her eyes were heavy and closed on their own.

It seemed like moments later that Allison awoke to a dark room. She reached for Daniel, only to find herself grasping at cool sheets. "Daniel?"

He padded into the room from the adjoining bath. "Right here, baby." He slid back into bed beside her and pulled her close. "Your heart is pounding."

"I was dreaming." She held him close, setting her cheek against his chest. "What time is it?"

"Early still. Go back to sleep." He stroked her back and then flattened his hand on her skin.

"What were you doing?" she murmured.

"Checking my phone messages. I didn't want to wake you."

"People left you messages in the night?" She lifted her head to rest her chin on his chest and stare into his deep blue eyes.

He nodded and tucked her head back against him. "Sleep. You're still catching up for lost z's."

"I must be. I sleep all the time."

She closed her eyes. When she opened them again, it was day. Light filtered into the room. She pushed herself to sitting.

Daniel sat on the love seat, his fingers traveling over the keyboard of his computer in rapid motion. He didn't notice her yet, and she took a moment to watch him.

He wore only loose shorts, his hair damp and slicked back. His naked chest beckoned her, but she shook the thought away. He had pressing issues to attend. His forehead was scrunched. Whatever he was working on didn't sit well with him.

Finally he paused and glanced up. He smiled. "You're up."

She nodded. "You never sleep."

"I do." He stood and set the computer on the coffee table to come over to her side. He sat on the edge of the bed and stroked his hand over her head and down her hair, tangling his fingers in the curls. "I love the way you look first thing in the morning. I'll never tire of it."

"You showered. I need to do the same."

"Yes. We should go get some breakfast. You must be starving." He nodded behind him. "I made coffee from the little room pot. You want some?"

"Sounds like heaven." She swung her legs out from under the covers and scooted to the edge of the bed. Her stomach growled. She hadn't eaten since the airport.

He drew his thumb down her spine. "You grab a shower. I'll bring you coffee. And then we'll go get a bite to eat." He kissed her and stood.

She watched his back as he walked away, his shoulders broad and muscular. She ached to grab them and hold on to him with both hands, as though that would stop time.

Instead she lowered her gaze and eased off the bed.

In minutes, she was showered and standing in the bathroom toweling off. She moaned when Daniel entered with a steaming mug of coffee.

Allison hung the towel on the rack and took the cup from his hands. The first sip was heaven. It made her eyes open a bit farther. "I needed that."

He smiled. "Get dressed, woman. Before I change my mind about breakfast and take you back to bed."

She followed him from the bathroom, grinning. "Don't tempt me." But she kept her gaze away from his body, knowing if she didn't put some clothes on fast, he'd make good on his promise. And as much as she preferred option number two, she knew he had pressing issues to take care of. He was meeting with the head of The Council this morning. And she was going with him. Maybe she would be able to shed some new light on things. Though she couldn't imagine how.

Breakfast was in the mess hall of the base. There were very few shifters around. It was late, the tail end of the meal. Allison took a seat with Daniel after they'd filled their plates. She scarfed down her food as though she were starving. In a way she was. Scrambled eggs, bacon, and hash browns went a long way toward making her feel alive again.

Just as she finished, a man approached their table. He extended a hand to Daniel. "Spencer. Good to see you again." And then he turned toward Allison. "You must be Allison." He shook her hand also. "I'm Steven Wightman."

Ah, right. A member of The Head Council. He'd been at the ranch when she'd first arrived, but she hadn't met him. She'd been interviewed by Alex Marshall that first day.

"Sorry we're running so late this morning," Daniel said.

"No problem at all. I expected as much. You got in late. Jerard is just arriving. I came to hunt you down and see if you were ready to meet with him."

"We are." Daniel stood. He took Allison's arm as she rose next to him. He grabbed both their plates and silverware and headed for the dish return.

Allison waited with Wightman.

"How are you doing?" he asked politely.

"Better every day." She smiled at him.

Her instincts told her he was someone she could trust, and Daniel had said as much. She shivered when she remembered he had met with her captor, however. Hell, he hadn't just met with the man. He was related to him. J.T. A guy who had never had a name in the year she'd known him. J.T. Wightman.

When Daniel returned, they both followed Wightman from the mess hall. Outside the sun was trying to poke through the layer of clouds. Men were moving around the base rapidly, each one nearly marching by on a mission. Allison grabbed Daniel's arm. This crazy rabbit's hole she'd fallen into just got deeper by the second.

What the hell was she doing hiding on a military base in the middle of Washington? She should have been at home in New York City getting the kids she cared for dressed and ready for studying. Her world had disintegrated over a year ago. She'd never see a glimpse of that life again.

She was mated now. To a man who would soon become a full-time member of NAR, if there was such a thing. Or did they call themselves something entirely different when they became full-time employees?

They reached a building that looked distinctly different from the others, modern, formal, even from the outside. Wightman opened the front door silently and held it for her.

Daniel followed on her heels. She felt his presence. Even if she closed her eyes, she would know if he was near. It calmed her nerves.

They proceeded down a long hall off the main entrance and entered what had to be a conference room. A long table filled the space. At the head of the table was an older gentleman who stood when they entered. "Spencer. Good to see you," he said to Daniel first before turning his attention to Allison. "And you must be Allison. Please, have a seat."

The man resumed his spot and pointed at the chairs closest to him. Wightman took up the seat next to the man she knew was Ralph Jerard on one side, while

Daniel pulled out a chair across from Steven for Allison. She was grateful. Her knees were about to buckle. It wasn't every day someone sat down with a member of The Head Council, and here she was with two of them.

"I trust you rested well? Were your accommodations sufficient?"

"Of course," Daniel responded.

"I know you've been called to active duty, Spencer, but under the circumstances, I think it would be best if you deferred your start date for a few weeks." He turned his gaze toward Allison. "I'm sure Ms. Watkins is fragile after what she's endured over the past year, and your time will be better spent helping her with her recovery before you turn her over to be mauled by the other military mates on base." He chuckled.

Allison held her breath, grateful for his understanding, but somewhat appalled by his description.

"Don't get me wrong. I'm sure you will fit in fine. But I know your road is challenging right now."

Allison nodded. "Thank you, sir."

Jerard leaned on his elbows on the tabletop, steepling his fingers and tapping them together. "As much as I hate to do this to you, we'd appreciate it if you would identify the man who held you captive."

She nodded again, with less enthusiasm.

"He's also being held on this base. We hesitate to consider him a prisoner because, although his actions were beyond the pale where you're concerned, his motives were well-intended in the end, and he has provided us with a great deal of inside information about the Romulus. Let's just say, he has been granted a sort of protected asylum here. He isn't free to wander around, and you won't have to see him face-to-face other than to identify him.

"But he isn't in a locked cell, either. He doesn't seem to pose a flight threat. If he were to leave this base, chances are the Romulus would hunt his ass down and kill him so fast he wouldn't even be able to see it coming."

Allison flinched at the description.

Daniel grabbed her hand under the table and held it tight against her thigh. She absorbed his strength as though he could pass his calmer demeanor to her through their contact.

"Are you sure he can be trusted?" Daniel asked.

"We can never be certain of anything these days. And I'll feel much better about his story after comparing it with Allison's accounting of what the last year entailed. And her visual recognition, of course." Jerard set his palms on the table and spread his fingers.

"Pardon my curiosity, but how safe is Allison here on the base?" He glanced around the room, and Allison had the suspicion he was asking the question more for her benefit than his own.

Wightman answered. "Extremely. This base has never been breached by anyone in all its years of existence, and that number is larger than you can imagine. You'll learn more when you start training full time."

Allison flinched at the mention of Daniel's permanent involvement. First she'd cringed at the idea of being claimed by a rancher, not wanting to leave the hustle and bustle of New York City. Now? Holy shit. She would give anything to retract that thought. It was an entirely different bag of dog poop to be mated to a man who was going to join the fight against evil.

And she was quickly growing to accept something huge and defining for her species was about to occur.

Jerard continued. "Suffice to say, no one is getting inside these walls, and no one is getting out that shouldn't."

Allison shivered. She twisted her hand to grab Daniel's, her fingers digging into his palms. She was among the shifters not leaving this base. Not that she had any intention of doing so. The risk was too great. But still, it rankled.

Daniel nodded. "Understood."

Jerard stood. "Well, I just wanted to introduce myself and assure you in person you'll be in good hands here." He spoke those words directly to Allison. "Wightman will take you to identify your captor. And he will also speak to you more thoroughly about the details of your captivity. Please keep everything related to this case strictly between the very small group of people involved. Myself, Wightman, Evan Harmon, and Alex Marshall. You met him in Texas, right?"

"Yes." Daniel stood as he responded, his hold on Allison's hand bringing her with him.

"I'm sure you've been informed we have a mole. Until we know who it is, don't speak a word to anyone." He narrowed his gaze. "That includes any wives you meet. As far as they will know, you came here to live because you're a military spouse. Any other information will just fuel the rumor mill and make it that much harder to keep inside information tight."

Allison nodded. She could barely think straight anymore. This was more serious than she ever imagined.

CHAPTER 11

As Daniel followed Steven toward a row of buildings, Allison gripped his hand so tight he knew her fingers would be sore. He couldn't blame her. If he were in her shoes, he'd be at least as panicked. In fact, he was impressed she hadn't broken down in tears yet or frozen with the fear of seeing the man who'd held her.

At the end of the long row of gray buildings, Wightman opened the front door and let Daniel pass with his mate first. He'd seen the letter D on the side of the building. He made a mental note never to take Allison on any quest near that building again.

Wightman spoke in a low tones as they walked down a long hall. "This is essentially a holding cell. Not a prison exactly, but more of a place for those we're keeping an eye on. No one leaves this building without permission. J.T. won't be leaving here for any reason in the near future and certainly not without notifying you first. If we even so much as move him to another location, we'll inform you. Your safety and sanity are a far greater concern than his comfort."

Allison nodded so slightly even Daniel could barely sense it.

Wightman turned toward them as he opened a door on the left. "This is a lineup room. You will see J.T., but he won't be able to see you through the one-way mirror."

Allison exhaled and her shoulders fell.

Thank God. Daniel had worried about the arrangement. His mate could live through that.

"Go ahead and take a seat. I'll have several people brought in to ensure you have a fair group to identify J.T. from." Wightman paused at the door and turned toward them. "J.T. is my nephew. That's no secret. But please understand I never even knew I had a nephew until this week when he showed up at my doorstep. He seems on the up-and-up, and I believe he is telling the truth, but my loyalties do not lie with him until his motives are proven. And even then, I will always have one eye open when it comes to him.

"He has done a horrible thing to you, Allison. I'm on your side. Never doubt that."

Daniel pulled her close as Wightman left the room. Her heart beat so fast, he tried to soothe her. He kissed her temple and then sat in a chair, tugging her into the one next to his.

She perched herself on the corner of the seat, leaning into him more than not. "Jesus, I'm nervous."

"I know, baby. I am too. And I'm so sorry. I hate you having to do this."

She nodded. "I know, but it must be done. If any information I can provide will catch these guys before they capture a new batch of women, I'm all in."

"You're the bravest, strongest woman I know." He stroked her back, his fingers grazing over her soft hair. "I love you."

She leaned into him farther, practically in his lap. He didn't give a damn. Fuck propriety. She was his mate and she was rightfully scared out of her mind.

Lights came on in front of them, bringing the room behind the mirror into view. She buried her face in his chest and gripped his shirt with the hand over his chest, balling the material in her fist. She breathed heavily at first and then controlled each inhale and exhale.

Daniel watched as six men filed into the room and stood against the white wall. A chart painted on the wall in black lines indicated each man's height. "Baby, it's time."

Allison took a deep cleansing breath, released her grip on his shirt, and lifted her gaze to his. She twisted her face toward the window after staring into his eyes for several seconds.

He did his damnedest to reassure her with his look.

For several heartbeats she looked from one man to another, back and forth, over and over until he feared she didn't see the man she was looking for. It wasn't as though she would have trouble identifying him. This was only a precaution. She'd lived with him for a year. She wasn't looking for a man in a lineup she'd seen grab someone's purse and take off running.

The door behind them opened and then closed with a soft snick. Daniel sensed Wightman behind him.

Allison didn't move anything but her gaze with a subtle turn of her head.

"Is he there?" Wightman asked gently.

Allison shook her head. She turned to them both in confusion. "He isn't."

Wightman nodded. "No worries. There are more."

Daniel flinched. *Jesus.* They'd brought out six of the wrong men? Why? Were they concerned about Allison's ability to judge?

The men filed out of the room and moments later six more came in. How many would they traipse through there to prove Allison was sane?

Allison went rigid as the men took their spots against the wall. She didn't glance around this time. Her gaze landed straight ahead. She barely gave anyone else in the lineup a fleeting glance. Finally she spoke, her voice squeaky. "Number three." She pointed at the man she identified.

"You're sure?" Wightman asked.

Allison turned toward him. She stared at him for several seconds. Daniel thought she might lunge at Wightman or shout something sarcastic. He actually couldn't blame her. Was she sure? *No, asshole. She isn't sure. She can't quite remember what the man she lived with for over twelve months until last week looked like.*

She nodded finally. "It's him."

Daniel hated the thoughts running through his head. Wightman seemed like a nice enough guy, and he was only doing his job. His words were words that would be spoken to anyone viewing a lineup. But it was hard to think of Allison as just anyone or the bastard who'd held her as less than a complete criminal who deserved to die for what he did to Allison.

Wightman nodded and eased out of the room. The lights went out once again, leaving Daniel and Allison alone in the near darkness. They sat there for several moments as Daniel tried to compose himself. It should have been Allison in distress. Instead she seemed much calmer than him. Daniel wanted to go through the glass and ring the guy's neck or alternately punch Wightman in the face, whether or not his current rage was founded.

Allison filled the silence with her sweet voice. "I forgive him." She relaxed in Daniel's grip.

"What?"

She settled into his chest, resting her cheek once again against his shirt. All her stress left her body as though it leaked out her limbs and rolled away into the corners of the room. "I forgive him," she repeated. "He is just as much a victim as me. Can you see that?" She lifted her gaze to meet Daniel's.

He shook his head. He had no idea what the hell she was talking about.

"I've heard all the details, Daniel. He was a rogue wolf who got that way only by fault of birth. This Romulus took him in under false pretenses and brainwashed him. He didn't know what he was keeping me for."

Daniel wasn't buying it.

Allison took his face in her palms and held him.

"He didn't hurt me, Daniel. He didn't beat me or yell at me or…rape me. He simply guarded me as he was told. He fed me my share of the pitiful rations we were given."

"He locked you in a closet and left you there for days on end." Daniel's voice was high-pitched, unrecognizable to his own ears.

Allison shook her head. "He needed to be sure I wouldn't escape when he was away. There was no other way to keep me unless he handcuffed me to the bed frame or something. In retrospect it was the most humane thing he could come up with."

"He left you for dead!" Daniel was shouting. *Has she lost her mind?*

"But he didn't kill me." Her voice was calm. Reasonable. As though she were discussing the weather and he was the insane half, conversing about a murdering, useless waste of life.

Daniel took deep breaths as she held his cheeks. She set her own face alongside his and waited patiently for him to calm. And she got her wish. He was still fighting angry, but he had to let it go for her benefit. If she was willing to forgive the bastard, who the hell was he to deny her that sense of peace?

By the time Wightman returned to the room, Daniel had gripped his mate's head with both hands and was staring into her calmer gaze in the dim light of the room. Her breathing stilled his own. Her heartbeats slowed his own. She seemed to have enchanted him with her strange tale of forgiveness.

He loved her so much in that moment. And he knew

he would spend his life striving to be worthy of her affection.

～

Allison held Daniel's hand tighter as they left the D building. She shivered, hoping she never had to return to that location.

She'd spent the last two hours answering questions she'd already answered many times in the last week. She wasn't angry. She realized it needed to be done. If any tiny detail of her story helped locate the Romulus and put an end to this nightmare, she would do anything in her power to assist.

Now, she was exhausted from rehashing her captivity and the sterile facility she'd been taken to for testing. She wished she could remember more details, but to be honest, very little else would probably come forth because she had been blindfolded or sedated most of the time she was there.

Daniel pulled her closer as they entered the busy mess hall for lunch. She followed him through the line and let him select a sandwich and drink for her. Her mouth was so gritty from the bad taste of reliving her captivity, she didn't think she could swallow food. But the water bottle he handed her made her groan. Her parched lips were grateful.

After she picked at her sandwich for a while, they left. Daniel had been quiet during lunch, eating his own sub while keeping his gaze on her.

"I'm fine," she whispered as they stepped back

outside. "Stop worrying."

He shook his head at her. "I'm beginning to wonder who's stronger, you or I."

As he finished, his cell rang and he grabbed it from his jeans pocket. "It's the ranch. My brother Drake," he told her as he answered. "Hey."

Allison stepped off the sidewalk with him so they weren't blocking the path as he talked. The bits and pieces of his muted conversation didn't sound good. His brow was furrowed, and he plugged his free ear as though having difficulty hearing. "Did anyone see him? Are you sure everyone is safe? How many reserves are there?" He ran his hand through his hair as he questioned his brother. "Yeah, that worries me… No, she's fine…" He glanced at Allison. "I haven't met with the commander in charge yet. I'll speak with him this afternoon and get back to you. Is Evan still there? Okay. Yeah… Please stay safe. If you need to, send Kenzie and the baby somewhere else." He flipped the phone closed.

Allison waited a beat before commenting. "What happened?" She set her hand on his chest.

"An unknown wolf was nosing around in the woods. They chased him off the property, but everyone is nervous."

Allison grimaced. "I hope they aren't looking for me."

Daniel shook his head. "I get the feeling there's more to it than that. I just can't put my finger on it." He turned toward her. "I have to attend some meetings this afternoon."

She nodded. "Of course. I'll be fine." What she really

wanted to do was run away with him and hide out somewhere where no one could find either of them, but that wasn't reasonable, and she stood taller, trying to keep her chin up as Daniel led her back to their room.

He left her there, promising to return as soon as possible and pleading with her to stay inside. Even though they were on a secure military base, Daniel was stressed, and she readily agreed in order to ease his concerns.

∼

Tarson Jones leaned against a large tree, trying to catch his breath while simultaneously tugging his boots on. He needed to get the hell out of the area fast. Thank God his car was still waiting just inside the tree line. He'd worried it might have been found and towed away while he'd been gone.

Without tying the laces, he bolted for the car, jumped inside, and started the engine. He glanced out the rearview mirror as he sped away. This mission had been far more dangerous the second time than he'd expected, and the information he'd gathered had not been what his superiors were hoping for.

That damn dude ranch was still harboring most of the women he had photos of. But worse than that, it was surrounded by members of NAR, who were maintaining a perimeter in wolf form. It was going to take some serious forces to break into that camp and recover those women, if that's what the Romulus had in mind.

Tarson doubted it was worth it. He couldn't imagine why the Romulus was so set on retrieving the damn women. They were just a bunch of weak females, after all. Who the fuck cared if they got away? Let them go it alone, as far as he was concerned.

He shook his head as he steadied his hands on the steering wheel and let up on the gas. The last thing he needed right now was to get pulled over for speeding.

When his cell rang, he hit the hands-free button and answered over the Bluetooth. "Tarson here."

"Jones. Jesus, man. Where have you been?"

His immediate superior of course. The entire organization was set up like a pyramid. Every man answered to someone, but it seemed no man was privy to enough information about the Romulus to know just who they were dealing with.

Tarson glanced in his side mirror as a car passed him, going far too fast. His chest beat so hard he thought he'd have a heart attack, but the vehicle moved away as fast as it had approached. *Where the fuck do you think I've been?* He ignored the question. "The place is surrounded. You're not going to get anyone out of there without a lot of manpower if that's what you had in mind."

Tarson had been in the woods traipsing around for two days. This was the first human contact he'd made. "I didn't see the woman you were looking for specifically anywhere. The one named Allison. Never saw her this time."

"She's not there anymore."

Whatever. It wasn't Tarson's problem. Getting paid

and doing his job was all he cared about. *But how the hell does he know that? Jesus, is the man psychic?* Tarson shivered. This bastard had way more intel than he was sharing with Tarson, whose life he was putting on the line.

"Did you see any of the others?"

"Yeah. All of them. And then some. There are at least fifteen women currently on the ranch. A few seemed to be members of the family, though. The rest have moved into some sort of bunkhouse now."

"How many men are guarding the place?"

Tarson chuckled. "Men? Dude, these guys mean business. They were all in wolf form. At least a dozen of them. They trade off, canvassing the area thoroughly. They were military for sure. NAR." Tarson hated NAR as much as he hated women.

The caller sighed. Tarson didn't even know the man's name. Only his voice.

It wasn't particularly strange for the guards to be in wolf form. As long as they weren't expecting an armed battle, it was far easier to track and scent anything out of the ordinary in their natural form. However, a dozen shifters milling about the ranch meant there were no humans on the premises. No way would they risk detection if there were.

"Okay. Return to the motel. I'll inform you of your next step soon." The caller disconnected, his deep voice still ringing in Tarson's ear. *Fuck.* He hoped he wasn't in trouble. He needed this job. It meant a steady paycheck. And for once he was on board with people he agreed with. In his experience, they were few and far between.

CHAPTER 12

Daniel slipped into the room late that night, breathing a sigh of relief the day was finally over and he could climb into bed with his mate. Her scent filled the small space, and he had to stifle a groan to avoid waking her. Not that he intended for her to sleep right now, but he wanted to ease her into consciousness in his own way.

As he stripped, he stared down at her relaxed face. Golden curls hallowed her cheek. Her mouth was parted slightly. She squirmed against the sheets for a moment, snuggling deeper into the covers. God, she was so peaceful in sleep. His gut clenched imagining being without her for even one night if he had to leave Seattle to participate in any combat missions.

Daniel rounded the bed and slid under the covers at her back. He wrapped his top arm around her and drew her against his chest, inhaling the scent of her shampoo that lingered on her damp curls. She must have showered in the evening.

She moaned. "You're so late."

He kissed her temple and splayed his hand over her bare stomach until his fingers grazed the underside of her soft breasts. "I know. I'm sorry. I missed you," he murmured against her temple.

A whimper escaped her lips as he thumbed her nipple. The bud tightened and poked into the pad of his thumb as he stroked the sensitive skin.

He nestled his leg between hers, nudging them apart until his thigh pressed into her moist heat. "You're already wet for me."

"Mmm." She ground herself on his leg, her delicious body squirming for more contact.

Daniel lowered his hand from her breast and gently caressed her clit.

She arched her neck and grabbed his wrist. "God, Daniel. You make me so horny so fast. When will it subside?"

"I'm hoping for never." He chuckled. "I love how you respond to my touch." He wiggled his fingers between her pussy and his thigh and pressed into her. She was so wet. And he felt her pulse increase immediately.

Under normal circumstances he couldn't imagine a woman being this ready for him this fast. But since the claiming, normal had flown the coop. Allison never needed any coaxing or encouragement to have sex. Her body hummed when he touched her, shooting to the top of the peak in a heartbeat every time.

Daniel lifted her top leg with his knee, opening her pussy and filling his senses with her sweet smell. He closed his eyes and breathed her in for a moment, never wanting to forget her scent when she was aroused.

Repositioning himself to nestle at her entrance, he thrust into her to the hilt.

Allison groaned so loud, he swept his hand up to cover her mouth. "Shhh, baby. You're going to alert the neighbors," he teased.

She breathed heavily. "I don't give a shit about the neighbors. Please, Daniel, move."

He grinned at her insistence and the way she grabbed his hand with hers and dug into his palm with her nails. He heeded her suggestion, setting up a rhythm that drew them both to the edge in minutes. He longed for the day he could fuck her for hours instead of minutes, enjoying the delicious sensations longer. But newly mated couples didn't have that luxury.

Daniel lowered his hand from her lips to rest his palm over her breast. He toyed with her nipple, waiting for the moment when he knew she could take no more.

She stiffened, pressing herself onto his cock. Her mouth opened wider and her eyes slid shut. *Now.* He pinched her nipple hard, shocking her and pushing her over the edge. Her body writhed against him as she came, grasping his cock and forcing him to grit his teeth in order to watch her reaction before his own orgasm took over his senses.

His plan lasted seconds. And then pure bliss, a sensation he would never tire of that always accompanied his orgasms with her. As he came deep inside her, he seemed to separate from his body to float above them in the room. The euphoria was that intense. Every time.

When he was finally sated, at least temporarily, he

held her for long minutes, his cock still buried in her sex. Finally, he eased out on a sigh and stood on wobbly legs to grab a washcloth for Allison.

He cleaned himself up and then returned to her side. She lay on her belly, her arms wrapped around the pillow above her head. She hadn't moved to pull the covers back up. He admired her skin, so smooth—covered with the pink splotches that accompanied her orgasms.

Daniel climbed between her legs, nudging them apart and then wiping her pussy with gentle strokes. She squirmed in protest, but he wasn't thwarted until he was satisfied.

Tossing the cloth aside, he straddled her ass. A tiny stream of light from the streetlights outside landed across her back. He brushed her hair away from her shoulders and neck and set his palms on her muscles to massage the tension from her body.

He grinned. She was anything but tense right now. More like a rag doll after the way he'd fucked her into ecstasy. But he knew her muscles would be tight underneath from the stress of weeks, months, hell a year of tension. Beginning with her lower back, he kneaded his way up her torso, making sure he addressed every knot along her spine and under her shoulder blades.

When he reached her neck, she tensed.

"So tight, baby. Relax." He pressed his thumb into the rows of muscles until each one released its tension. And then he moved to the top of her spine, right under her hairline. "Where did you get this scar?" he asked as he worked the knot at the base of her skull.

"What scar?" she mumbled into the pillow.

"This one. Right here." He stroked his finger over the tiny line running parallel to her spine.

She shrugged. "You must be seeing things. I've never had stitches anywhere."

Daniel leaned in farther and narrowed his gaze, thankful for his wolf vision that allowed him to see even in the near darkness. She'd definitely had at least one stitch there. He could see the cross mark.

Gently, he probed the area.

"Ouch." She flinched as the single word squeaked out.

"Sorry." He didn't touch that spot again. In fact he couldn't continue. His hands were shaking, and it was all he could do to control his breathing so she wouldn't be alerted to his fear.

What the fuck did they do to you, Allie?

Instead of sharing his thoughts, Daniel slinked down her body and pulled her into his chest. "Go back to sleep, baby." He clenched his fist on the mattress in front of her to avoid trembling.

In moments Allison was peacefully oblivious. Daniel was going to experience a long night of chasing his fears as the clock ticked. There wasn't anything he could do about whatever was under that scar tonight, anyway. It would have to wait until morning.

~

Allison blinked awake when she heard the shower running. The bathroom door was open a few inches and steam seeped through the gap. She stared at the ceiling, wondering what new shit would hit the fan today. Every day was full of surprises.

When the water turned off, she pulled herself from the bed and padded to the bathroom. She leaned in the doorway, watching her mate dry off, his head tucked as he toweled his hair.

He lifted his gaze to meet hers. "I could smell you as soon as you entered the room." He leaned forward and kissed her forehead. "We have an early appointment. I was just about to wake you."

Allison's smile faded. Could they not have one leisurely hour together? She tried not to protest outwardly. The seriousness of what they were dealing with outside the bedroom needed to outweigh her desire for sex. It was tough to chase away the call to his body most of the time, but they would have their whole lives together. This period of time would be a blip on the radar in the end.

Allison stepped into the shower and quickly washed. Before Daniel was completely dressed, she was back in the room, the towel wrapped around her middle.

He looked up. "The towels they have here are way too big." He dragged his gaze from her feet to her neck. "Are you even under there?" he teased, buckling his watch.

"Ha ha. If we didn't have to meet with so many people every hour of every day, I'd gladly forgo the towel for my birthday suit." To make her point, she dropped the terry cloth on the floor and stepped over it, knowing what her nudity would do to him.

Daniel groaned and turned away. "You slay me."

"Whatever. Obviously not enough to get you to change your mind about leaving this room." She shrugged into her clothes, choosing jeans and a light sweater over her bra and panties. As soon as she finished slipping on her shoes, she returned to the bathroom to comb through the curls in her hair. "I haven't worn makeup in days." She stared at herself in the mirror.

"I love you that way," he said as he came up behind her and watched her work. "You're so pure." He stroked a finger down her shoulder until she shivered.

She rolled her eyes at him. "Bet that's what you tell all the girls."

"Only the ones I'm mated to."

He was stiff. His usual jovial self completely absent this morning. She hadn't noticed that last night when he'd come in. But on the flip side, she'd been rather preoccupied the entire time she'd been awake in the darkness. Something must have happened yesterday to put him on edge. And whatever it was, he wasn't in a mood to share it right then.

Allison followed him from the room, glancing at the coffee pot and wishing she'd at least had one cup before heading to the mess hall.

Daniel held her hand as they walked. He didn't stop at the dining room, however, and she sighed, wondering when he was going to snap out of it and feed her. Instead, he walked at a fast clip until he came to a building she hadn't been in before. He opened the door and wrapped his arm around her until they reached what looked like a doctor's office inside. "Sit over there." He pointed to two adjacent chairs. "I'll be right back."

She watched him speak to the receptionist quietly while she nodded and replied just as softly.

Allison could hear better than any human. All shifters could. But the only words she managed to pick out were appointment and her name.

Daniel headed toward her, but just as he reached her side, another door opened behind him and a cheery woman popped out. "Allison Watkins?"

Allison flinched. She narrowed her gaze at Daniel. "What are we doing here?" she whispered.

"I have some concerns," he replied without any details. "Don't worry. I'm sure it's nothing."

They followed the kind woman with the dark ponytail to a room. Allison couldn't wait for her to leave so she could pounce on Daniel-the-silent and drag answers from him.

Instead, the room they entered next already had someone in it. And that someone turned around to greet them as Dr. Wilburrow. His smile was too big as he shook hands with first Daniel and then Allison.

"I haven't mentioned to her what I found," Daniel said. "I didn't want to scare her unnecessarily."

Dr. Wilburrow turned to Allison, who could feel her face turning beet red. They were discussing her as if she were a child or not in the room. "Found what?" She transferred her gaze from the doctor to Daniel and back.

"Remember last night when I came in late?"

"Yes." How could she have forgotten that?

"I found a scar on your neck that you didn't know anything about."

She reached her hand under her hair to feel her neck, a tingling running down her spine and threatening to let her collapse as his words shook her to the core. "I've never had any injury to my neck." She'd tossed his words out the door last night, thinking he was seeing things. She would know if she had a scar, wouldn't she?

"May I take a look?" the doctor asked.

Allison turned around and lifted her hair with the shakiest hands she'd ever experienced. Even Daniel's normally calming touch on her shoulder didn't soothe her. What the fuck was going on?

Dr. Wilburrow poked the spot in several places, making her flinch. "Does it hurt?"

"Only when you hit it just right." Inside, her heart was racing. Daniel stepped in front of her, and she leaned her bent head against his chest for support. He took over holding her hair, and she let her arms fall to his waist. She felt light-headed. It would be a miracle if she didn't pass out.

Subtle movements from Daniel told her he was nodding at the doctor as they engaged in a silent conversation of facial expressions.

Allison didn't move, even though the doctor stepped back. She was afraid to see either of their faces.

Finally, Daniel lifted her face and met her gaze. His

cheeks were red. His brow scrunched, his lips tight. "We think they implanted something inside your neck."

"What?" She meant to scream the word, but her voice came out more of a crackly interruption. She slumped forward, and Daniel caught her.

He lifted her onto the narrow bed in the office and laid her on her side. He smoothed her hair from her face and held her bicep firmly. "We have to get it out. Whatever the hell it is, I don't want it in you another minute."

She nodded, her mouth dry, her head pounding, her vision blurring. She tucked her hands between her legs to keep from shaking.

He did his damnedest to console her, but she could only hear groups of words that didn't seem to go together as he spoke. She concentrated on breathing, but it seemed she wasn't inhaling enough oxygen.

"She's in shock," the doctor said. He slipped something over her head and pulled it across her face to nest under her nose. *Oxygen*. Thank God. She was choking.

And then papers were being passed around. Daniel signed some forms. He never took his free hand off her, anchoring her to this world as best he could. Not enough, though. She was going to float away. She could feel her body lifting off the bed and then moving. She widened her gaze to find out it wasn't an illusion. They'd moved her to another gurney and were rolling her down a long hall.

"Look at me, baby." Daniel's voice was firm, in

control. Freaked the fuck out. "It's going to be okay," he said next, even though she hadn't glanced his way.

Allison stared instead at the ceiling as she rode down the hall. She wanted to count the tiles, but they were moving too fast. Everything was in high speed, and she needed to slow down. The tiles... How many had there been? She needed to know.

"I love you," Daniel whispered in her ear.

That was the last thing she heard before darkness descended.

~

Something heavy was weighing her down. Allison tried to lift her arm but found it trapped. Her eyes were too heavy to open. Her mouth was dry. She couldn't control her tongue to lick her lips. And her head was pounding.

Movement to her left made her turn her head a fraction, but it hurt too much and she winced.

"Allie... Baby... You're okay. Don't move yet. You're just coming out of the anesthesia." Daniel's voice filtered into her mind, but where was he? She couldn't see him.

Oh, right. Her eyes. She blinked them open finally and found him hovering over her.

She found she could wiggle her fingers, but her arms still wouldn't obey her commands, or she didn't have the energy to lift them.

Daniel stroked her forehead and smiled at her. His smile was fake, but she noted relief that hadn't been there earlier. What had happened? It was coming back to her. The doctor... The scar on her neck... Something was inside her...

She shivered. "Did they get it out?" she finally managed to mutter.

"Yes. Easy peasy. No problems."

She scented another man as he entered the room. Her gaze wandered to the newcomer. Dr. W-something or other.

"Hi. You did great." He smiled at her and patted her leg. "You'll be fine in a few minutes. Just let the anesthesia wear off, and you'll feel much better."

"I can't move my arms." She tilted her gaze down, not wanting to risk moving her head again. *Oh.* Heavy blankets covered her.

"You were so cold, baby. Just rest a minute." Daniel stroked her arm through the layers. At least she could feel his touch.

"What was it?"

"A chip. They must have been using it as a GPS."

"That's all?" She stared at his face, gauging his response. If he lied to her...

"Yes." He didn't flinch. "Promise. Nothing more than a tiny GPS locater. Nothing drug related."

She swallowed hard, and Daniel reached for a cup of ice on the side table. He set a few small chips on her lips, and she moaned around the cool, melting water. "More."

"Take it slow at first," the doctor said. "Some people have difficulty keeping things down after anesthesia."

She nodded, regretting the act immediately. "Are you sure there aren't more foreign items inside me?"

The doctor lowered his notes and met her gaze. "Positive. We did a full-body scan to make sure. That was the only one. It was very close to the surface. You were never in any danger. The tiny cut I made didn't even need more than a butterfly Band-Aid. It took two minutes. The only reason you feel like you do is from the anesthesia. I didn't want to risk keeping you awake without knowing for sure what I was dealing with."

Allison took a deep breath and closed her eyes to center herself. *You're okay. It's out.*

She still shivered at the thought of the invasion.

And then her eyes shot wide open. "Shit. Now they know where we are." She glanced at both men, having declared something they both already considered.

Dr. Wilburrow, that was his name, smiled. "Yeah. Can't be helped. If we're lucky, they haven't specifically tracked you here yet. The second we removed the chip and examined it, a team of men took it and left. Hopefully it will buy us some time, leading the Romulus in another direction. The longer we can keep them thinking you're somewhere else, the better.

"Hopefully, they will believe you came to Seattle to meet with The Head Council and then left by car to go somewhere else. They're going to drive that chip around all over until we can pick a good place to stop and lure the bastards in."

Allison swallowed. It was a good plan.

The doctor patted her leg. "I'm going to leave you now. I've got rounds to make. Take it slow, but as soon as you can get around, you're free to leave."

"Thank you," Daniel managed. He stood and shook the doctor's hand before turning back to her.

"I thought only a handful of people knew what was going on?"

"Yeah, well, Dr. Wilburrow is now a member of that group. Everyone is doing their best to keep it small, but it's growing by the hour. Not much can be done to avoid it. Within days, they're going to have to put full-time military troops in place and arrange for any eventuality."

Daniel gave her another spoonful of the ice. His face grew serious as he spoke. "I'm sorry I didn't say anything to you before we got here. Part of me hoped I was full of shit and overreacting. The other part was afraid of how you might react when you found out there was a foreign object in your neck."

"Under the circumstances, I'm going to thank you, but please don't coddle me, Daniel. I'm a grown woman." She finally managed to lift her arm and draw it toward her chest. She rolled her head gently from left to right.

"I know. Sometimes I think you're stronger than me." He frowned. "Especially when it comes to anything related to your health and safety. I freak out a bit."

She squirmed her arm free and grabbed his hand. "I understand. Just know I feel the same way about you, and keeping details from me that involve me won't win you any favors." She pushed the covers down to find herself in a hospital gown. "If it was no big deal, why all the ceremony?"

"We couldn't be sure. Just in case there were any

complications." Sweat rose on his brow as he watched her move around.

"You were really scared."

"Out of my mind, baby."

"Help me sit."

"Are you sure you're ready?"

She rolled her eyes. "I had a tiny piece of metal under the surface of my skin. I think I can sit."

Daniel kissed her forehead and helped her ease off the bed, supporting her back with one hand and grasping her arm with the other.

She swung her legs around to hang off the side. "Did you undress me?"

"With the help of a nurse. I was all butterfingers."

She set her palm on his cheek and waited for him to meet her gaze. "I'm fine."

"I know."

"You're shaking."

"Yep." He kissed her palm and then stood upright. "Don't scare me like that again." He pulled her into his chest and hugged her tight.

"I'll keep it in mind." Her voice was muffled by his shirt, but she wrapped her arms around his waist and held him just as close. "I'm starving."

"You're going to have to stick to mild foods for a few hours."

"Well, find some of them and feed me. I don't care what it is right now. I just need to eat."

CHAPTER 13

While Allison slept off the last of the anesthesia, Daniel stepped outside their room and called Evan. He paced on the sidewalk while he listened to the ringing from his end.

"Hey," Evan answered. "How are things in Seattle?"

"Well, interesting."

"What happened?"

"Last night I found a small scar on Allison's neck."

"Fuck."

"Yeah. I took her to the clinic this morning, and they removed a tracking device."

Daniel could hear Evan's heavy breathing as he continued.

"A team of men immediately left Seattle with the chip. We're hoping it was soon enough that the Romulus hasn't already descended on this location. It's a long shot, but maybe if they see it moving, they will think she and I are on the move again."

"Perhaps. It's worth the effort, anyway."

"They're going to keep moving until we come up with a plan about where they should stop, assuming a nice battle will ensue at that final destination, and it's conveniently under our control now as long as the Romulus doesn't catch on." Daniel leaned against the outside wall, keeping his voice low.

"Shit. These other women…"

"Exactly. The Head Council is sending a team there on the next flight to check out each of them and determine the best course of action. Don't say anything yet. No need to cause a panic."

"God no. Didn't Allison go through the roof with worry?"

"I didn't give her a chance. I never told her what I was thinking until we were in the medical building about to remove the damn thing."

Evan chuckled wryly. "Bet she loved that."

"Yeah. She's not super pleased with me right now, but I can handle it. Imagine what she would have done all night if she'd known it was there?"

"Probably would have clawed it out of her neck."

"Exactly… Anyway, I just spoke with Jerard. He's coming up with a plan, but as it stands, he's thinking we remove any devices we find on the other eleven women, separate the chips from the women and send them away from the ranch in different directions."

"Should work, at great risk to your family and their home," he reminded Daniel.

"Yeah, at this point there's no way they would do anything less than that to save those women. You won't hear any dissention among members of my family."

"I know. They've been a godsend. But I hate having to do this to them. This was only supposed to be a retreat for abused women, not Fort Sumter."

"No one could have foreseen any of this. It's not anyone's fault. We'll do what we have to do for justice." Daniel righted himself once again and stepped across the path to avoid the ears of a few soldiers walking by. "Did my brother's wife get away?"

"Yes, she and the baby went to her mom and dad's."

"Good. And how's your mate?"

"Stubborn," Evan said.

Daniel chuckled. "Really? I've never met a stubborn woman. How shocking."

"Yeah, we moved in with your parents, so at least she's with your mom most of the time instead of alone at Drake and Kenzie's place. But now that you've informed me about the tracking devices, I won't give her an option. I'll get her out of here."

"Evan…" Daniel began. He bit his lip before continuing. He hated what he needed to say next. "Make sure she doesn't have anything on her, either."

Evan sucked in a deep breath. "Yeah. You're right. Fuck."

"I know it's been over a year since she was rescued, but we don't know when these chips were put into place. I'm telling you, the incision site was so small it's a miracle I noticed it."

"On her neck, you said?"

"Yeah, right at the base of the skull, under the hairline. But that doesn't mean everyone would have it in the same place. That's why three guys are coming out there equipped to investigate each person. They have a wand that works like a metal detector with them. Just to be certain they don't miss anything."

"Good. Well, I won't say anything to anyone until they get here."

"Good plan. They should be there later this afternoon. I'll keep you posted, either me or Jerard or Wightman."

"'K, later."

"Bye." Daniel hung up the phone and stuffed it in his pocket. When he slipped back in the room, Allison was just waking up.

She moaned and pulled to a sitting position. "I feel like I've slept twenty hours a day since we met."

"You need to. You've been through tremendous trauma." He eased onto the bed next to her. "How do you feel?"

"Fine." She prodded the back of her neck, wincing, but not too bad. "It's sore, but nothing more than what a cut would feel like. I'll be fine."

"We're going to move into the large housing facility in the middle of the base this afternoon."

She nodded. "My being here has put the entire base at risk."

"You can't think of it like that. You had no way of knowing it. None of us did. Besides, this base was already at risk. There has to be a mole inside. I don't believe for a moment the Romulus doesn't know exactly where this base is. I'm sure they're watching it. I'm more concerned about your safety right now."

"Why do we need to move?"

"It's safer. We won't have a door directly to the outside, and we'll be more sequestered in the middle."

Allison stood and padded over to the bathroom. "I'm going to shower first, okay?"

"Yeah. No rush. I'll start gathering our stuff."

They hadn't traveled with much. Two large suitcases was all they had when they left the ranch. Allison only had clothes she'd borrowed from Kenzie and what her parents had brought her. Daniel had known he'd not need much in the way of civilian attire in the near future. Getting his mate to a more secure location was the most important thing on his mind. If there was such a place these days…

~

Evan stepped up to the front of the room where he'd gathered all twelve women, including his mate. He hated what he had to say. Had dreaded it all day, ever since receiving the call from Daniel. But it couldn't be helped and the three official, somber-looking medical people from Seattle were ominous all by themselves. Every eye in the room was wide and worried.

"There's no easy way to tell you all this, but it's come to our attention that some or all of you could have had a GPS tracking device inserted in you somewhere."

A collective gasp filled the room as the women stiffened. A few grabbed hands.

"Unfortunately, they found a chip on Allison this morning. So, these men are here to make sure none of you are bugged and deal with it if so." Evan held his mate's gaze as he finished. He hadn't mentioned anything to her or any of the women so they didn't have a chance to panic prematurely.

The three men in khaki combat gear organized the women into groups to scan their bodies. Meanwhile Evan stepped up to his mate. He pulled her to standing and wrapped his arms around her. "That includes you, baby," he murmured against her head.

"I figured." She shook as she responded to him and gripped his shirt with both hands.

Evan held her close while they waited for all the others to go first. The trauma they'd been through was more recent. They deserved answers as soon as possible. Ashley could go last.

Evan waited, holding his breath. They'd already chased off one shifter in the woods. It was possible in creating this haven for the women, they'd inadvertently led the Romulus right to their door. How bad did those fuckers want these women and why?

The room was quiet considering how many people were gathered. In the end, half of the women had chips in them, all located in the same spot in the neck. Ashley wasn't among them, thank God. But she kept a strong front through the entire process and worked with one of the other device-free women, Heather, to help calm the six who needed the chip removed.

Heather had been a nurse before she'd been captured. Fortunately she'd only been held for a few weeks. Her mind had cleared faster than the others because she hadn't received nearly as much of the drug combo. She was sharp and strong and always willing to help the others.

She and Ashley made their way from one woman to the next, holding their hands while the doctor made the tiny incision to remove each chip. Each one was identical, and sighs of relief were palpable in the room as they were extracted.

It gave Evan the willies just thinking about having that foreign object inside him and not knowing about it. Such a violation. He couldn't keep his hands from shaking. Ashley was far stronger than him in this situation, but then he'd never have survived half of what she'd gone through for years under the abuse of her captor.

When it was over, he was exhausted. He helped secure the chips in a plastic bag and then put them in a cardboard box until it could be determined what the next step would be.

The most important thing would be to get the six women affected out of town ASAP.

Evan placed the call to Jerard as he stepped outside, inhaling deeply of the oxygen that had seemed to be depleted in the room. "Sir."

"How'd it go?" Jerard asked.

"We recovered six. Everyone is clear now."

"Good God. This is insane."

"Yeah. I was thinking of a few harsher words than that, sir. But insane will work." Evan walked as he spoke. Jerard was considerably older than Evan, and the man rarely lost his cool.

"Okay, so I've arranged a safe house for them. No

sense bringing them here since the entire base in Seattle has been compromised." Jerard sighed. The man had to be tired. "Do you think after sundown you can get them all out safely?"

"Yes. We haven't had any other unwanted guests lately."

"Good. Maybe they lost interest when they saw the size of our operation there."

Evan doubted that. The Romulus had proven to be far more powerful and extensive than he'd ever expected. A dozen shifters from NAR on guard surrounding a dude ranch wasn't exactly a challenge considering the amount of intel Evan had gathered about the Romulus.

"We'll make sure the area is secure and get them out of here in the night. Just let me know where and I'll handle it."

"Great. And I'll get back to you in a few hours about moving the chips too. I don't want the six women left to become targets, and I don't want that ranch to become a battle scene, either. We'll leave about a twelve-hour gap between moving the people and then the chips."

"Sounds good." Evan glanced around at the peaceful haven he'd grown to love. The idea of this place being destroyed by the Romulus made him sick to his stomach. Besides capturing women and sticking them with needles, what else was the Romulus capable of? Was it possible they were an otherwise peaceful group of shifters? *Ha.*

Tarson paced while he listened to his next instructions. Although pacing might have been an overstatement in the tiny motel room he occupied. He'd had a bad taste in his mouth for weeks, and it wasn't getting any better. Fear? Anger? Distrust?

"You do understand the importance of this mission, don't you?" the voice asked.

"Yeah, yeah, I got it." Tarson ran his hands through his hair.

"Those women must be brought to justice."

"Of course." *Right? I mean the audacity of the females in this world is appalling. Who the hell do they think they are?* He understood that part. And then there was The Head Council. Bastards. He would do anything he could do to help against those mother fuckers.

Hell, the reason he'd gone rogue himself so many years ago was to avoid having to deal with the politics of the damn shifter community. So many fucking rules and regulations. He could hear his mother's nasally, sing-songy tone from when he was a child. "Most importantly, don't let any humans catch you shifting."

Whatever.

He'd left that shithole of a life first chance he could, and he'd been on his own for years. When hard times hit bad, he'd been approached by a group of drifters and offered a job. It had been all sunshine and roses for months. He'd finally found people he could agree with. Their mission was something he could get on board with.

He didn't know everything about the Romulus. He'd never even been to their main headquarters, but he knew enough. They were a growing power against The Head Council and its stupid politics, and they had the good sense to realize women were not superior to men. Fucking humans and shifters alike had succumbed to that line of bullshit.

Crazy bitches needed to know their place. Especially these damn women he'd heard had banded together and left their mates. Who the fuck did they think they were?

If the Romulus intended to bring them back into the fold and teach them a lesson, he was in. But it was going to take a hell of a lot more manpower than Tarson alone to get the job done.

"We need you to go back to the ranch one more time and scope things out some more."

"You realize I'm going to need help with this, right? That place is swarming with shifters, and they have the military on their side." Though why the hell NAR would be inclined to get involved with a bunch of fucking runaway women, he had no idea.

"Yep. And you'll have it. But first, I need specifics. I need to know how many shifters are there, how many men, how many women, how many children. We can't make a move until we're sure about that. Any specific details you can provide would be helpful."

"Why not just let them go, the ungrateful bitches?" Who'd want them back anyway?

"Their actions are considered criminal. Or at least they should be. Not only did they steal from their mates, but some of them are with child. Can you imagine some bitch running off pregnant with your offspring?"

Was this guy kidding? Tarson couldn't imagine anyone even producing him any brats. The last thing in the world he wanted was some damn crying babies to go with some damn whining bitches.

"Anyway, we're counting on you to give us the lowdown so we can prepare."

"Got it. I'll get out there first thing tomorrow. I can't get very close, though. Damn close call last time. I wasn't expecting all those fucking military dudes." Nor had he been expecting everyone present to be shifters.

"Take binoculars and do what you can. We need good surveillance in order to proceed."

"I'm on it." Tarson hung up when the line went dead. He set his head in his hands and tried to think. How the hell was he going to gain enough intel to be worthwhile with all those guards circling the place?

CHAPTER 14

Allison unpacked the last of their things for the second time in a few days and turned toward her mate. "I feel helpless," she said as she approached him and sat next to him on the love seat.

He was working on his computer, reading through page after page of information, but when she touched him, he put his arm around her and turned his head in her direction. "You shouldn't. You're key to this crazy mess. Without you we wouldn't have half the information we have."

"You mean like blurry sketches of some white room I may or may not be imagining in a place I can't describe and never saw? That kind of information? Cause that doesn't seem helpful to me. I don't even know what state it's in!" She raised her voice and then quickly lowered it again. If they'd lacked privacy in the first place they'd stayed, which had been more like a motel room, this room was ten times worse.

Now they were inside an enormous building. The

room they occupied was about the same size and configuration, but they were surrounded by other rooms on every side. She needed to keep her voice down.

Daniel pulled her closer and leaned back. "Baby, you can't think like that. It doesn't work that way. You're safe now, and that's what matters most. Every minute detail you've given NAR and The Head Council is important. What may seem trivial to you could be a key piece of intel later."

"Okay, but I'm not useful here now, and you're about to go off and join NAR yourself full time. I came here wearing a chip that surely has led the Romulus to The Head Council's front door. As soon as they figure out they've been had, they're going to freak."

"What are you trying to say?" He narrowed his gaze at her.

"I think I should leave."

He shook his head, more in disbelief than negation. "And go where?" He grasped her biceps with both hands and held her at arm's length. "What do you mean?"

"I think I should go to New York, spend some time with my parents."

"Are you kidding? No way. Do you think for a moment the Romulus doesn't know where your parents live? Allie, we have members of NAR watching your family even now. You wouldn't be safe there at all."

Allison shrugged free of Daniel's grasp and stood. She needed to move around while she reasoned with him. The deflated look on his face alone made her pause. But she needed to speak her piece. "Daniel, listen to me. I've met for hours with everyone related to this case. My services are no longer needed. I'm of no use on this base to anyone—"

"That's *insane*," Daniel shouted as he stood, setting his computer on the coffee table and bumping his knees against the edge in his haste. "First of all, you're my mate and I've only had you for about a week. I can't stand the idea of you being out of the room for one minute, let alone out of the state for an indefinite length of time." His head was shaking as he spoke, his hands fisted at his side.

She let him keep up his rant for a bit longer, knowing he would need to state his case. If he didn't, he wouldn't be able to hear reason.

"You're my life, Allison. I can't breathe right when I'm not with you. I know it's normal and it will ease with time, but a week isn't enough. I hope to God you feel the same way about me?" He lifted a brow in accusation. "If you don't, please enlighten me. Because I don't know how the hell you could even entertain the idea of leaving me, let alone plan it out to the point that you'd approach me with a proposal."

"Of course I feel the same way about you," she calmly replied. "You know I do. And I realize that under ordinary circumstances, mates tend to hibernate together for weeks until they can stand to be around other people. But, Daniel, these are not ordinary times."

He shook, his fists tightening as he stared at her in shock.

She looked around the room and held out her arms to encompass their surroundings. "Daniel, the shifter species is about to go to war. You know that better than I do. And there's a good chance now that I've been here on this base wearing a GPS device that war is going to start right here." She pointed at her feet. "On this base. In this city.

"NAR and The Head Council can shuffle their feet all they want trying to move those damn chips around the country, luring the Romulus to some faraway locations in order to preserve the secrecy of our species. But the reality is eventually all that's going to happen is that the Romulus is going to be fucking pissed off when they figure out they've been duped.

"Sure, they'll send a few men to track my chip, but what do you think is going to happen when they figure out I'm not there? Their infrastructure has to be enormous. They aren't stupid. This was the last place they tracked me.

"Same goes true with the other chips from the women in Texas. You can lead the Romulus on a wild goose chase for a few days, maybe a week, but the clock is ticking. Sooner or later, it's all going to come back to here. This base. They know I'm here. Or that I was."

Daniel flexed his hands. "I can't stand the idea of you being outside of the safety of this location. It's heavily guarded. You're with me." He shook his head. "You can't just jump on a plane and go to New York for a little vacation. I would freak out with worry every second. It would be too distracting."

Allison took a deep breath. "Daniel. Think about what you're saying. I'm so distracting to you here you can't do your job. The Head Council said they would give you a few weeks to get adjusted, but that was before the situation escalated. Already you're working night and day on this. And I'm distracting the hell out of you just by being in the room.

"My presence here is far more detrimental to this mission than if I left. You would be able to devote yourself entirely to the task, and when the Romulus descends on this base—when, not *if*—you won't have to worry about my safety.

"I'm not carrying a GPS device anymore, Daniel. No one will trace me."

"Is this what you want?" he asked, his face scrunched in pain.

Allison stepped toward him and wrapped her arms around his stiff waist to hold him while she looked up at his face. He didn't move his arms from his sides. "No. What I want is for the last year to never have happened and for me to have met you on a normal sunny day while picnicking in Central Park.

"What I want is for us to have seen each other from a distance, known we were meant to be together, and walked off into the sunset hand in hand to spend the rest of our lives staring into each other's eyes and planning every day like it was better than the last."

Daniel gave a wry chuckle and rolled his eyes.

"Hey, I'm a romantic." She smiled up at him, waiting for him to soften. "But I can't have any of that. I was dealt a different hand. I'm the luckiest woman alive—"

"How can you say that?" he interrupted.

"Because in spite of what I've been through the past

year and the fact that I never intended to ride a horse in this lifetime and there's a war about to erupt that threatens our very existence and my mate is going to fight that battle scaring the shit out of me every single day... Despite all that, I found you, anyway. I wouldn't trade a single minute of hard times from the past or the future if it meant I couldn't have met you and known as much happiness as I've known in the hours we've spent together.

"I love you. I will always love you. And I'll be with you in spirit no matter where we are. Until this mess is sorted out, you have a job to do. And I'm getting in between you and your work."

Daniel set his forehead on hers first, his breath coming out in short gasps. After he stared into her eyes for a few moments, a metaphorical clock ticking the seconds away in her mind, he finally wrapped his arms around her and held her tight. "I hate the idea of you not being where I can see you every day."

"I know."

"Why do you have to be right?"

She smiled. "I'm not right. I'm practical."

"I want you with me."

"And I want to be with you. Don't doubt that. I've thought about this a lot. Staying here is selfish of me. It puts us both in danger."

He groaned and closed his eyes. "Okay." His shoulders slumped. "I can't deny you aren't safe here. I'm not for one moment worried about your presence here making others unsafe. We're way past that. The Romulus has at least one mole on the inside. They know exactly where this base is and what happens here. You have nothing to do with that.

"However, in the interest of your safety and my peace of mind, I agree you should be moved. Not New York, though. Let me think about it."

The next thing she knew he swept her off the ground and took long strides across the room to the bed.

Allison squealed as he tossed her on the bed.

Daniel pulled his shirt over his head and dropped it on the floor. He wriggled out of his jeans next, stopping only to remove his shoes before he could step out of the denim. His cock peeked out the top of his underwear, and Allison watched as the first bead of precome leaked from the head before he lowered that last piece of clothing to the floor and stepped out.

He nailed her with his gaze. "You just going to lie there?" he teased. "How about you get undressed too, and then I won't feel so silly."

"You were listening to me before, right?"

"I was. But your damn intelligent brain made me horny. I need to be inside you now. Can we examine the living arrangement crisis further after?"

She smiled, but narrowed her gaze. "This isn't over."

"Of course it isn't. I would be disappointed in my stiff-spined mate if I believed otherwise."

"You will take me seriously."

"I will." He sobered, but he also climbed onto the bed and tapped her nose. "Naked."

Between the two of them they managed to divest her of her clothes also.

Daniel lay in the V of her legs and kissed her senseless. When he lifted his face minutes later, his forehead was scrunched. "Is your neck okay?"

She nodded, licking her lips and tasting him. "Of course. It's just a scratch. Can't even feel it now." Bless him for thinking of it, though. She knew for a fact his little head was in charge right then. The evidence of it was pressing into her thigh.

"I love you," he whispered, brushing a lock of hair from her face.

"I love you too."

He dipped his face into the curve of her neck and nibbled up to her ear.

She tilted her head to give him better access, moaning softly as a shiver raced down her arms.

When he lifted his gaze to meet hers again, she had trouble focusing. That happened a lot around him. He scrambled her brain and hazed her vision. "I want you to come so hard, you won't ever forget it."

She swallowed at his words. What the hell did he think she did every time they were together?

Daniel stared at her for long moments before finally settling loosely between her legs and inching down her body just enough to gaze at her chest.

Her heart beat wildly as she watched the top of his head, his gaze moving back and forth between her nipples. They hardened further into stiff peaks. She squirmed.

"Lie still, baby." He grazed a finger over her nipple so lightly she barely felt it.

The tip puckered anyway, and his breath wafted over it next, making her groan at the intensity.

He switched to the other breast, swirling his finger around the nipple, but not making direct contact.

"God, Daniel. Stop teasing." Her breath came out sharp and ragged. She grabbed his shoulder and nudged him to move farther down her body.

"Uh-uh. Stay still." He shrugged her arm off him and circled her wrist. "Set your hands over your head. Let me explore. Don't rush me." He winked at her. He was evil.

Her hands shook, but she lifted them both anyway, clasping them above her head, which forced her breasts higher on her chest.

"So fucking sexy, baby." Daniel caressed the underside of each breast, alternating back and forth. He spiraled around each one until he reached the center, but not with enough pressure. She wanted more.

A burn began in her belly and her pussy clutched at nothing. Wetness leaked, cooling as it ran between her butt cheeks. She held her breath to steady herself.

Daniel licked his tongue over one nipple, and she arched.

He set his hand between her breasts to hold her down while he did it again and then switched to torture the other stiff bud.

Allison closed her eyes and concentrated on his touch. Without watching, her arousal heightened. Each caress, each lick, landed in unexpected spots. Finally, when she thought her head would explode, Daniel eased down her body and settled between her legs. She was growing to realize he was a huge fan of sucking her off.

She took deep breaths as he pushed her thighs open wider. After several seconds, she opened her eyes and lifted her head to see what he was doing. His gaze was locked on her face. He'd been waiting on her. He pulled her lower lips apart slowly and held her sex open. When he dipped his head, he blew against her wetness.

Allison writhed. He wasn't even touching her and she writhed.

But Daniel held her thighs tight, not giving her an inch. He lowered his lips to her skin and kissed the inside of one thigh. His tongue landed on her sensitive skin and trailed toward her pussy, skipping over the swollen, needy area to reach the other thigh. Even the contact on her leg made her hornier.

When he nibbled a path toward her sex, she gasped. Her legs shook. She needed him that bad.

One finger trailed between her lower lips, forcing a short, high-pitched squeal from her lips.

"You have to stay quiet, baby. These walls are thin."

She moaned. She had no control over her vocal chords.

"I don't want you to come. I want you to feel. Got it?"

He chuckled low and deep when she didn't respond. Not come? Was that a choice?

The finger returned to press into her pussy, and she tried to lift her torso to meet it. To no avail. He gathered her wetness and trailed it down to circle her lower hole. Even though he'd touched her there before, she still stiffened. She wasn't used to that kind of attention. It feel unnatural...and fucking awesome in a forbidden sort of way.

Daniel's finger went back and forth between her pussy and her rear, over and over, circling the tight hole closer with each pass. His breath on her skin sent a chill down her shaky legs.

Finally, he pushed his finger into her tight hole, a gradual thrusting that left her wanting more. She gritted her teeth, silently begging him to let her come. She needed more contact with her sex, her pussy, her clit, even her nipples. All those spots were on high alert with his finger in her ass.

She dug her heels into the mattress but couldn't get purchase with his hand holding one thigh open and his shoulder on the other. At some point he'd flung his left arm across her belly to hold her open, leaving his right hand free to explore.

She rolled her head to one side. *Breathe.* Could she come without him toughing her anywhere else? She was beginning to think so.

"Don't come, Allie," he commanded. "Not time yet."

With his index finger inside her tight hole, he pressed his thumb into her pussy.

Oh God.

When he rubbed the two fingers together, the walls of her pussy the only barrier, she stiffened. She'd never been this aroused in her life. So close with no promise of release. Like a fantastic romance novel read with no vibrator available in the house and her arms tied behind her back.

She panted, thinking she could come from this strange new touch. And his fingers disappeared.

"Not yet, baby." He stroked her inner thighs again, his finger dancing lightly over the skin, almost too lightly.

When his tongue landed on the skin surrounding her clit, she grasped the sheet above her head with both hands, squeezing the linen. *Please*.

"Your skin is so soft," he muttered against her. His voice was filtered, probably because her ears were ringing.

He licked her outer lips, tasting her everywhere, but not with enough pressure and not long enough in any one spot.

Her arousal mounted, but every time she grew closer, he pulled back. For long minutes he did nothing but circle her clit, her pussy, and her lower hole in figure eights, lazy slow torture that drove her mad. Every once in a while he pushed his finger into her pussy or her ass, but not for long.

Her belly clenched, aching. Her mouth was dry from breathing so heavily and not having the energy to lick her lips or swallow.

"So damn sexy," he whispered.

"God, Daniel. You're killing me."

"I know. And it's gorgeous. Your skin is all splotchy." He trailed a finger over heated areas of her belly, her breasts, her thighs, his touch landing everywhere in random order.

He'd said she would come harder than ever before. After this much foreplay, she believed it.

The sweet, sweet agony of denial. It sent her brain in every direction. He manipulated her senses, making every touch seem more hypersensitive than the last.

Daniel's fingers moved faster, reaching inside her and stroking around her pussy over and over as her arousal rose higher.

As she reached a point where she knew orgasm was imminent, he released her sex, scooted up her body and thrust into her before she knew what was happening.

And just as quickly she came, her eyes rolling back into her head, her mouth open on a moan, her body too limp to wrap around him. Pulse after pulse of her orgasm grabbed his cock. Even though her clit had received no stimulation, wave after wave rolled through her, surprising her with the intensity he had promised.

Before it ended, he moved, in and out, his cock seeming larger than ever, her pussy grasping at it firmly. One orgasm became two as she wrapped her arms and legs around him and pressed her clit into the base of his cock on each pass.

"That's it, baby. God you're sexy." He brushed a curl from her face as she tried to lick her lips. Her mouth was too dry. But he kissed her, his tongue coming out to tangle with hers instantly, his lips moistening her dryness.

He thrust faster as he kissed her.

She dug her nails into his back, realizing she was sailing higher once again. She couldn't lift her eyelids. It didn't matter. She could feel everything, and that was all she cared about right then. Every thrust of his cock drove her back toward the peak.

When he finally stiffened deep inside her and came, she launched into a third orgasm. Or maybe the three had really just been one long drawn-out experience. She couldn't be sure.

What she knew, as she came back to reality, was no one would ever be able to make her feel the way Daniel did. She was one with him in a way only mates could understand. She'd known that for days, of course, but the stakes just went higher. If she had any doubt about Fate's plan for her life, she would toss it out the door. He was hers and she was his. They would work things out and get through this rough patch in history and live long and happy together.

They had to.

CHAPTER 15

Daniel leaned against the back of the small couch and put his feet on the coffee table as he answered his cell. "Evan, tell me something good."

"Well, depends on your definition of good. My mission is to save the lives of innocent women, so if by good you mean, did I get six women out in the middle of the night and secure them in another location, then yep, I did that." Evan paused. His voice was more upbeat than it had been in days. "And then I moved six motherfucking GPS trackers in the opposite direction about an hour later in an armed car with two members of NAR. So that mission is a success so far also."

"Good." Daniel breathed a sigh of relief. "And no more signs of spies in the area?"

"Nope. Not a single human or shifter has been spotted."

"Well, don't lower your defenses any. I don't trust these guys."

"Agreed."

"Are the other women leaving also?"

"Not yet. We'll wait and see what Jerard thinks later today. So far no word on what the best course of action is yet. Since they don't have any chips on them, maybe they aren't as valuable to the Romulus, but I'm not willing to take any chances yet. I just want them safe."

"I hear you."

"How's Allison?" Evan asked.

"She's good. She's not too pleased with my involvement in NAR, and she has this wild, harebrained idea that she needs to go to New York until this blows over." He smiled at his mate where she sat at the tiny kitchenette table as she lifted her gaze to meet his with a glare.

"New York is a bad idea. The Romulus would likely pick her up there in a heartbeat. But now that her chip is removed, it's not a bad idea to send her to a safe house. No one should be able to track her."

"Jerard said the same thing earlier. I've been thinking about it. I'm trying to see logic here."

Evan chuckled. "Well, it's impossible for you to see things logically in your sensitive state."

"Ha ha. And just what is my sensitive state?"

"Whipped, dude. It happens to all of us when we claim a mate." Evan chuckled.

"Whatever. I'm considering her request, but every time I think about it I get sweaty palms." He stared at her and held out his hand for her to see while he raised his eyebrows.

"I can imagine. Listen, after I met Ashley, I stepped aside for six months. Trust me, it wasn't easy. Granted, I hadn't actually claimed her yet, but it was still tough knowing she was out there, remembering her scent, thinking about her every hour of every damn day. But she's with me now. And Allison will be with you too. What you want to consider above all else is her safety."

"Damn you all and your sensible ideas." Daniel smiled.

"Yeah, someday you'll get reasonable too. I hear after about five years, we tend to calm down on our irrational concerns for our mates."

"Oh, good. That sounds fantastic."

"All right. I've gotta go. I'll catch you again later. Let me know what you decide."

"Will do. Thanks." Daniel hung up the phone as Allison stalked toward him. *Oh, man.* Either she was pissed about his easy-going attitude about her suggested departure, or she couldn't stand another moment without touching him. He was hoping for the latter, but the look in her eye could go either way.

She padded in his direction with her brow furrowed, but when she reached his side, she took his face in her palms, stared into his eyes, and then consumed him in a kiss that made him glad he was sitting.

～

Two days later Daniel's cell rang in the early hours of the morning. He was growing tired of hearing the ring tone. Every time he picked it up it filled him with nothing but stress. He held Allison tighter as he lifted the damn phone to his ear. The clock was ticking. Everyone, including Jerard, agreed it was time for Allison to leave the base. It wasn't safe for her there. And in spite of Jerard's promise to give Daniel a few weeks with his new mate, they needed him on active duty ASAP. Every able body was being mobilized in quick order. That included Daniel.

"Hello?" He hadn't bothered to glance at the caller ID before answering.

Allison made a small noise and squirmed against him.

"Spencer. It's Jerard."

Daniel sat up straighter. He'd spoken several times with Jerard, but not usually before the sun came up. He waited.

"The jig is up concerning the chip."

"Shit. What happened?" Daniel had hoped it would take the Romulus longer to track the moving chip no longer attached to Allison and/or at least longer to care enough to go after her.

"Three of our men placed it in a remote location in the middle of Utah and then surrounded the site and waited. It didn't take long after they stopped moving for half a dozen men in camouflage to creep up to the house. The Romulus must have been tailing our guys the entire time, just waiting for us to stop moving."

"Was anyone hurt?"

"No. Not NAR anyway. Those six bastards are going

to be hurting when they wake up, though. Transport is on the way back here with them secured in a detention vehicle. We'll question their asses first chance we get."

Daniel waited for the next shoe to fall. "Go on."

"I spoke with Evan earlier too. A shifter was lurking around the dude ranch again. Evan says his people believe it was the same guy. When that guy reports back, things could get ugly in a hurry."

"Do you think the ranch is in trouble?"

"It's possible. I was hoping we would head that off by moving the women who'd been tracked to a secure location. But I don't trust these guys. You never know what might happen."

"Why didn't our men just snag the spy and bring him in?"

"Seemed prudent not to let the Romulus know we were onto them. Instead I sent more troops there to protect your family's property. Another dozen are en route now."

Daniel cringed when he glanced down to find Allison staring up at him, her hand over his chest.

"It's time to move Allison."

"I know." He swallowed as he looked into her eyes. He knew she could hear every word Jerard spoke.

"I'm sending a car in fifteen minutes, Daniel. We can't risk it anymore. We don't have any idea what the Romulus is capable of, and we can't risk her life to find out."

"I know," he muttered. "She'll be ready."

"Okay. I know this is hard. We'll go with the plan you and I discussed yesterday."

Daniel nodded, even though Jerard couldn't see him. What mattered most was Allison at this moment, and the fact that he had about thirteen minutes left with her before she left.

"After you see your mate off safely, I think you should head home also. Make sure everyone is safe. I'll contact you again later." Jerard hung up.

Daniel set the phone on the bedside table and turned to take Allison in his embrace. For the first time since he'd been a full-grown man, he swallowed a lump of aggravation so tight in his throat it threatened tears. He wouldn't let them fall in front of her, of course, but they were just beneath the surface.

"It's going to be okay," she mumbled into his chest. She lifted her face to his. "I need to get dressed."

He nodded but didn't move to release her. Instead he settled his nose in the crook of her neck and inhaled deeply as though without that he might forget her scent as soon as she walked out the door.

Realistically he knew this was the best course of action. He couldn't keep her safe here. No one could. There was every possibility war would break out right on this base. Besides, he needed his head entirely in the game if that happened. And to do that, he needed to be training alongside everyone else every day. Not hanging out having sex with his woman.

Allison wiggled free of his clutch. She smiled as she scooted to the edge of the bed and dressed quickly. He hated every second that another inch of her skin got covered in clothes. It was cool outside, and besides, she needed to dress warmly for any eventuality.

Daniel stood on the opposite side of the bed, pulled on his jeans and a T-shirt and grabbed his tennis shoes. His gut clenched as he sat on the edge of the bed to tie the laces. He hated this moment more than any other in his life. It hurt so bad his chest felt tight.

Allison came to his side after she finished dressing. She wrapped her arms around his middle and eased between his legs. She pulled his head to her chest. "I'm going to be fine. And so are you. Just keep yourself alive for me, please."

Daniel lifted his gaze and grasped her waist tighter than necessary. "Nothing will happen to me. I promise. Please always stay alert. I need to know you're safe at all times."

"I will." She nodded and then kissed his forehead as a knock sounded at the door.

Daniel flinched as though the visitor were unexpected. He took her face in both hands and kissed her soundly before releasing her to stand and step over to the door.

He never let go of her hand, even as he grabbed the bag they'd packed two days ago from beside the door to their room.

When he opened the door to the hall, a somber man in full gear stood outside. They nodded at each other, and Daniel followed him down the hall and into the elevator, still grasping Allison with one hand and her duffle with the other.

When they stepped outside, he led her to the awaiting car. The sun was starting to peak over the horizon. Not an unreasonable hour for anyone to be leaving the base. Many cars would leave at the same time, some as decoys to ensure no one possibly watching outside the base could discern any particular pattern.

Daniel kissed Allison briefly beside the car. Neither the man who'd led them outside nor the driver of the vehicle paid them any attention, thankfully giving him a moment with his mate.

"I love you," he said as he stared into her eyes again.

"I love you too." A tear slipped from one eye, and he wiped it away with his thumb.

Allison didn't say another word as she climbed into the back seat of the car and then squirmed down onto the floor. The plan was for her to remain out of sight as they drove away so no one would suspect a solitary member of NAR driving a plain car home at the end of his shift.

Daniel shut the back door, his hands shaking. Lord, how he wished for another time and place. If the universe would please just open up a rift and let him slide into a different dimension with his mate right now, he'd be grateful.

But he didn't get his wish, and he stood rigid as he watched the car drive away until it rounded the corner and he could no longer see it.

Only he and Jerard knew where Allison was headed. Even the driver was on a need-to-know basis right then. New York had been totally out of the question. But there were safe houses around the city, and Daniel felt confident they'd made a good choice.

Tarson gasped to gain his breath as he paused. He'd been running in wolf form for over an hour. He'd known the risk of returning to that fucking ranch was great, but he'd done the job anyway. What other choice did he have, really? And his support for the Romulus grew every time he spoke to his superior.

These bitches thought they could run off and leave their mates had a lesson coming to them. Unfortunately he didn't think anyone higher up the totem pole at the Romulus was going to be pleased to find out how little he knew.

At least he'd escaped their clutches again. He'd remained at a great distance this time, relying heavily on the binoculars he wore in a pack around his neck until he could get close enough to shift and spy on the ranch without being detected.

He waited until he'd reached his car, shifted, dressed, and had put several more miles between him and the ranch before making the call to his superior.

"Tarson. Thank God. I've been waiting on you. I was growing concerned."

"I'm fine." Though Tarson doubted that was what his superior meant when he said he was concerned.

"What'd you find out?"

"Several of the women seem to have left. Only six remain that I saw."

"That's exactly what I suspected."

"How could you?"

"I have other intel also. Always good to have confirmation, though."

"Well unless some of them are hiding on the property and never come outside, only six are left."

"Will you be able to identify which six are still there if I give you pictures?"

"Maybe."

"How many shifters are still guarding them?"

"Interestingly the same number. It didn't appear their security was any more lax than last time I went."

"Good job, Tarson. You've done a great service. You're information is invaluable."

"That's all? I'm done?"

"Yep. I'll get you photos of the women ASAP so you can try to identify them."

Tarson glanced out the rearview mirror to make sure he wasn't being followed. He was headed straight out of town. He wouldn't stop until he reached his hotel and dropped into bed to sleep for twenty hours. He was that exhausted.

∽

Henry hung up with Tarson and immediately hit the speed dial for his superior.

"Yes."

"Sir, six of the women are missing."

"Any idea which ones?"

"No. But I'm sending photos to my man to see if he can identify which ones are still at the ranch and which ones left." Henry flipped the pen he held in his hand around and around his fingers. When his nerves got the better of him, it fell to the desk.

"Shit." The older man paused, probably thinking.

"Do you suppose we've been duped?"

"Oh, I don't suppose anything. You don't need to send photos to your man. I know exactly who is on that ranch and who isn't."

"How do you know for sure?"

"Allison was on the move again. She spent several days in Seattle and then took off. I sent six men to follow her. When she finally came to a stop, they called to say they had her surrounded and were moving in." The man took a deep breath. "That's the last I heard from them."

"Fuck." Henry stood and began to pace. "What the hell?"

"I imagine it was a setup. Either NAR figured out that woman had a GPS tracker and led us out there to capture my men. Or worse. They could have even removed the chip and left the woman behind."

"Which means she's probably still in Seattle. Did you get an exact location in Seattle?"

"I did. It's an enormous military base used by NAR, their headquarters. I've been there many times. If Allison Watkins is inside that base, there's very little chance we can get her back easily. I'm sending men to the outskirts to watch all outgoing vehicles, but it's a long shot. Chances are we've lost that battle."

"What if she tells them too much?"

"At this point, I think we're so far beyond that small problem. What we need is to get mobilized and do it fast. This is war now. I need my men ready ASAP. The longer we wait to take down The Head Council and this military base, the more difficult it will get."

Henry stared out the window of his office. He could see his men training in the courtyard below. "What about the men you sent after Allison?"

"They're probably dead. If not, they don't know enough to cause any harm. Forget them. Just get my army ready and do it fast."

"Yes, sir."

"The first thing I want to do is send a group of men to that ranch and retrieve those women. You said there are about a dozen NAR troops there?"

"Yes, sir." Henry froze. Was this guy serious?

"It's time to go to battle, Henry. If we let those bastards think they can get away with this, they will walk all over us. A show of strength will go a long way toward earning us the respect we deserve."

"What do you have in mind?"

"Send a dozen men in to take those women back from the ranch. Our men are stronger and better able to fight. Plus they will have the element of surprise on their side. That should be plenty."

"Do we really need those women, sir?"

"No. We need respect."

The line went dead before Henry could say another word.

Henry held the phone stiffly in his hand, and he lowered it to his side. Because of those jackasses at The Head Council not minding their own business, the timeframe Henry had been hoping for had shrunk.

Until now, the Romulus and its entire organization had remained under the radar, a secret. They'd intended to surprise NAR and The Head Council and take them out easily. Now the situation wasn't as foolproof. *Damnit.*

CHAPTER 16

The second Daniel landed, his phone was ringing. As he listened to the messages left by Jerard while he was in the air, he started running toward the front entrance of the airport. "Shit," he muttered under his breath.

He listened to three messages with his cell tucked under his chin and his feet pounding the floor to avoid trampling anyone.

As he finished hearing all the details, he popped outside and immediately spotted the car sent to pick him up. Relieved to recognize the driver as a man he knew well from the local group of recent recruits to NAR, he flung himself into the front passenger seat as the driver did the same on his side. "Hey, Devon. Thanks for picking me up. Hurry, man." Daniel couldn't bring himself to express much in the way of pleasantries right now. His family and their ranch weighed heavily.

"On it," Devon responded as he sped away from the curb and made his way toward the highway.

Daniel's heart raced. He gripped the handle above the door to avoid slamming into the side. Luckily Devon was actually a cop. He slapped a button on the dashboard and lights started flashing, easing his path and warning other drivers to get out of the way.

Time stood still anyway as Daniel called his brother. "Drake. Dude. Pick up. Come on. Come on." He waited while the line rang several times.

Finally it connected. "Daniel." Drake was out of breath.

"What the fuck is happening?"

"The place is surrounded by shifters. About a dozen. It isn't pretty."

"But you have enough man power from NAR to take them all out. What's the problem?"

"These aren't ordinary shifters, man. I've never seen any like them before. We aren't sure what they're capable of, and we're in a standoff so far."

"What do you mean? They aren't wolves?" Daniel glanced at his watch and then the road. They were still half an hour away.

"Oh, they're wolves, but they're huge and unnaturally feral. And they have demands."

"What sort of demands?"

"They say they aren't going anywhere until we turn the women over to them."

"Fuck."

"Exactly. We hate to fire any shots. If the neighbors are alerted to the altercation, it will compromise our entire existence. These guys don't look right. I don't know what they're capable of. They appear to be genetically altered."

"What the fuck? That's crazy."

"Yeah, well wait until you see them. How far away are you?"

"I'm getting close. Which angle should I come in from? Maybe I can take them by surprise from behind. Scatter them a bit."

"Check with me at the last second. Probably the west. You'll have to leave the car about a mile away. Don't come any closer. Shift and strap your cell on you so you can reach me."

"Got it. I'll be in touch." Daniel ended the call, but before he could set it on his lap, it rang again. "Jerard."

"Where are you?"

"On my way to the ranch. About fifteen minutes out." He glanced at Devon, who was paying so close attention to the road he didn't appear to have heard.

"Listen. I have new info."

"Go ahead." What the fuck more could there be?

"The men were brought in that had followed the chip decoy. I didn't realize one of them had been shot. They brought him to headquarters on a stretcher. He was in a lot of pain. We used that to our advantage, insisting we wouldn't treat the wound until he gave us information.

"So get this. We put that bastard in a cell in solitary and he shifted, of course."

Naturally. In wolf form the man could speed up the healing process himself. He couldn't make a bullet disappear, but he could ease the pain, stop the bleeding, and help the wound begin to stitch itself back together.

"So now he won't talk?"

"This dude is enormous. And fucking strong. He even dented the bars of the cell. Luckily they're too solid even for him, but if any of the wolves sent out to the ranch are like him, we could have a problem."

A chill raced down Daniel's spine. What the fuck were the Romulus up to? "Already talked to my brother Drake. He said the same thing."

"Damn. I was just about to call Evan and warn him next. I guess I don't need to."

"No. I'm going to shift about a mile to the west and head in. I'll have my phone on silent and check it periodically. I'm hoping to come up from behind and sneak through. They can't possibly have the entire place surrounded with no holes. And I know the land better than any of them. When can we expect backup?"

"I mobilized more troops, but they haven't arrived yet. I'll see what I can find out. Be careful. Stall if you can."

After Daniel hung up, he held on to the door to keep from getting jostled while he started to remove his clothes. He'd leave them in the car when they reached their destination. Devon could really handle a car. Thank God. Daniel stuffed his cell in the small pouch he always carried and grabbed the door handle, ready to make a move. It didn't take long to direct Devon to the spot he wanted, and he leaped out with no more than a thank you and shifted so fast he was practically on the run before he had his bearings.

By the time he got close enough to see the enemy, his heart was pounding. He could scent the bastards before he spotted them. And fuck they were indeed huge. Nearly twice his size. Were they normal-sized in their human form?

They didn't notice him or they didn't give a rat's ass. Either was a possibility considering how intent they were on surrounding the ranch.

Daniel crept into a heavily wooded area with rough terrain and made his way toward the north side of the property, where he imagined he could slip up behind the dorm building and enter from the rear.

As he approached, he gazed around the area. He could see several of the large wolves pacing, but none that appeared to be in human form. They could give chase when they spotted him, but the important thing was they couldn't shoot at him in shifted form.

Daniel dropped his phone pouch from his mouth and shifted to catch his breath and alert his family. He hit speed dial for Drake.

"Daniel. Where are you?"

"Coming up from behind the dorm. Shouldn't have any trouble getting through. I don't think these bastards care much about adding another hostage to their siege."

"Okay. I'll be watching for you."

"Good. Later." He shifted back, chose his moment, and took off at an incredible speed.

The larger wolves growled, and he could smell them congregating in dissatisfaction, but none bothered to chase him down. In moments he was at the back door, and the door whipped open to allow him entrance.

Drake handed him a pile of clothes and waited while Daniel shifted and tugged on jeans and a T-shirt. "Is Allison safe?"

Daniel lifted his gaze as he buttoned his jeans. "Yes. Snuck her out this morning to go to a safe house."

Drake exhaled. "Good idea."

"So what are we up against? I don't like the size of those bastards, and not knowing what they're capable of makes me nervous."

"No shit. And I can't imagine why they're bothering with this great show of force to retrieve six women."

"I'm thinking it's simply because they can and they want us to know it."

"All this is just posturing?"

"Maybe." Daniel's phone buzzed in the small pack he'd carried in his mouth for the last sprint to the dorm. He grabbed the cell and answered with "I'm in."

Jerard exhaled. "Good. Now tell me what you think? How many of them are there? And can we fight them?"

"Maybe a dozen and I have no idea. What else have you found out from the ones you captured?"

"Nothing yet. Sit tight and I'll call you when I have more information. Until we know what the Romulus is capable of, it wouldn't be prudent to attack."

"Agreed. How long before we have backup?"

"Within the hour."

"Good." Daniel flipped the phone closed and followed his brother down the hall to the main living area of the dorm. His entire family and the six women were all together there. Thank God they'd congregated in one spot. Fighting against these guys from more than one front would have been far more dangerous and disorganized.

Daniel hugged his mother, reassured his parents about Allison, and then joined Drake and Evan hovering over a table where Drake was pointing out the lay of the ranch on a wide map. "Ashley?"

Evan lifted his gaze. "She left to join Kenzie."

"Good." He relaxed his shoulders. At least all three mates were safely elsewhere. By now Allison would be at the safe house. He would call and check on her soon.

Daniel's brother Scott also joined the group. Only two years younger than Daniel, Scott was itching to join NAR himself. Daniel hoped he would hold off for a while. Their parents were going to be pushed to the edge of sanity if two sons left the fold, even if it was to protect their way of life.

"So you think we can get these six women out of here safely?" Evan asked.

Drake shook his head. "I don't see how we can sneak them by at this point. We're either going to have to talk these bastards down or fight. And I fear the latter."

When there was nothing else to do, they paced. Daniel ran his fingers through his hair and watched the standoff outside, a dozen NAR shifters in human form surrounded by a dozen Romulus in wolf form. It was eerie. He couldn't wait until more NAR showed up. It would raise his comfort level considerably.

Finally Daniel's phone rang and he yanked it from his pocket. "Jerard, give me something."

"I'll give you several things actually. We've been questioning the men we picked up earlier all day.

They're powerful, Daniel. And the guy that got shot is almost totally healed, although the bullet lodged in him is still there. They can do a lot of damage in wolf form. You don't want to go head to head with them in a fight.

"I don't think these guys even know what they were given to alter themselves, but I don't see any evidence it extends to their human forms. If they decide to move in and attack, there is little that can stop them. Our bullets will hardly slow them down."

"Shit."

"Yeah, well, there's more. They aren't hanging around there just for shits and grins. Apparently one of the women you rescued was promised to their leader. And that bastard wants her back."

Daniel turned toward the women. "Does she know that?" *Which one?*

"Doubt it. She probably never met the man. Or didn't realize it. I'm not even sure which woman she is. The point is, these guys aren't going away until they have her. They have orders to retrieve the women alive."

"Okay. I'm going out to talk to them. Maybe I can make them see reason."

"You can try that. It can't hurt. Backup will be arriving any minute." Jerard sighed. "Keep me informed."

"Got it."

"Daniel."

"Yes?"

"One more thing."

Daniel squeezed the cell tighter. He wasn't going to

like what Jerard said next. He could sense that much in the man's tone and reluctance. "Go ahead."

"We got more extensive results back from the blood work taken from the women."

Daniel held his breath.

"Half of them have a unique genetic makeup distinct from the others."

"Let me guess, the half with the GPS trackers."

"Yes. Including Allison."

"What does that mean?"

"No idea. We'll have to research this further. I'm no doctor. Something about the Alu element in their DNA. I don't have time to understand it completely today. When you get back, we'll sit down with the medical professionals and get a better picture. I'm going to assume the Romulus is messing with the gene pool."

"That would explain these fucking enormous wolves."

"Exactly."

"Okay, I'm going out to talk to them."

"Be careful."

Daniel hung up and turned to his brothers and Evan. "I'm going outside. I'll see if they're willing to talk."

"I'm going with you, then," Drake said.

"Me too." They both turned to look at Scott. "Hey, it's my home too. I'm as capable of protecting the property as either of you."

Daniel couldn't argue with that. But they weren't exactly equals. Neither of his brothers had the combat training he had. Nevertheless, a front of three would improve their odds against the enormous wolves. "Fine. But let me do the talking."

The three of them went out the back door, their parents on their heels. At the last second, their father followed them. "Let's see what we're up against, boys."

They walked halfway across the clearing next to the corral and stopped, hoping the enemy would send a contingency to meet them. Members of NAR moved in tight, fully-automatic rifles at the ready.

Daniel spoke first, his voice loud so everyone in the vicinity could hear. "This will go much easier if a few of you would shift. We can hardly negotiate without verbal communication."

Several of the larger wolves approached in a V pattern. The center one dropped a huge pouch from his mouth and shifted. He shrugged his tall lanky self into a pair of jeans and then met the Spencers several yards away. Brown hair fell over his brow, in desperate need of a cut, considering the last time he'd had a trim it seemed to have been with a pair of safety scissors in the dark. "There is nothing to negotiate. Like we told your posse here..." he nodded at the NAR contingency "... we're here to retrieve the women you folks kidnapped from our men. By any standard of law, that would be considered illegal."

"And the fact that your people kidnapped them in the first place over the years is above the law?" Daniel gave a sardonic chuckle. "I think you must be confused."

"If those women told you they were taken against their will, they lied." The man spread his legs wider and set his hands on his hips. "If you people allow yourselves to be steamrolled by a bunch of fucking women, you're stupider than dirt."

"Then I'd say we have a problem, boys." Daniel glanced at each of the wolves fanning out from their leader. "I have to take the women at their word. And besides, even if they had gone with your people willingly in the first place, the fact that they don't want to return trumps everything else you have to say."

"You can't win against us, jackass. We're powerful. Each of my men could take out three of yours without breaking a sweat."

Daniel decided to call his bluff. "Is that so? The intelligence I have from the group of your trained animals captured by us in the night would have me believe otherwise."

The leader of these fuckers flinched. Good. Daniel had never seen the man before, and he didn't care who he was, as long as he backed down and got the hell off his family's property.

"Look, guys. There isn't a chance in hell we're ever turning those women over to you, so I suggest you go back where you came from before the North American Reserves get impatient and start killing off your men. No one has to die here today."

The skinny man smirked. "We aren't as easily harmed as you seem to think."

"Oh, I'm aware of your strengths." That wasn't entirely true, but this jackass didn't know it. "Nobody is invincible, though. A bullet to the heart is a death sentence even for the hardiest of creatures."

The lanky man hesitated.

A shot rang out.

Daniel ducked low next to his family, unsure where the shot had come from or what its target was. Considering the posture of the enemy, Daniel realized someone from the other side had fired a weapon. Which meant not all of them were in shifted form and the asshole staring at Daniel had anticipated the gunfire.

"That was a warning shot, Spencer. Send the women out now or my men will start aiming at people."

Another shot rang out. This one did startle the fucker. Daniel lifted himself to standing while the leader of the enemy turned around to scan the area.

"Man down!" someone yelled.

The skinny man turned back to Daniel's family. "You want a war? Fine." He shifted so fast, his jeans flew up into the air in tatters. Teeth bared, he advanced toward Daniel, his eyes feral, the rest of his enormous shifted men closing in around him.

Without hesitation, Daniel and his family shifted in an instant also, their clothes scattering around them in shreds. Every enemy wolf was much larger than the average shifter, but Daniel had no intention of backing down. He growled deep and loud as he advanced. *Come on backup. Now would be a good time to arrive.*

If the fuckers wanted a fight, they were about to get one. They might have been larger and had uncanny strength, but they weren't half as intelligent if they thought to win this battle. Shifters emerged from everywhere. It was easy to discern who the enemy was by their size. And NAR troops outnumbered the

Romulus. Daniel glanced both ways during the initial standoff. About half of the good guys were shifted. The other half held their weapons drawn.

Someone shouted above the growls. "Stand down unless you fuckers have a death wish. I don't care what your agenda is, you will die here today if you don't get your asses off this property and go back where you came from.

Suddenly a high-pitched scream filled the air, chilling Daniel to the bone. When he scanned the enemy, he quickly found the source of the voice.

His heart leaped in his chest. He'd known what he would find, but he still couldn't believe what he was seeing. Allison. A huge man held her back against his front. He'd removed his hand from her mouth only long enough to let her disrupt the beginning of the battle, and then he'd silenced her.

Her eyes were glazed over and huge with fear. Tears ran down her face. She didn't look right. Those fuckers had drugged her. Probably to keep her from shifting.

Daniel inched forward, holding his breath. These large wolves were going to die.

Before he could fully wrap his mind around what was happening, Daniel lost sight of his mate. The larger wolves bounded forward, initiating the battle. In an instant the clearing was filled with wolves attacking one another. The enemy was larger, but so many members of NAR shifted that they were outnumbered two to one, making the field more even. Daniel's heart pounded as he tried to squeeze between the tumble of snarling wolves toward where he'd seen Allison.

If they hurt her…

It took what seemed like forever for Daniel to escape the battle and come out on the other side. The same moment he laid eyes on his mate, still held around the middle by some mother fucker with a death wish, another shot rang out. The asshole holding Allison collapsed to the ground, blood running from a perfect shot to the head.

Daniel raced forward, his paws not moving fast enough. He watched as Allison shuffled backward, using her feet to scoot away from the fight. Thank God she had enough of her faculties to react.

Shift, baby. Shift and run. He willed her to escape, but he knew she would if she could.

And then the leader of the enemy suddenly appeared at her side, once again in human form and naked. He grabbed her by the neck and held her against his chest. "Stay back, Spencer. Unless you want this pretty little thing to die of asphyxiation, I suggest you make this madness end right now and turn over the women you're harboring."

Not a chance in hell, you asshole. Daniel continued to inch forward, only yards separating him from his mate.

"I'm not going to warn you again. Step back or watch her suffocate." The fucker squeezed her neck harder. She was turning pale, her eyes huge, her hands gripping his forearm. But she was no match for him. When he dragged her to her feet, he held her so high, her toes barely touched the ground.

Daniel stood very still for a moment. If he hesitated much longer, her life was over. Fury made his adrenaline pump until it boiled over. Still he stared, waiting for the right moment.

And then he got his opportunity. The asshole, deciding Daniel had chosen to see things his way, relaxed his stance marginally. Daniel leaped into the air, higher than normally possible, his jaw clamping down on the fucker's arm and yanking it so hard he pulled it free of Allison's neck.

Allison slumped to the ground, gasping for breath on all fours. He could hear her sputtering for oxygen, but he continued to rip into the leader of this insane group of assholes who dared to attack his family's property.

Having been caught off guard, the son of a bitch didn't have the opportunity to shift. In human form, he was no match for Daniel, who saw an opening and went for the man's jugular. It took just seconds. Blood filled his mouth as he bit through the vein that would bring a quick ending to this asshole's life.

Daniel dropped the lanky man to the ground, spat out the disgusting taste of his blood, and watched as his life ebbed away. He stared up at Daniel with huge eyes for several moments, his body twitching. And then he relaxed as he succumbed to his fate, his gaze still pointed at Daniel.

When he knew it was safe, Daniel leaped toward his mate, finding her huddling against the ground in a ball of fear. Her huge brown eyes stared up at him before she opened up and wrapped her arms around his furry neck.

Daniel nudged her away, nodding toward the barn at

her back. She released him and took the hint, scrambling to stand and then running toward the safety of the structure.

She plastered herself against the door, her shoulders slumping as though she were struggling to remain upright, but she didn't enter. He couldn't blame her, and he was glad she was still in his line of sight.

Daniel turned around to find wolves everywhere, their fur and paws and jaws the only thing visible. He scanned the surrounding area. NAR troops had the entire clearing surrounded, guns drawn. The Romulus may have made their presence known, but they would not win this battle today.

In a matter of moments, every enormous wolf had a human figure standing over him with a gun to his head. Thank God for the arrival of the additional troops.

He turned toward his mate and bounded in her direction. The moment he arrived, he shifted, grabbed her hand, and tugged her into the barn. He pulled her into his embrace and held her tight as she heaved for breath and sobbed against his chest.

Daniel lifted her face with both hands. "Are you okay?"

"I am now."

He lowered his lips to hers and closed his eyes. When he pulled back, he set his forehead against hers and sucked in a deep breath. "Scared the fuck out of me."

"Me too." Her eyes were still huge dark spheres.

"It's over now."

"I hope so."

CHAPTER 17

The following morning, Allison rolled over in Daniel's embrace and held him tighter. She hadn't released him for the entire night, and she had no intention of doing so anytime soon. "Someone fixed the window," she muttered as she kissed his pec.

"Yeah, my family doesn't waste much time." He kissed her forehead. "Did you sleep?"

"A little. I kept jerking awake in a nightmare."

Daniel chuckled. "I'm aware of that."

"Do you think this madness is over?" She bit her lip as she waited for his response.

He hesitated before he shook his head. She lifted her gaze to meet his. "We can't be sure of that. Just because we took several of them into custody yesterday doesn't tell us how many there are in total and what their long-term objective is.

"I'm just relieved none of our men were killed. My family is safe. Their wounds will heal."

She shivered. All of the Spencer men had been in the

midst of the battle. Each had received a variety of injuries before NAR had stepped up their involvement and taken over. None had life-threatening wounds. The women were all safe. Natalie had been the only female family member to stay behind, and she was a blessing now that the battle was over, soothing the nerves of the six women still in their care.

There was no way to be sure of anything, but for now, NAR was still present and hopefully everyone had been able to get some sleep.

"Your brother Scott is going to enlist."

"I know. He made that perfectly clear last night."

"I think Drake is torn."

Daniel nodded. "Yeah, but he has a baby to consider now. If I weren't already committed, I have to say it would be difficult to make that decision now that I have you."

"If you hadn't enlisted last year, there's a good chance I would be dead now, or at least back in their custody." She shivered. The idea was never far from her mind. She owed Daniel her life.

When her vehicle had been stopped on the way off the base and she'd been snatched from the car, she had never expected to survive. Six of these huge feral wolves had been no match for one small woman and the shifter driving her. When those massive beasts had stepped into the road and blocked the car, Allison had nearly swallowed her tongue. She'd lifted her face when the car came to an abrupt stop and gaped at the size of those wolves.

In a heartbeat, two of them shifted, overtook the car,

shot the driver, and yanked Allison from the back. She'd squirmed from their clutches, but she was no match, and moments later she'd felt the deep penetration of a needle.

She'd expected to be knocked out, but instead, she realized she was unable to shift.

But much to her surprise, the men who snatched her drove her straight to an airstrip and loaded her onto a small plane. They hadn't said a word. She'd been surprised when they landed in an unknown location and then driven her straight to the ranch.

And then she'd learned the reality of her predicament. They needed her as a pawn, intending to use her as a way to get the Spencers to back down and deliver the six women sheltering in the dorm.

She knew that would never happen. And then fear over her fate had crept into her system and shook her to her core. She would die, but not in vain. Her life wasn't worth an exchange for six other women.

As the madman had held her neck, she'd kept her gaze locked on Daniel, knowing she would never see him again and willing him to remain strong.

Instead, back up troops arrived and the tables had been turned. She was still in shock, even the next morning.

Daniel eased his hands down her body and hauled her on top of him. He kissed her gently before he spoke again. "I have to return to Seattle."

She swallowed and nodded. "I know."

"Jerard would like me to leave you here under the protection of NAR with everyone else."

She nodded again.

"I can't do it."

She exhaled.

"I love you." He threaded his fingers through her hair and held her head in a firm grip.

"I love you too." A tear escaped her eye, unbidden.

"I would never be able to concentrate on my job if I had to worry about your safety halfway across the country. You'll go back to Seattle with me. Okay?"

She inhaled sharply. "Thank God."

"NAR is figuring out another safe place to hide you, either on base or nearby. You'll be safer with me."

Thank God, she repeated in her head. If she'd been left behind as she expected, she wasn't sure how her sanity would hold out.

Daniel stared at her and opened his mouth to speak. "There's more."

"Lord, what else?"

"When the twelve of you were initially rescued, your blood work was sent to a lab for further testing. Apparently it wasn't a coincidence that half of you had GPS chips. Those of you with tracking devices have a different genetic makeup than the others."

"What the hell does that mean?"

"We don't know for sure. But I'm betting it isn't a coincidence. The Romulus wants you for a reason. And they didn't want to misplace you, either."

"You think it has something to do with those giant mutated wolves?" She shivered to consider the possibilities.

Daniel nodded, his face serious. "I do. But whatever

they intended to do with you, they will never get the chance now. No one is going to snatch you again. I'll make sure of it." He pulled her tighter into his embrace. "I don't know jack about genetics, but whatever the fuck the Alu element is, apparently yours is distinct."

Allison jerked from his embrace and bolted to a sitting position. She stared down at him, shaking. Her mind grasped at what he'd just said.

"What, baby?" He touched her arm.

"Did you say, Alu element?"

"Yes. But I was just repeating what Jerard learned. I can't tell you what it is."

"I've heard that before."

Now Daniel stiffened, his grip on her arm hardening. "Where? When?"

"I don't know, but at some point in moments of lucidity at that strange facility they took me for testing, I heard them discussing that. Something about genomes and the Alu element. I never could have come up with it on my own…but now that you say it, I remember."

"Jesus." He pulled her back down against his chest. "That's good, baby. Don't worry. We'll figure it out."

"What if there's more I can't remember?" She spoke against his firm pecs.

"I'm sure there's plenty. But don't stress, our professionals are on it. At this point, whatever you could remember would be so loaded with medical terminology, it would be a jumble. Our guys will figure it out."

They lay in silence for a few minutes. Allison willed her heart rate to slow. It made her cringe to think she'd been intended for some genetic research. Or had already been used for it. Either way, she hated the notion.

Blocking visions of the past year from her mind, she concentrated on her mate beneath her.

Daniel lifted her face, kissed her soundly, and then shocked her by rolling her onto her back and nestling himself between her legs. "We have to leave soon," he muttered.

She could hear him adding to that sentence, but not the words. While he gave her the details of their departure, he lowered his hand and lifted his body to stroke through her folds. She instantly needed him. Whatever he was rambling on about became white noise in the background as her body readied itself for his cock. All she cared about right then was escaping reality in his embrace.

He chuckled and she let her gaze land on his. "Are you listening?" He pressed two fingers into her.

She shook her head and arched her neck.

"Good. Then I'm doing my job."

The next thing she knew, he had thrust into her to the hilt. *Home*. That was her only thought. It didn't matter where they went or how many places she hid. When he was with her, she would be home.

AUTHOR'S NOTE

I hope you've enjoyed this fifth book in the Wolf Gatherings series. Please enjoy the following excerpt from the sixth book in the series, *Betrayed*.

BETRAYED

WOLF GATHERINGS, BOOK SIX

"I don't like it, Dad. He's my only child."

Shit. Marcus had stepped onto his parents' front porch seconds before he heard his mother's voice. Just his luck it was warm enough out today to leave the front door open and let the breeze blow in through the screen door.

And thank God, because the last person on earth Marcus wanted to face was dear old Granddad, Melvin Cunningham.

"That's entirely the point, Lora. You're *my* only child also. Which makes Marcus the only person alive capable of carrying on the family genes."

Marcus cringed. He hated the way his grandfather spoke to his mother. He'd never treated her like an adult. And keeping with tradition, his father treated her no differently.

As if on cue, his father spoke next. "Listen to him, Lora. He knows what he's talking about."

Great. They were all gathered in the living room

discussing his future, or what they expected to make of it, without his input. Figured.

His grandfather cleared his throat and continued. "Carl's right. Things have changed. Medical research has made drastic improvements in the last two years. My people have isolated specific chromosomes that make up our DNA and give us the ability to shift. Do you know what that means?"

His mother must have shaken her head because he didn't hear anything from her before his grandfather continued. He could picture her staring wearily at her father. He'd seen the look many times. It hadn't done him any good growing up, however. She'd never had the balls to actually stand up for Marcus and keep his father and grandfather from tampering with him.

As a kid he'd spent summers at military camps with other shifters. His grandfather had encouraged his mother to "toughen him up."

In his late teens he'd felt like a guinea pig when his grandfather had shown up with a vial of some horrific substance he insisted would make Marcus stronger. "You're far too scrawny," he said. "This will beef you up, boy."

Marcus hated the drug and the subsequent series of medicines he'd been given over the next several years. Nothing had made him stronger except time. The pile of drugs had only altered his state of mind and infuriated him.

"It means we're on the cusp of a breakthrough. It means everything to our species, Lora."

"What do you have in mind, Dad?" Marcus's father

spoke now. He'd never had a good relationship with his own father and called Marcus's grandfather Dad for as long as Marcus could remember.

"I'll need to bring him in to our facility in Minnesota. After a bit of testing, he should easily be a candidate for gene therapy."

"Dad, he's a grown man. Twenty-six years old," his mother protested. "You can't haul him off to Minnesota for medical research. He'd never agree to it."

"He doesn't have to, Lora. No one mentioned anything about agreement." His father's voice was cold. Calculated.

Marcus cringed. *They have to be kidding.*

He'd known his parents were involved in something less than stellar for a long time, but he'd never expected this.

His mother was right. He was no child now. He was a grown man. He'd been significantly shaped by his strange childhood. Even though he'd been small as a boy, he learned to fight. He learned to use weapons. He took what he learned at military camp and applied it in positive ways. He was never what his grandfather had hoped, but he became a stronger, more self-sufficient adult as a result of his training.

"The drugs you gave him over a year ago didn't work correctly. You said so yourself. And you nearly caused us undue embarrassment at The Gathering by encouraging him to mate with more than one woman. I don't know how we will be able to show our faces at the next Gathering. The Davises must be furious," his mother said.

His father fielded that one. "Lora, nobody cares about the damn Gathering."

"Those are our friends, Carl. The people we've enjoyed the company of our entire adult lives."

"Those relationships are trite, Lora," his grandfather said. "I don't give a shit about those pansy-assed, lower-class shifters."

His mother gasped so loud, Marcus could hear her. He held his breath, not daring to move a muscle.

His stomach clenched thinking about Kathleen and Mackenzie Davis, the two sisters his grandfather encouraged him to mate with at The Gathering last year. Every day he struggled to block the weekend out of his mind.

"Listen to me, Lora." Granddad's voice rose. "Those damn gatherings are over. We're about to go to war. Don't you realize that?"

"Why would we do that? Against whom?"

"It's a wolf-eat-wolf world now, girl. Survival of the fittest. Last week those bastards snatched twelve women from their mates and stole them away to the Spencer Ranch in Texas. Did you know that? Our people must mobilize."

"What are you talking about? 'Our people.' What does that mean? We're all shifters. There isn't a *them* and an *us*."

"There is now," his father said. "And we're going to be on the winning side of this battle, Lora. I intend to fight for our survival as a species. I have to agree with your father. And Marcus needs to man up and do his duty for our side. If those bastards want a war, they'll have it."

"What bastards? Who are you talking about?" she asked.

His grandfather cackled maniacally. "Anyone working for The Head Council." The man sounded exasperated. "Listen to your husband, Lora. This is war. Marcus is strong. He works in construction. He's an asset to our team. Even with his limited military experience, he's got what it takes now that he's fully grown. I need him."

Military? Even after ten summers at military camp, Marcus had never considered joining any armed forces. The primary branch of military for shifters was called NAR, North American Reserves. They were under the jurisdiction of The Head Council. However, except for occasionally hearing about the organization, Marcus knew very little about them. They weren't the group he'd trained under. The camps Marcus had been sent to as a child had been private.

And he could see why now. Apparently his grandfather and his father were opposed to The Head Council. No wonder some of the tactics he'd learned at those military camps had seemed excessive.

Had his grandfather been grooming him all those years? Had he been training with a secret subversive force?

Marcus closed his eyes. He felt sick to his stomach.

His mother gasped. "Just because he's strong doesn't mean you have the right to shuffle him off to some medical facility for experimental drug treatment."

"It means exactly that. After he got out of his teens, when I thought he'd end up scrawny and weak, he's made up for it in spades in recent years. Precisely the sort of man we need on our team."

Marcus cringed again at his grandfather's insistence. The last thing he wanted to do was join dear old Granddad at some strange medical facility in Minnesota.

With the exception of the nasty interlude at The Gathering last spring, he'd been living his own life for over six years. It had taken him a while as a teenager to realize he didn't want to take anything his parents or grandfather prescribed, but eventually he'd started hiding the pills anywhere he could and pretending to do as they requested.

Instead of bulking up with drugs, he'd worked out. Hard. The physique he had today was thanks to his own hard labor, not some steroid or mind-altering drug.

The Gathering had been an exception out of his control. His grandfather had cornered him and jabbed a needle into his thigh before he could protest. The entire weekend had been a series of stupid actions while he'd been under the suggestive drugged state. He'd been horny as hell, his cock rigid for forty-eight hours. So when Granddad pointed out first one woman and then another as his mate, he'd easily succumbed to temptation.

He'd known something was off, but he'd been helpless to stop the madness. And two sisters had suffered under his ruthless insistence. Nothing could erase the memory and the guilt. Since that weekend, he hadn't dated anyone, human or shifter.

He forced himself to concentrate on his grandfather's words instead of lamenting the past. "Get in the game, Lora. You're either with us or you're against us. Those damn law-abiding rule followers are in for a rude awakening when they find out what we're capable of. We hadn't intended to mobilize so quickly, but the Romulus is ready. And we've been backed up against a wall with this mass kidnapping."

Who the fuck is the Romulus? He'd never heard of them.

"Are you trying to tell me the Spencers actually kidnapped a dozen women against their will? I can't believe that. I've known Natalie and Jerome for years. They're the kindest people I've ever met." His mother's voice faded as she spoke. She must have turned away or lowered her voice.

"That's exactly what I'm saying. Well, not the Spencers themselves. They're just harboring the women. But we're moving in and will beat them at their own game in no time."

"You intend to fight them? On their property?" Her voice trembled.

"Yes. And I expect you to keep your trap shut and get your mind in the right place," Granddad said. His threat was clear.

Marcus cringed as he pictured his mother cowering in front of her father. Bile rose in his throat.

"Melvin has created a superwolf, Lora. Unstoppable." His father's words were filled with pride as though he were discussing some educational accomplishment rather than some strange subversive military coup planned by his grandfather. What were they called? The Romulus? Marcus's spine stiffened as he pondered what a superwolf might be.

"What's a superwolf? Why?" his mother asked, voicing Marcus's exact thoughts.

Melvin spoke again. "They're larger and stronger than the average shifter. Lora, I'm tired of taking orders from others. I'm sick of living in hiding. We've lived below the radar as a species for centuries. I have the financial backing now to make this possible. There are humans in high places who know about us. They're helping me. In return, I'll assist them."

Whatever the fuck his grandfather had planned, the details made Marcus go pale. His body shook with rage. He needed to get out of there, and fast. The last thing he wanted to do was to get caught and hauled into this mess.

How he'd lived twenty-six years oblivious to all this shit was beyond him, but he didn't have to live another minute on the wrong side of justice knowing what he now knew.

"Where's Marcus now?" his grandfather asked.

"Probably on his way over. I invited him for dinner," his mother said.

Thank God he'd gotten off work earlier than expected and come straight to his parents' home. He hated to think what might have happened if he'd been ten minutes too late for this powwow.

"Then I'll wait. We'll either convince him to come in, or take him against his will if need be."

Marcus eased away from his spot against the outside wall. He prayed not a single board in the porch squeaked to give him away as he inched toward the side railing. He didn't dare go back down the front steps. With one hand on the banister, he leaped over the top and landed firmly on the ground. Seconds later he was running into the woods behind his parents' house.

He couldn't take the chance of going home. Besides, he wouldn't be able to take anything with him anyway. He wasn't going to take a casual drive in his car to escape. The only option he had was to shift and go completely under the radar. Rogue.

He managed to dash more than a mile into the trees before he paused to shed his clothes and shift. The last thing he wanted was for anyone to easily figure out he'd run by encountering his clothing. He found a dip in the ground, buried everything he had, and covered it with debris and leaves. Over the years he'd run in these woods so many times, there was no way anyone would be able to track him. His scent was everywhere.

Shifting was quick and easy, and then he was on the move.

He lamented the loss of the life he'd built for himself over the last few years. His job as a contractor would quickly be snatched up by someone else when he didn't show up for work. It couldn't be helped.

Marcus was a grown man. No drugs had been in his system for six years, with the exception of that one weekend. He'd worked hard to build his life the way he wanted it, giving everything he had physically and emotionally to overcome his weird childhood. And he wasn't about to lose the ground he'd gained. Not even for family. Not for anybody.

He ran. Hard. His destination easy.

Texas.

Like his mother, Marcus would never believe the Spencers had anything to do with the kidnapping or harboring of anyone. His best option now was to go see for himself.

ALSO BY BECCA JAMESON

Blossom Ridge:

Starting Over

Finding Peace

Building Trust

Feeling Brave

Embracing Joy

Accepting Love

The Wanderers:

Sanctuary

Refuge

Harbor

Shelter

Hideout

Haven

Surrender:

Raising Lucy

Teaching Abby

Leaving Roman

Choosing Kellen

Pleasing Josie

Honoring Hudson

Nurturing Britney

Charming Colton

Convincing Leah

Rewarding Avery

Surrender Box Set One

Surrender Box Set Two

Surrender Box Set Three

Open Skies:

Layover

Redeye

Nonstop

Standby

Takeoff

Jetway

Open Skies Box Set One

Open Skies Box Set Two

Shadow SEALs:

Shadow in the Desert

Shadow in the Darkness

Delta Team Three (Special Forces: Operation Alpha):

Destiny's Delta

Canyon Springs:

Caleb's Mate

Hunter's Mate

Corked and Tapped:

Volume One: Friday Night

Volume Two: Company Party

Volume Three: The Holidays

Project DEEP:

Reviving Emily

Reviving Trish

Reviving Dade

Reviving Zeke

Reviving Graham

Reviving Bianca

Reviving Olivia

Project DEEP Box Set One

Project DEEP Box Set Two

SEALs in Paradise:

Hot SEAL, Red Wine

Hot SEAL, Australian Nights

Hot SEAL, Cold Feet

Hot SEAL, April's Fool

Hot SEAL, Brown-Eyed Girl

Dark Falls:

Dark Nightmares

Club Zodiac:

Training Sasha

Obeying Rowen

Collaring Brooke

Mastering Rayne

Trusting Aaron

Claiming London

Sharing Charlotte

Taming Rex

Tempting Elizabeth

Club Zodiac Box Set One

Club Zodiac Box Set Two

Club Zodiac Box Set Three

The Art of Kink:

Pose

Paint

Sculpt

Arcadian Bears:

Grizzly Mountain

Grizzly Beginning

Grizzly Secret

Grizzly Promise

Grizzly Survival

Grizzly Perfection

Arcadian Bears Box Set One

Arcadian Bears Box Set Two

Sleeper SEALs:

Saving Zola

Spring Training:

Catching Zia

Catching Lily

Catching Ava

Spring Training Box Set

The Underground series:

Force

Clinch

Guard

Submit

Thrust

Torque

The Underground Box Set One

The Underground Box Set Two

Wolf Masters series:

Kara's Wolves

Lindsey's Wolves

Jessica's Wolves

Alyssa's Wolves

Tessa's Wolf

Rebecca's Wolves

Melinda's Wolves

Laurie's Wolves

Amanda's Wolves

Sharon's Wolves

Wolf Masters Box Set One

Wolf Masters Box Set Two

Claiming Her series:

The Rules

The Game

The Prize

Claiming Her Box Set

Emergence series:

Bound to be Taken

Bound to be Tamed

Bound to be Tested

Bound to be Tempted

Emergence Box Set

The Fight Club series:

Come

Perv

Need

Hers

Want

Lust

The Fight Club Box Set One

The Fight Club Box Set Two

Wolf Gatherings series:

Tarnished

Dominated

Completed

Redeemed

Abandoned

Betrayed

Wolf Gatherings Box Set One

Wolf Gathering Box Set Two

Durham Wolves series:

Rescue in the Smokies

Fire in the Smokies

Freedom in the Smokies

Durham Wolves Box Set

Stand Alone Books:

Blind with Love

Guarding the Truth

Out of the Smoke

Abducting His Mate

Three's a Cruise

Wolf Trinity

Frostbitten

A Princess for Cale/A Princess for Cain

ABOUT THE AUTHOR

Becca Jameson is a USA Today best-selling author of over 100 books. She is well-known for her Wolf Masters series, her Fight Club series, and her Surrender series. She currently lives in Houston, Texas, with her husband and her Goldendoodle. Two grown kids pop in every once in a while too! She is loving this journey and has dabbled in a variety of genres, including paranormal, sports romance, military, and BDSM.

A total night owl, Becca writes late at night, sequestering herself in her office with a glass of red wine and a bar of dark chocolate, her fingers flying across the keyboard as her characters weave their own stories.

During the day--which never starts before ten in the morning!--she can be found jogging, running errands, or reading in her favorite hammock chair!

…where Alphas dominate…

Becca's Newsletter Sign-up

Join my Facebook fan group, Becca's Bibliomaniacs, for the most up-to-date information, random excerpts while I work, giveaways, and fun release parties!

Facebook Fan Group:
Becca's Bibliomaniacs

Contact Becca:
www.beccajameson.com
beccajameson4@aol.com

- facebook.com/becca.jameson.18
- twitter.com/beccajameson
- instagram.com/becca.jameson
- bookbub.com/authors/becca-jameson
- goodreads.com/beccajameson
- amazon.com/author/beccajameson

Printed in Great Britain
by Amazon